THE LEAI

GILLIAN FREEMAN was born in London in
honours in English literature and philosopk
in 1951 and afterwards worked as a copywi
literary secretary to the novelist Louis Golding before embarking on a literary
career of her own. In response to an advertisement placed by the fledgling
literary agency of Anthony Blond, Freeman submitted the manuscript of her
first novel, *The Liberty Man*, which went on to be published by Longmans and
was one of the best-reviewed novels of 1955. By 1961, Blond had his own
publishing house and wanted to publish a 'Romeo and Romeo' novel with
working-class gay protagonists; the result was *The Leather Boys*, published
under the pseudonym of Eliot George. The book was well received and went
into numerous paperback printings in the US and UK during the 1960s and
'70s before Gay Men's Press reprinted it in 1985 as part of its *Gay Modern Clas-
sics* series; it was also adapted for Sidney J. Furie's Golden Globe-nominated
1964 film, for which Freeman wrote the screenplay.

Freeman's other novels include *The Leader* (1965), a disturbing 'what if'
story about a Fascist's rise to power in Britain; *The Alabaster Egg* (1970), a his-
torical novel whose title refers to a gift from the gay King Ludwig II to his
lover that later finds its way into the possession of a young woman in Nazi
Germany; *Nazi Lady* (1978), the fictional diaries of a woman of the Third
Reich; and *An Easter Egg Hunt* (1981), the tragic story of a young girl in Edwardian England who disappears from a boarding school on Easter Sunday.
More recently, Freeman's *His Mistress's Voice* (1999) and *But Nobody Lives in
Bloomsbury* (2006) have been published by Arcadia Books.

In addition to her novels, Freeman has written a number of screenplays,
including *That Cold Day in the Park* (1969) and *I Want What I Want* (1972). Her
nonfiction works include the influential study of pornography *The Undergrowth of Literature* (1967) and *Ballet Genius: Twenty Great Dancers of the Twentieth Century* (1988), the latter co-authored with her husband, the novelist and
ballet critic Edward Thorpe. Freeman also wrote the scenario for Sir Kenneth
MacMillan's immensely successful ballet *Mayerling*, which premiered in
London in 1978 and which has since entered the repertoires of ballet compa-
nies all over the world.

Gillian Freeman and Edward Thorpe have two daughters and live in
London.

ALWYN W. TURNER is a historian and writer, whose work centres on British popular culture in the 20th century. He is also the author of a trilogy
of books on British politics from the 1970s to the 1990s. His website is
www.AlwynWTurner.com.

By Gillian Freeman

FICTION

The Liberty Man (1955)*
Fall of Innocence (1956)
Jack Would Be a Gentleman (1959)
The Leather Boys (1961)*
The Campaign (1963)
The Leader (1965)*
The Alabaster Egg (1970)
The Marriage Machine (1975)
Nazi Lady: The Diaries of Elisabeth von Stahlenberg, 1933-1948 (1978)
An Easter Egg Hunt (1981)
Love Child (1984) (as Elaine Jackson)
Termination Rock (1989)
His Mistress's Voice (1999)
But Nobody Lives in Bloomsbury (2006)

NONFICTION

The Story of Albert Einstein (1960)
The Undergrowth of Literature (1967)
The Schoolgirl Ethic: The Life and Work of Angela Brazil (1976)
Ballet Genius: Twenty Great Dancers of the Twentieth Century (1988)

SCREENPLAYS

The Leather Boys (1964)
That Cold Day in the Park (1969)
I Want What I Want (1972)
The Day After the Fair (1986)

* Published by Valancourt Books

GILLIAN FREEMAN

THE LEADER

With a new introduction by
ALWYN W. TURNER

VALANCOURT BOOKS

The Leader by Gillian Freeman
First published London: Anthony Blond, 1965
First Valancourt Books edition, January 2014

Published by Valancourt Books, Richmond, Virginia
Publisher & Editor: JAMES D. JENKINS
20th Century Series Editor: SIMON STERN, University of Toronto
http://www.valancourtbooks.com

ISBN 978-1-939140-90-6
Also available as an electronic book.

Cover by M.S. Corley
Set in Dante MT 11/13.6

INTRODUCTION

'Great Britain has lost an empire and has not yet found a role,' declared Dean Acheson, the former U.S. Secretary of State, in December 1962. He was talking specifically about foreign policy, but his remarks were sharp enough to provoke a debate about the future of the post-imperial nation.

Even as he spoke, however, there was the first sign of a new Britain being born. 'Love Me Do', the debut record by an obscure Liverpool group, the Beatles, which had been released two months earlier, was on the threshold of the top twenty singles chart. From that humble beginning was to come a cultural revolution that would sweep the world, make London 'the swinging city' (in the words of *Time* magazine), and provide a new identity for an old country.

Yet the bright, shiny optimism of the 1960s was not the whole story; there was also a darker undercurrent in British popular culture. Less than a generation earlier, the country had only narrowly avoided a Nazi invasion, and those memories were hard to dismiss. In 1964 the film *It Happened Here* presented a vision of what London would have looked like had that invasion taken place. That year too the BBC's leading science fiction series *Doctor Who* had told the same story in metaphorical form with the hugely popular story 'The Dalek Invasion of Earth'. Meanwhile Robert Muller's novel, *The Lost Diaries of Albert Smith* (1965) documented the advent of fascism in contemporary Britain, and neo-Nazi groups were to be seen in television series like *The Avengers*, *The Saint* and *The Baron*.

Between them, these and other works suggested that Britain's new mood of confidence was perhaps not as stable as it would wish to believe. The international success of the Beatles and the Rolling Stones, of Mary Quant and James Bond, could not entirely conceal the unease; these phenomena were too novel to seem permanent, too shallow to be secure.

Gillian Freeman's novel *The Leader* was another to articulate the disquiet. 'England needs a leader, just as Germany needed one in the thirties,' argues its protagonist, Vincent Wright (né Pearman). 'On the surface everything looks good, prosperity, welfare service, employment. But underneath it's rotten. Who are being employed? Niggers. Who by? Jews. For whose benefit? Their own, not the country's.' Like others in the fiction of the time, he too wants a revolution, to be led by his nascent Britain First Party.

Where Freeman's version stands out is her characteristically acute depiction of the net-curtained misery of lower-middle-class suburbia. Wright is a deluded, frustrated bank clerk, fuelling his fantasies of significance with records of Wagner. Asthma ruled him out of National Service, he worries about his lack of physical stature and, in his mid-thirties, he has only just moved out from his mother's house, though he still visits to be fed tea, tinned salmon and chocolate cake.

There is no glamour to be found here, just a shabby, seedy failure of a man. He attracts followers, but he knows how unimpressive most of them are, and can't forget that he has to pay some of them to buy their loyalty. The more common response is that of his bank colleague, Miss Glass, who he imagines is in love with him, but who rejects his party on the grounds of what she terms British tolerance: 'It's just like the Nazis,' she tells him; 'don't think you're pulling wool over my eyes.' He seethes about those who are 'sentimental about Belsen', yet – lacking the courage to be honest – he has no answer for them, save deceit.

Wright was drawn from life. His language, his attitudes were widely shared in a Britain that had over the last decade or so experienced a rising wave of immigration from the West Indies and the Indian subcontinent. Two years after *The Leader* was published, several groups on the far right of politics merged to form the National Front, which soon became the most electorally successful fascist party Britain had seen. More significant still was the emergence in 1968 of Enoch Powell, a former cabinet minister whose anti-immigration speeches made him the most popular – if also the most reviled – politician in the country. The same year the newspaper proprietor Cecil King made an abortive attempt to persuade Earl Mountbatten to lead a coup against the Labour government.

The appeal of Powell and of the National Front was precisely to those who felt, like Wright, 'humiliated by the country today' and who objected to the presence of those 'who can't even speak our beautiful language, who believe in primitive gods and have very, very different values to ourselves'. These were the people, still dreaming of a time when Britain had both an empire and a role, who were untouched by the Swinging Sixties.

Yet ultimately there is no escape from the world ushered in by the Beatles; Wright rails against 'a culture based on pop art', and still finds himself persuaded to recruit a rock band to record a single for Britain First. That tension between the primary colours of a cultural revolution and the shadowy fringes of disaffection is one of the many reasons why *The Leader* remains such an intriguing novel.

ALWYN W. TURNER

November 30, 2013

THE LEADER

For Piers Jessop

Chapter 1

THE plastic butterflies were the size of birds. They clung to the wall on suction cups and quivered if one touched them. Vincent flicked at a Red Admiral with dusty antennae and it suddenly sprang away from the wall and fell on to the floor. He picked it up and pressed it back exactly on to the pale circle left on the wallpaper. As he did so he felt a congestion in his chest, the first symptom of an asthmatic attack. It must be the dust in the room. Quickly he took his inhaler out of his overcoat pocket and putting the glass mouthpiece between his lips he pressed the rubber bulb. He felt a fine vaporous spray against the back of his throat. Within a few seconds his breathing became easier. Then he walked to the door and looked down the hall to the half-open kitchen door where Madame Vera was drinking tea with a friend.

'Madame Vera!' he shouted irritably. He heard a chair scrape the linoleum and a teaspoon against a cup.

'Won't keep you long Mr Pearman. My friend's just going.' He went back into the room and crossed to the window, staring out at the lorries which passed endlessly along the road shaking the window frames.

She had no right to keep him waiting. She should attend to him whatever time he arrived, whether he had an appointment or not. One of the net curtains had caught on the cardboard notice propped on the sill, and maliciously he moved the notice so that the curtain fell in front obscuring it from the street. It was the notice that had first attracted him two years ago, symbolically on Christmas eve, perhaps his final rejection of Christianity; a foggy night with an imminent snowfall icing the air. He had called without an appointment then, and had caught Madame Vera in a baggy black skirt and floral overall making tea in the small scullery; and there he was for the first time on the other side of the swagged curtains with Madame Vera, psychological palmist, giving him a cup of tea

and a cream horn, pulling out the folding table and covering it with
a red velvet cloth, taking his hand and scrutinizing the lines which
took on the depth and magnitude of a relief map. She told him he
must make a change, that he had great potential which was being
restricted by his environment, that a woman was stifling him with
too much love. Until then Vincent had only toyed with the idea
of leaving home. After his visit to Madame Vera he moved. Since
then he had never made a decision without her.

He had told no one about his visits. There was no one to tell.
Certainly not his mother who would not have understood. Certainly not Miss Glass at the bank who would have disapproved.
Tampering, Miss Glass would call it. We shouldn't tamper with the
unknown. At the beginning it had occurred to him that if he had
been able to discuss it he would have felt less compelled to make
visit after visit. But after the first month or two when he still held
reasonable doubts, he had become convinced that there really was
an unknown force within him that would have remained dormant
but for Madame Vera, that without her guidance and faced with
a choice he would make the wrong decision. When he read his
horoscope in the morning paper, humorously at first, he related it
to what Madame Vera had told him on his last visit and let it influence him during the day. Once, when the paperboy was ill he had
waited until half past nine, hovering by the front door with his hat
and coat on, giving himself just five minutes more at home, then
another five, then one, and finally leaving for work without having
read his stars – he was Gemini – and with no time to stop on the
way because he was far too late already. He lied about his late-
ness and lied again so that Miss Glass exchanged her earlier coffee
break for his and he was able at last to buy a paper. His rational
sense told him that he was being silly, that millions read the same
paper, millions read other papers with conflicting horoscopes, and
yet he couldn't laugh at himself, not any more. The extraordinary
thing was that his horoscope was usually right, the daily trends
of setbacks and luck and conflicts-to-avoid really did tally with his
own days. He wasn't superstitious as his mother and Miss Glass
were. His mother wouldn't walk under a ladder and Vincent made
a point of doing so. Miss Glass wouldn't wear green or pass Vin-

cent on the stairs to the strongroom. Vincent was amused by her. He was amused by the almanac he had bought from a man who came to his door and even brought it to work to show Miss Glass. He had bought it because the man who was selling them had had one hand blown off in the war. The almanac cost twopence and Vincent gave him sixpence. It was worth the sixpence, he told Miss Glass, just to read the advertisements for lucky charms. 'Since I have carried Joan the Wad I have had two wins on the pools' ran testimonial after similar testimonial. 'That's what people think luck is,' he said, 'money on the pools.' How limited they were. He knew now that luck wasn't acquired by carrying a charm, that one's good luck and bad luck were navigated by one's own actions which in their turn were influenced by astral forces.

'Well,' said Madame Vera, coming into the room and closing the door behind her. 'Worried, are you?'

'I do need guidance,' answered Vincent sitting down at the table and placing his hand on it, palm upwards.

'I do wish you'd make an appointment Mr Pearman. It's very embarrassing when I've got company.'

'You get enough money out of me,' he said, 'and I don't always know in time to send a card. You ought to be on the telephone.'

'Oh well, you're here now.' She sat down opposite him and took his hand. 'A meeting, is it?'

'That's right,' he curbed his irritation. 'What are the signs? Good or bad?'

'I'll just turn up the cards,' she said, getting up and taking a pack from the mantelpiece. 'Very good, Mr Pearman. The signs are very very favourable. Do I see a lady?'

'No, it's a man.'

'Of course dear. Here he is, right on top of the pack.' She laid out the cards. 'Be cautious. But on the other hand don't hesitate unduly. This week-end, Mr Pearman?'

He nodded.

'I thought so. This is going to be an important meeting. I think there's a letter.'

'Probably,' Vincent nodded.

'Do as it says. That's all I can tell you today.'

Vincent stood up. 'I'll try and drop you a postcard next time.'
He took out his wallet. 'What do I owe you?'
  'Half a guinea.'
He gave her the money and she followed him to the front door.
'Probably next week then,' he said.
'All right, dear. Cheerybye.' She closed the door behind him.

He got off the bus near his mother's house. She lived in a tall
terraced house in a long road. There were two hundred houses
of a similar design, with pointed porches adorned with elaborate
stone work, slate roofs and brick chimneys with revolving cowls.
Inside the porch of his mother's house the walls were tiled in glossy
brown and yellow, and there were two panels of amber glass set in
the front door.
  She had left it open for him and as Vincent entered the hall
he was engulfed by the smell of the house. He had only become
aware of it since he had left. The smell was predominantly a stuffy
dryness that seemed to come out of the walls and the woodwork.
It was the kind of smell that came when you picked up an old
book in a second-hand shop and turned the pages, and it mingled
with the smell of the floor-polish and the strong lavender-scented
disinfectant that Mrs Pearman sprinkled so lavishly in the sink and
downstairs lavatory.
  Vincent closed the door.
  'I'm in the dining-room darling, just laying the tea,' called his
mother.
  He took off his coat and hung it on one of the pegs by the door,
went along the passage and down the two shallow steps to the
dining-room. His mother had put a cloth on the table and was
taking food from the kitchen hatch. She always went to a great
deal of trouble when Vincent came to see her, buying special food
that she thought he liked, tinned salmon, chocolate cake, pork
chops. In fact he didn't care much about his food at all, hadn't a
very developed sense of taste because he suffered from catarrh,
and really he had grown out of tinned salmon and chocolate cake
at the age of twelve. There was a chocolate cake on the table today
and when he saw it, sitting on an elaborate doily, he knew that he

would be carrying a large piece of it home with him, in a brown paper bag with the sticky doily inside.

'Kettle's on the boil dear. Will you make the tea?'

It was a ritual which irritated him but gave her comfort, as if he still lived here and took part in the daily chores. He was suddenly filled with such loathing of the familiar black and gold tea-caddy, the plastic measure, the teapot with its additional rubber spout that for a moment he thought that if he let himself he might easily become uncontrollable and smash the teapot and spill the tea. Then the feeling passed and he forgot it, handed the tea through the hatch to his mother who sat down at the table and waited for the tea to brew and Vincent to join her.

The food made Vincent relax, and he talked to his mother about the bank and Miss Glass, about his flat and his expedition down the Portobello road last week-end, with all the pointless details that she liked, and later the two of them watched television in the over-furnished living-room which Mrs Pearman called the drawing-room. The television rested on a damask table-runner on top of the small grand piano. Beside it were two photographs, one of Vincent at the age of six, and another of his father, taken on a seaside holiday only a few weeks before he had died suddenly from a heart attack. On the wall above there was a framed reproduction of the Bridge at Arles painted by Vincent's namesake and after whom he had been christened. There was a glass-fronted bookcase containing a Bible, a set of the Encyclopaedia Britannica 1929 and six assorted novels which arrived in the year Vincent had given his mother a book club subscription for Christmas. There was also a copy of Tiger Tim's Annual. The piano stool, on which Vincent rested his feet, was covered with a grospoint picture of a water mill worked by Mrs Pearman when she was pregnant. A bowl of goldfish with ants' eggs floating on the surface stood in the centre of the window-sill. Vincent knew it all so well his eyes no longer registered it.

Sometimes he went upstairs and looked at his old room and that he saw freshly and couldn't believe he had slept in it for thirty-five years. He knew his mother dusted it everyday in case he came home. She had confessed that she hoped he would, that the novelty of independence would become as tedious to him as it was to her. Why should they both live separate lives, she had asked. After all, they only had each other now. She didn't like to think of him alone, she said, evening after evening in that uncomfortable sitting-room in Prince's Mansions, where he hadn't even a television, just his old gramophone, and no one there to rub his back when he had an attack. Bless him, she thought, looking at him now with his feet on the piano stool, how he's enjoying the programme.

As soon as it ended, at half past eight, Vincent said, 'I must go home now. It was a lovely supper.'

'Oh, it's so early,' Mrs Pearman protested, trying not to sound too disappointed but her eyes, encircled by the green spectacle-frames, showed her feelings. 'Stay and watch the play.'

'I've got work to do,' said Vincent standing up.

'Bank work?' asked his mother.

'That's right.'

'You need to relax when the day's over,' said Mrs Pearman, 'you have to have some time to call your own. Can't you have a word with the manager, darling. You'll be ill if you overwork.'

'I've never been able to sit around doing nothing,' said Vincent. 'I like to work.'

He put on his coat in the hall and his mother came close to him and said, 'I wondered if you would like to come to church with me next Sunday?'

'I can't this Sunday,' said Vincent.

'Vicar asked me if he was going to see you. He thinks it funny you don't come.'

'Sorry mother, I've made arrangements.'

He had made them deliberately, he hated the two or three yearly occasions when he was forced to go to church. He didn't share his mother's gratification when he accidentally met the Vicar in the street, didn't want to be an integral part of the local community. His mother knew them all – the vicars from the churches she didn't attend, the health visitor, the district nurses male and female, the shopkeepers. He had found it difficult to avoid churchgoing when he had lived at home, the reproachful look when she had brought up his breakfast tray on Sunday mornings, the recounting of the sermon later over lunch. It impinged too much on his inner life, this having to show interest, repress guilt, argue, protest. He couldn't share her many and often trivial interests, he didn't want to decentralise his own thoughts.

'You have so many secrets nowadays,' she said. 'I suppose you don't want to tell me what your arrangements are.'

'Oh mother,' he said impatiently, 'it wouldn't interest you. But if you must know I'm going down to Kent to see some things I might buy.'

'Antiques?' she asked.

He nodded, kissed her, then closed the front door behind him and heard his mother immediately turn the key and put the chain across.

He walked along the dark road, lit at intervals by sodium lamp light, past the maternity home where he had been born, past the Salvation Army chapel, past the houses belonging to his mother's friends where he used to play. As he passed each one he could visualise the kitchens, the bedrooms, the back gardens. Of course the bedrooms he used to know were redecorated now. Few mothers were as sentimental as Mrs Pearman, keeping their children's bedrooms intact. Binky, Vincent's particular friend, had lived at number sixty-four. He still thought of it as Binky's house. It was really odd how one lost all point of contact with old friends, people like Binky who at one time had been such an integral part of his life that he never did anything without consulting first and reporting afterwards. Binky was in Rhodesia now with three lovely children according to Mrs Pearman who saw the photographs. Was the link quite severed? No more than a set of shared experiences in a particular decade? Had they both progressed beyond any need of one another? Had the experiences contributed to the adult person, the Vincent Pearman who was now walking home to Prince's Mansions and the Binky Potter in Rhodesia? When an adult suddenly achieved a strong conviction, as he had, was his past responsible for it, would he have acquired the belief if his life had been lived in similar but not exact circumstances?

He turned the corner and walked quickly past the empty shops. Miss Glass obviously still depended on sharing every experience.

Why else did she tell him that she had cornflakes for breakfast, that the waste-pipe of her sink was blocked and she had forgotten to buy any caustic soda, that she had laddered four pairs of stockings last week? Miss Glass seemed to find reality only when she had communicated each dreary item, and each day regaled him with some long and tedious domestic account.

He came to the church his mother wanted him to attend on Sunday. It was red brick, like everything else, Gothic-trimmed like his mother's porch, in fact it seemed at this moment a huge replica of the porch, pointed, ornate, leading into the same stuffy airlessness he found at home. The block of flats where he lived was next door. There was a flight of stone steps up to the front door with stone lions – the left hand one mono-pawed from an accident on a moving day – supine at the top, flanking the glass-panelled doors; inside the doors more steps to the lift. The walls of the corridors were brown. As the lift rose Vincent could see the dustbins by the front doors ready for the porter's morning collection.

His flat was on the fifth floor where the corridor windows were smaller than on the lower landings, and the rent cheaper. He took out his keys and unfastened each of his two locks. Then he went in, and like his mother had done, put the chain across into its keep.

Always after a visit to his mother he felt an extra pleasure in coming home. He had escaped. Putting the chain across the door was a symbol of freedom, locked in but free. She was locked out. No one in the world knew what he was doing now, unimportant as his actions were, they were his secret. His mother didn't know that he was standing a foot away from his kitchen door unbuttoning his coat. There was no telephone. She couldn't contact him. She had begged him to have a telephone, even offered to pay the bills 'Just to know that I can say good night to you, darling.' No telephone, a locked door, this was liberty and independence. He didn't have to share his life.

He went into the kitchen and made himself a pot of tea. The task that had been so irritating in his mother's house was now pleasurable, making tea to drink alone in the comfort of his own privacy. Wonderful British drink, he thought, a national drink. He had once said this to Miss Glass. 'Our men drink beer,' she had

ventured timidly. She didn't understand. Tea was for emergencies, for courage, for body-heat, for camaraderie. Give a drink of
hot sweet tea it said in first aid books. People drank it during air-
raids, after funerals. He made it with his usual care, the pot well
warmed, the water really boiling, two good spoonfuls of tea, a stir
before putting the lid on.

   He carried the tray into the sitting-room, placed it on a table and
sat down in his only armchair. The tea was strengthening under the
cosy. The room was his own. He leaned back. Timing five minutes
by the clock he poured a cup of tea and drank it, then chose a
record from a pile on the shelf and put it on the record player. He
must wash his shirt. He took off his jacket and tie and laid them
on the sofa, humming with Isolde's Liebestodt. He unbuttoned his
shirt and took that off too, examining the collar and cuffs to see
if they would stand scrutiny for a second day. No, not really, not
when he was virtually under inspection there behind the counter.
A cashier needed to be spotlessly clean. One couldn't emanate
that air of authority wearing a soiled shirt. He carried it into the
kitchen and immersed it in a plastic bowl of soapy water. He had
his routine. He allowed his shirt to soak until he was ready to go
to bed, then he rinsed it, put it on a hanger over the bath so that it
could drip harmlessly, did up the buttons, put the collar stiffeners
back in. By the morning it would be dry but because he never wore
any of his outer clothes two days in succession, he would fold it
and put it in the airing cupboard on the landing. And wear it the
day after.

   The music was loud. He liked it loud and there had never
been a neighbour's complaint. He loved this rich, dark, romantic
mythology, the grand passions, the violent deaths. In his own life
there was absolutely no passion, no violence, just the ordered
days of a bank clerk who lived a short distance from his work.
But lately he had found something of a romantic element as he
touched the future with Madame Vera. He would have loved
to have been Wagner, to have lived in Munich in the nineteenth
century, to have been permitted to indulge an extravagant sensi-
tivity; a room draped in yellow silk, the ceiling hung with satin.
As Vincent Pearman, a citizen of North London in the twentieth

century, it was pointless even to consider a foible of this kind. One must be a Wagner to have one's whims admired and not despised, to have artificial roses on the pink silk draping the picture frames accepted as adjuncts of genius, of personal importance.

Very suddenly he stood up. He put one foot on the rust coloured velour of the sofa, his hand on the arm, and hoisted himself up so that he was standing on the middle cushion. It was difficult to find his balance, and he spent a moment adjusting his position, and then he kept quite still so that the springs twanged and sank into silence. He stared, unblinking, at himself in the glass above the mantelshelf opposite him, examining each of his features in turn; the thinning hair, brushed forward to conceal the thinness, the brown eyes – 'violinist's eyes' his mother called them – the nose, long and with a fleshy centrepiece between the nostrils, the chin small with a dent that had once been a dimple, the neck short, with hairs at the throat. Vincent was not tall enough to see further, except for the white shoulders of his vest sleeves. He made a sharp movement with his arms and almost fell. He rested his calves against the back of the sofa and leaning there, lifted his arm high up, slanting it above his head. He clenched his fist and brought his hand forward in a communist salute. He unfolded his fingers and extended them, the fascist salute. He brought his arm close to his head, paused and thought, then bent it from the elbow, the forearm across his forehead and clenched his fist again. He smiled. No one had thought of that.

Chapter 2

VINCENT turned the little black stand so that the side facing the clients read Till Closed. It was four minutes to eleven. Miss Glass continued to cash a cheque for Mr Burgess, adding, Vincent observed, another thirty pounds to the already large overdraft. He smiled at Mr Burgess, despising him. Standing behind the counter on the raised floor he was taller than Mr Burgess. He knew that in spite of the new car, the well-cut suits, the casual conversation about shares and holidays, Mr Burgess was poorer than he was.

Miss Glass followed Mr Burgess to the door and shut and locked it after him.

'He always has a very nice appearance, hasn't he?' she said.

'That's about all he has got,' answered Vincent sourly. 'I'm surprised Mr Fowler lets him go on like it.'

'Oh well, he has his income,' said Miss Glass, returning to her till. 'He usually gets a cheque in March. It's late though.'

'He needs it.' Vincent began to count the money in the drawer beside him. 'What would he do if there was a credit squeeze? He'd be in a spot then.'

She turned her name-stand round so that the name, Miss B. Glass, was towards her. It was one of the typically stupid actions that gave Vincent intense irritation. The bank was closed. Obviously therefore, her till was closed. Besides, the customers had all gone. The initial stood for Beryl, she had been called, she said, after the stone in her mother's engagement ring. Mr Fowler, the manager, found it an inspiration for endless feeble jokes and puns. Miss Bristol Glass, he called her, when she wore a bright blue, cable-stitched jumper, Miss Burning Glass when she lit a cigarette. She smoked tipped cigarettes and her lipstick was always imprinted on the butts in the ashtrays, the exact colour combination of Vincent's mother's linoleum which had a so-called oriental pattern.

Miss Glass was forty-one and had worked in this branch since she was seventeen. She still lived with her mother. It was amusing to Vincent that a woman as stupid as Miss Glass should know such intimate facts about people vastly superior to her, should know, for instance, all the details of Mr Burgess's income when Mrs Burgess lived in ignorance of them, lived under a complete misconception it seemed, judging from the daily arrival of her cheques.

Vincent enjoyed this kind of secret knowledge. It gave him a privileged position, a peculiar insight. When he met a client in the street he saw through the elaborate persona the client liked to present, just as this morning he had failed to be impressed by Mr Burgess's sixty guinea suit. He wasn't deceived by outward signs of poverty either. That often concealed an inherent meanness. He not only knew what people earned, but what they spent, and even the way they spent, sometimes a disproportionate amount on theatre tickets or clothes or photographic equipment. He knew Christian names, which in any other such limited personal contact would be remarkable. He knew how much a client allowed his wife and to what his insurance policies amounted. It was as revealing in its way as knowing a medical history or sitting on the receiving side of a confessional. When a doctor, washing his hands up to the wrists, said 'Undress and lie on the couch, will you?'; when a priest, looking intently through the grill asked, 'What have you to tell me, my son?'; the relationship was as stark between man and doctor, between man and priest, as it was between cashier and client. The only difference was – and this was what gave it an added relish – in this case the client was unaware of the intimacy. It gave Vincent an enjoyable sense of power, just as he savoured the extra height the raised floor seemed to give him. He doubted that silly Miss Glass was conscious of *her* power.

When the strongroom had been ritually locked for the weekend – there were four separate key holders, he was one of them – and Mr Fowler had put on his velvet collared overcoat and soft hat and left for his home in Friern Barnet, Vincent took his own coat from the little cloakroom and left by the back door. Usually he travelled home with Pamela, the youngest and newest of the four machine operators. She had acne and a deep fringe and lived a street away from Vincent. But today he was going to Victoria station to catch an early afternoon train to Kent.

Because he was sitting opposite a nun, Vincent was too embarrassed to read the copy of *Psychic News* he had bought at the station bookstall. He and the nun sat alone in the carriage, suddenly lit by the spring sunshine as the train pulled out of the station. Atoms of dust became apparent on the window ledges and on the floor and on the glass facings of the photographed views of Dover Castle and Folkestone sands. They were especially visible all over the nun's black clothes. As bridges and buildings and stations cut out the rays of sun, the silvery dust on the nun's shoulders was extinguished and illuminated like a million minuscule glow-worms. One was always reading about radio-active dust, thought Vincent, and this was what it must look like, actively shining. The nun's presence made him uncomfortable. He tried not to look at her too obviously. She had a round plain face with a double chin which was severed by the absolutely white wimple, half the chin trapped inside, a fugitive fold reposing on the starched exterior. The wimple had a row of buttons up the side in a straight line, like the buttons on a boot. Her eyes were very small, blue and watery. She took a prayer book out of a little velvet bag and began to read it, mouthing the words. The heavy cross on her bosom moved imperceptibly with each intake of breath. If he hadn't been staring at it Vincent wouldn't have been aware of that fractional rise and fall. He lowered his gaze to her boots, huge – bigger than his own – cracked and brilliantly polished. Up on the rack was a black plastic hold-all with some horse chestnut sticks wrapped in a plastic bag.

Vincent unfolded his *Psychic News*. On the back page was a head-line – Church Events. He held it towards the nun defensively, then was suddenly furious with himself for this mental genuflecting in the face of a religious symbol. He didn't like Christianity. His own false respect mirrored a weakness in society. He opened the paper so that the front page with its striking caption Medium Contacts Mars faced the nun too. But when he looked over the paper at her she had closed her eyes. There was no reason really why spiritualism shouldn't be absorbed into her religious doctrine. Perhaps she wouldn't be shocked after all. But it was difficult to predict her attitude. One wouldn't have thought, for instance, that convents would have given sanctuary to Jews in Europe during the war; that nuns would travel as tourists as some American orders seemed to do, with expensive cameras slung over the voluminous black cloaks; or drive cars; or beg. This one was either praying or asleep. The train stopped and three girls stepped up into the carriage, giggling, and the nun opened her eyes and sat up straight again.

'I'd never 'ave believed it of 'im,' said one girl between her giggles.

' 'E got a nerve,' said another.

'I told 'im, you bloody shut up, mate, or you're in dead trouble,' said the third, giggling again.

Vincent looked sharply at the nun at the word 'bloody' but she seemed unmoved. Lost in her inner thoughts, Vincent said derisively to himself. He looked at the girls. Two were blonde and one was dark. One blonde was very nubile and had big sweat marks under the arms of her patterned jumper. On her big cushiony bust a tiny silver cross lay almost horizontally. The thin dark one had hairy legs. The smaller blonde wore jeans and a leather belt with brass studs on it. In spite of his braces, quite hidden by a knitted waistcoat and pinching his waist, Vincent wore a wide leather belt too.

⋆   ⋆   ⋆

Vincent had imagined a country cottage, exposed beams and uneven tiles overlapping on a low roof. He sat in the taxi as it bumped along the narrow lane, enjoying the view of the fields and trees all sprouting buds and shoots of practically edible green.

'Not far now Sir,' said the taxi driver. He wore a navy blue beret at an angle and a paisley scarf tucked into the neck of his shirt. It was his own car, he told Vincent, he polished it inside out every other day. The upholstery was soft brown leather and did shine. There was a net suspended under the felt roof and there were several maps and folders in it. The driver reached up and took out a folder and gave it to Vincent. It had the driver's name and telephone number on it and the prices charged by the small hotel he owned as well as the taxi. 'The wife runs that side of things,' he said, as he stopped the car. 'You'd find it very comfortable.'

The house was not at all what Vincent had expected. Although its location was rural it might have been a town house. It was Victorian, built of red brick and three storeys high. The paintwork was dark green – unblemished on doors and window frames, but rusting on the gutters and pipes. Vincent paid the driver and stepped out of the taxi on to the gravel drive. The quietness was impressive, not a sound except a bird singing. 'It does seem quiet after London,' said Vincent.

'I expect it does, Sir,' answered the taxi driver, closing his door and switching on the engine again. But even that sound was soft and gentle, and blended in with all the other sounds of which Vincent was now becoming aware, a distant tractor, a dog yapping inside the house, humming telegraph wires, and the stones and twigs bouncing and crackling under the wheels as the car drove away. He walked the few steps to the front door and rang the bell. Immediately the dog's yapping became hysterical, but when the man opened the door there was a fat tabby cat with him that pressed against his legs and walked between them several times, its tail up straight, as the polite conversation took place.

'Mr Pearman?' the man said, extending his hand. 'I'm William Fox.'

'How do you do,' said Vincent, shaking hands. 'It seems so peaceful here after London.'

'I loathe London,' said Fox. He stood to one side. 'Come in.'

The cat walked slowly into the garden and stood sniffing the air. Vincent followed Fox into the house and waited while he shut the door. He took Vincent's coat and hung it on a mahogany coat stand, the only piece of furniture in the hall. The floor was bare and polished, but there was a strip of worn carpet on the stairs.

'I expect you'd like a cup of tea, wouldn't you?' Fox indicated a door and Vincent walked into the room. A small pug dog growled from a chair.

'Don't mind him, Mr Pearman, he's just old and cross. But harmless. Please sit down.'

There were only two armchairs in the room and the dog was on one of them. Vincent felt embarrassed taking the other, but Fox waved him in to it and went and stood by the mantelpiece. There was a fire burning, but it was banked with coal dust and didn't give a great deal of heat.

'I'll go and see about the tea,' said Fox. 'We'll talk shop afterwards.'

There was a long silence before Fox left the room. Vincent searched desperately for something to say, but Fox was looking reflectively out of the window, obviously not feeling any desire to talk. He was tall and upright, unquestionably an ex-army officer, even if Vincent hadn't received his letter with (Col. retd.) after the neat schoolboyish signature. His moustache was sand-coloured, slightly grey. His hair was greased flat and his eyes were reddish brown, Van Dyke brown in Vincent's paintbox. He sometimes painted birthday and Christmas cards, neat little street scenes, coloured the houses with Van Dyke brown; country views, with Van Dyke brown churning under the wheels of the plough, or gleaming on a horse's back. Fox's brown eyes were extraordinarily bright and at the moment, as he stared out of the window, the pupils were as small as pin-heads.

He brought in the tea a few minutes later, an odd teapot, cups balanced, digestive biscuits still in the packet. When Vincent compared it to his own flat, everything here was bare and spartan. This was the living-room, but there was nothing to make it comfortable, no table lamps, only one central one hanging on a foot of flex, with a slightly torn parchment shade; no cushions; no carpet. The tea was very strong and the digestive biscuits soft.

'Do you live alone?' Vincent asked.

Fox spooned sugar into his tea. 'I have a lady who does for me, but otherwise there's just myself and Monty.' He nodded towards the snoring pug. 'And the cat.'

'It seems a big house for one person,' said Vincent.

'My grandfather built it for his wife, servants and five children. It seemed silly to sell it. I like it. I like the scenery. It's a good part of the country to live.'

'Beautiful,' agreed Vincent. Out of the window he could see the cat jumping over the long thick grass of the unkempt lawn. The black buds on the apple trees were breaking. 'It must look wonderful in summer.'

'It's bloody marvellous,' said Fox. *'Kent, in the commentaries of Caesar writ, is termed the civillest place of all this isle.'*

'Who said that?' asked Vincent, knowing by the way Fox flung his head back that he was quoting. He added, 'It's not a part of the country I know well.'

Fox finished his tea and put the cup back on to the tray. He ignored Vincent's conversational gestures. His tone changed abruptly, as if, with the completion of the tea ceremony, all overtures were at an end. 'Come upstairs,' he said, 'and have a look at the collection.'

Vincent followed him into the hall and up the stairs. The carpet – the only carpet – stopped two steps from the top. The landing was bare except for a big oak chest of drawers with dust on top and a jug containing some papery everlasting flowers which looked as if they would crumble and add to the dust if anyone touched them.

'This is all shut down,' said Fox. 'I sleep upstairs.' He turned the key in one of the doors and opened it for Vincent to see inside. There was a pile of boxes in a corner and a bed covered with old newspapers, a looking glass and a picture lying face upwards on them. Nothing else.

'My mother's room until she married,' said Fox. 'Extraordinary when you come to think of it. Look at it now.' He locked the door again and they went upstairs to the top floor.

'This is my bedroom.' He paused. 'I like to live simply, as I expect you've observed.'

The room was furnished with a similar chest of drawers to the one on the landing below, a hard chair and an army truckle bed. Beside the bed was a control panel with several knobs labelled *Bass, Treble, Volume*, in Fox's neat writing. From it wires straggled up to the picture rail and looped round the room to the two speakers and the electric motor and turntable in a plain wooden box. There

were racks of gramophone records on the floor, some of them
thick old shellac ones.

'Complete Gilbert and Sullivan,' said Fox. His suits hung behind
the door, there was no wardrobe. When he opened the door it was
prevented from swinging the full extent because the suits bumped
into the chest of drawers.

His books were on the landing outside, six long shelves, tightly
packed.

'Quite a library,' said Vincent, touching them with his finger tips
as he followed Fox. He ran his fingers across the spines like a child
dragging a stick along railings. Fox paused outside the door at the
end of the corridor, and then turned the key, waiting for Vincent to
stand beside him before opening it. Vincent expected him to fling
it wide with a flourish, but he did it very slowly, so that Vincent's
first impression was one of grey light and a damp cold dusty smell.

'Go on in,' said Fox. He stood aside for Vincent to pass him, and
Vincent walked into the room and stood just inside the door. In
front of him were three long trestle tables placed in a row, a few
feet apart. The light from the door illuminated the polished and
unpolished metal of the objects arranged along them.

'Put on the light,' said Fox.

Vincent turned and saw a man standing just inside the door. He
was absolutely still, his arms at his sides, his feet, in highly polished
jack-boots, a little apart, his eyes hidden under the shadow of a
steel helmet. Vincent felt himself go faint, he closed his eyes, his
heart thudded. The man was dressed in German field uniform of
the last war, grey breeches, grey-green jacket, dark green shoulders tabs with a lightning-flash insignia in silver thread, a black belt
fastened with a Nazi eagle holding a swastika in its claws.

'How do you like Klaus?' asked Fox, switching on the light
himself. 'Seventh Panzer Division.' He was smiling. 'Did you think
he was real?'

Vincent swallowed. 'For a moment.' It was a display dummy
with wax face and hands, about six foot tall, about Fox's height,
much taller than himself. There were blue glass eyes under the rim
of the helmet. He turned away, still unnerved, very angry with Fox
for tricking him.

The room was the width of the house. The windows had been boarded up in an amateurish way with pieces of box wood and deal. The light shone down on to the middle of the room but the extremities were in shadow. Opposite the door, between the two windows, was a large picture of a sandy beach, the striped bathing huts surmounted incongruously by fluttering Nazi flags. It was labelled *Holidays in Germany*. To the right and left of the windows were blown-up photographs, some of them pinned on boards and some framed in passe partout – photographs of party rallies at Nuremberg; of Hitler standing up in a half-tracked vehicle giving the Nazi salute; of smiling German soldiers; of Nazi youths in shirts and breeches, banging large drums and blowing bright shiny trumpets; of Hitler with a group of German Generals; Hitler and Mussolini; Hitler receiving a bouquet from a little girl in a white dress; Hitler with Goebbels, with Goering, with Doenitz; photographs of German aircraft; a large cut-away drawing of the *Gneisenau*.

Vincent began to walk between the trestle tables, looking at Fox's collection while Fox stood beside the dummy soldier watching Vincent. The first table was laid out with a series of daggers, ceremonial daggers, and swords, including a naval officer's presentation sword. Fox leaned across and picked up a black leather scabbard.

'This is the one I advertised.' Vincent took it from him and held it between his palms, pressing it hard wondering who had held it before him, someone like the mock Klaus over there.

'You can have it for a fiver,' said Fox.

'Yes, I'll buy it.' Vincent kept it as he continued to examine the collection. How small his own seemed in comparison, the buttons he kept in the box, the insignia, the belt he was secretly wearing. Fox had rows of buttons, some with eagles, some with swastikas; there were several belts with varying types of clasp, several iron crosses, several victory medals with Hitler's head on them, laurels and oak leaves and the ubiquitous swastika. There were three German field service caps, two sailor's hats with *Kriegs Marine* cap tallies and twin black ribbons at the back; two sets of field service knife fork and spoon clipped together, four pairs of boots of different sizes. Vincent picked up a Nazi flag, a black swastika on a white disc on a red ground. 'Very striking,' he said, 'very arresting'. He put it back in position beside a German naval flag, a small swastika in the centre of the black Maltese cross of the Kaiser's Imperial Navy. There were two pistols, a Mauser and a Luger, piles of service maps, piles of books and magazines and propaganda leaflets and a rack of gramophone records.

'I'll play you one of the speeches later if you like,' said Fox. 'Well, you've seen it. Let's go downstairs.' He put up his hand and switched off the light, leaving Vincent stumbling and peering in the dark, trying not to knock objects off the tables or to brush against the sinister Klaus.

'Well?' asked Fox, as they returned to the living-room. 'What did you think of it?' He sat down, pulling the pug off the chair on to his knee.

'Magnificent, really. Most impressive.'

Fox nodded. 'Why did you answer the advertisement?'

'I thought that was obvious,' said Vincent. 'You had some collector's items you wanted to sell. I was interested in this.' He held up the dagger in its black leather scabbard.

'And that was all?'

'What else?'

'Did you want to meet me?'

'I was interested of course,' said Vincent. 'One's always interested to meet a fellow collector.'

Fox stood up, dropping the dog back on to the chair, and went over to a big roll-topped desk. He opened a drawer and took out an enormous book, faded red, and Vincent thought at first it was a volume of the Encyclopaedia Britannica.

'Do you know what a shargar is?' asked Fox.

Vincent thought his mother wouldn't like the word.

'No. I've never heard of it.'

'It's more than a rotter. It's more than a slacker. It's an undisciplined and pappy example of young manhood. The type I wouldn't have stood for in my regiment.'

Vincent could see the title of the book now. It was the collected *Boys Own Paper* for the year 1904.

'I often read this,' said Fox, 'dip into it.' He opened it and flicked the pages. 'Of course some of it's out of date, like the words I used just now – rotter and slacker and shargar. Shargar's the one they use here, mostly. Bloody funny some of it. Look at this.' Vincent looked at the picture Fox held out to him, of a white hunter in a topee, a lion's paws on his shoulders, slavering jaws an inch from his face. The caption was 'A Dangerous Moment'.

'It's the attitudes which are admirable. The kind of attitudes which once made us a strong nation. The kind of attitudes that have been jettisoned by the youth of England today.'

'We're too busy licking America's boots,' suggested Vincent.

'Boots!' said Fox with a laugh. 'Listen to this.' He turned the pages of the book rapidly to find a particular place. 'This is part of one of the weekly newsletters; contains advice, a sort of solve your problems page.' He put the book flat on the mantelpiece and leaned over to read it. 'The editor calls himself Captain. I like that. It gives a definite feeling of leadership.' He found the page and began to read. 'Take plenty of exercise and fresh air. Do not inhale the filthy weed as shargars and degenerates do. Take a cold tub every day, even if it is necessary to break the ice on the tub first. Do not eat too much red meat.'

Vincent couldn't control a smile. 'What's the red meat supposed to do?'

Fox didn't smile back. 'Ideas were different. Red meat was con-sidered to make people intemperate and hot blooded. It's the general principles which should be adopted. Young men are pam-pered nowadays, all that central heating and ice cream, even at school, even in the army.' He shut the book with a snap. 'I have tried to embody some of these principles in a group I've formed. We call ourselves The Spartans. We go to camp in the school holi-days, canoeing and hiking. Sometimes we make a point of eating only fruit for a day or two. After a week or so in the open the boys are as strong as trained athletes, and I feel young and energetic. I'm over fifty Pearman, but I consider my physical fitness is due entirely to self-discipline. I don't indulge myself with rich food and alcohol and easy living.'

'You're quite right,' said Vincent excitedly. 'I'm very unhealthy by your standards. I get so little fresh air and exercise because I work indoors, in a bank. I was brought up badly. Do you know my mother wheeled me in a push chair until I was nearly five? She still gives me cakes and sweets.'

'I've never been constipated in my entire life,' said Fox.

'Mothers like mine build a race of sickly degenerates,' Vincent said, standing up and walking about the room. 'All those boys who think of nothing but clothes and pop music. I see them standing about in groups, all dressed up, when I go home.'

'Exactly.' Fox picked up the coal scuttle and poured more slack on to the fire. The flames disappeared beneath black dust. It reminded Vincent of wartime. His mother burnt this mixture of coal and coal dust and clinker during the war. Now she bought big pieces of shiny coal and her fire blazed and gave out a tremendous heat. 'There was a time when I wanted to start a school,' Fox said as he set down the scuttle. 'I had dreams of selecting only the right type of English boy and moulding him. But I hadn't the money to do it. If I was dependent on my pupils for an income I'd have to have taken the sons of Jewish business men and any jumped-up tradesman.'

Vincent walked to the window. It was practically dark outside, everything two-dimensional and in tones of black and grey. He felt a tremendous surging warmth in his chest, his breath was shallow, he knew his eyes were bright. Meeting Fox had acted on him like a catalyst; it gave him the impetus he needed; it helped him to shape his loathings and longings into coherent form. Fox stimulated him into an awareness of his own potential, something he had only realised as they had spoken together.

They must form some sort of unit which would further their aims to help build Britain into the strong, pure and self-sufficient country he knew it could and should be. Get rid of the muck and the filth and the degenerates which were polluting the British way of life.

'Blood and iron,' he suddenly said aloud, turning back to face Fox. 'Those were Bismarck's words.' The room was so dark that, looking away from the window, he couldn't see Fox for the moment. He blinked. Slowly the room emerged. 'We must build on British blood and British iron. We must stamp out the weeds

and cut out the rot that eats into our lives. Did you know that
Wagner hated the Jews? He wasn't so wrong, neither was Hitler.
I'm not saying his methods were right, mind, but he realised where
the canker lay.'

Fox still stood in front of the fire, not speaking, watching
Vincent.

'A lot of them come into the bank,' said Vincent fiercely. 'Some
think they've got away with it, they're so bloody British, with their
accents and their cars and the public schools for their sons. Britain's greatest mistake was to ally herself with the French. They
were always our natural enemies, and the Germans our natural
allies. 1914 was a tragedy. And stemming from that our abandon-
ment of Germany as a brother nation was the biggest act of folly
we ever committed. What a magnificent group of Nordic nations
we would have made!' He stopped, out of breath.

Fox said nothing.

'I believe,' said Vincent, surprised at his own fluency, that he
really could formulate his thoughts like this, 'that the time is ripe
to form a totally new group with new aims. I think the two major
parties in Britain are played out in their various ways – a heave, a
shake and the whole lot will fall down like rotten apples. I think all
we need is a little thought and a little effort, the setting out of basic
principles. A call to youth by a leader.'

'Who?' said Fox.

'Yourself,' Vincent retorted, then paused. 'Or myself. Or someone we've yet to discover.'

'We?' said Fox.

'Aren't you interested then?' asked Vincent flatly.

Fox drummed his fingers on the closed annual which was still
on the mantelpiece. 'Yes, I'm interested. You just seem to have
embarked on a gigantic idea in a rather sudden way. After all, we
hardly know each other, we're merely two people interested in
collecting the same sort of curios.'

Vincent came close to him. Outside the stars were visible. 'Yes,
but surely they mean something more than that? Surely they symbolise something more than just the objects they are. You can't
tell me that all that upstairs, the figure, the photographs, books,

pamphlets, is just a collection which might be so many stamps or birds' eggs? I'll be honest with you, when I see those things, when I hold this dagger . . .' he realised it was still in his hand and thrust it at Fox, 'when I look at my own bits and pieces, they bring back to me wonderful memories of a nation of steel, a nation which in less than a decade nearly dominated the earth, a nation full of pride and strength and greatness and aware of its destiny.'

'What was its destiny?' said Fox. 'A waste of rubble, a Wagnerian Valhalla?'

'Oh I know, I know,' answered Vincent, sitting down on the arm of the chair. 'That was the tragedy of it. And it need not have happened. That's the fatal weakness in the Germans of course, a sort of national death wish. But we don't have it.' His voice rose. 'We have the greatness of the Germans without their weakness. *If only we could be led.*'

'This is what you said just now,' Fox pointed out.

'All right, I'm repeating myself. But that doesn't make it any the less true. What I asked you was, doesn't your collection mean something more to you?'

'Yes,' said Fox simply, 'it does. And I agree with you. I just think you're becoming excited and fail to see the magnitude of the task. I wouldn't have thought, frankly, that you would have been the person to begin it.'

'Why?' asked Vincent hotly. 'Because I'm small? Because I'm a bank clerk? What was Hitler? A corporal in the army. What was Napoleon? The son of a civil servant, a second lieutenant. What matters is not one's social origins or one's physical appearance, but one's *vision*, one's determination, one's conception of the future. I may look what I am, but believe me, sometimes I seem to burn inside, knowing we could be a great country were it not for the Jews.'

'It's funny,' said Fox, crossing the room swiftly and switching on the light, 'but when I saw your name on the letter I thought you must be Jewish yourself.'

★   ★   ★

How could he have thought it? Would a Jew collect Nazi relics? Vincent was still shaken, he had actually trembled when Fox had made the accusation, and Fox had meant it to be an accusation.

'Do hurry,' he said sharply to the taxi driver, 'or I shall have to spend the night in your hotel.'

'Don't worry, Sir,' said the driver soothingly – Vincent knew his name now, it was R. Fayers, printed on his brochure – 'I'll get you there on time. You won't miss it.'

The last train left at half past ten. It was ten when Vincent realised the time. He had stayed for supper, which had been surprisingly good, mulligatawny soup and a steak-and-kidney pie, and Fox had drawn the curtains and poked the fire so that flames had at last burst through the barrier of coal dust. Vincent thought Fox was the very opposite to himself, unemotional, rational, probing and discussing both his own and Vincent's beliefs. Yet from the analysis emerged a real strength of purpose, that one had to begin somewhere and now might well be the time.

I must change my name, he thought, as Fayers drove into the station yard. Did other people think he was Jewish too, when they heard his name, or saw it on the counter when they came into the bank? Did he have a Jewish forbear? Was Pearman a Jewish name? There was a Pearlman who banked at his branch. What were the others? Landauer, Levy, Green – that was hardly indicative – Freedman, Brickman. Yes, it was the suffix 'man' that was Jewish. There was a Rothman too. But he couldn't drop it and call himself Vincent Pear. That was comic.

He paid the driver and said good night to Mr Fayers. How about Fayers? It was pretty uninspiring, he could do better than that. He ran up the steps as the train swung in beside the platform, climbed in an empty carriage and sat down panting. Another train tore through the station, with a clattering that grew in volume and diminished as it passed. That was Doppler's effect, he had learned it at school. Vincent Doppler? It sounded Germanic and too odd. His own train pulled out. Vincent Britain. Vincent Strong. You are now in the Strong country it said on the hoardings as one travelled to the South West. But that didn't matter, it sounded impressive. Only he wasn't strong, he was palpably weak and people would laugh. He hadn't given his health a thought until talking to Fox, but now he had definitely eaten his last chocolate and smoked his last cigarette. Vincent Glass? It was as ridiculous as she was. Fox? It was sly. Wasn't there a simple Anglo-Saxon name, redolent of strength but not obvious. Vincent Churchill? Church? No, certainly not Church; and Shepherd had a gentle Christian implication too. Straight could be rhymed with Hate and Fate, and it was advisable not to have a name that could be rhymed with disadvantage. Oh well, he'd think of something. He leaned back and shut his eyes, giving up the search for a new name. What an extraordinary meeting it had been. Madame Vera had been right when she spoke of its importance. Had she been fully aware just how important? He must go and see her tomorrow, now more than ever he needed to be guided in his actions. She didn't like to be disturbed on a Sunday but for once she would have to put up with it. It was fate that had made him begin a collection, fate that he had bought the particular copy of *Exchange and Mart* in which Fox had advertised, fate that he had answered the advertisement and fate that had taken him to Kent today.

The underground platform was empty when he stepped out of the last tube at his home station. A cleaner with a bucket and a broom disappeared, clanking through the arch to a door marked Private. Vincent stopped in front of a brightly coloured poster advertising a film. There was a picture of an all-American boy on a sleazy dockside. For almost a minute Vincent looked at the poster, and then he placed his ticket between his teeth and rapidly pulled off his right glove and stuffed it into his coat pocket. Looking up and down the platform he felt in his top inside pocket and took out his yellow ball-point pen. There was no one on the platform, only litter and sweet machines and the two dark tunnels at either end.

Still gripping the ticket in his bared teeth he stood very close to the poster so that his arm was bent and wrote JEW, in capitals, beside the director's name.

Elated, putting on his glove as he went, he ascended the escalator on his way home.

Chapter 3

'SUNDAY's my day of rest too,' said Madame Vera tartly. 'I've asked you before not to come on a Sunday.'

'It's three o'clock,' Vincent excused himself. 'I didn't expect to find you in bed in the afternoon.'

Madame Vera opened the door of her front room. The curtains were drawn and the atmosphere was stale. Vincent imagined he could see yesterday's cigarette smoke suspended in the air. Madame Vera shuffled across to the window. Her bedroom slippers were edged with dirty lambswool and she had trodden the heels down so that they flapped as she walked. She pulled back the curtains. In the daylight Vincent could see how grubby her kimono was. It was patterned with big mauve and pink chrysanthemums and pressed so tightly on her unsupported bosom that there were twin sausages of flesh under her arms.

'I wouldn't have come if it wasn't important,' said Vincent, sitting down on his usual chair.

She sighed as she unfolded the card table. 'It's always important. People don't realise how exhausting it is, dipping into the future. The concentration's terrible.'

'I don't know just how much of the future you see,' said Vincent significantly, 'but if you had any idea when you advised me last week, you'll know why I'm here now.'

Madame Vera looked shifty. 'I'm not divulging,' she said guardedly. 'You'd better tell me. That meeting, was it? It came off?'

'Yes,' answered Vincent. He wanted to sound calm. 'I've had the meeting.'

'Well, go on, dear.' She took his hand. 'It's marked here that you've reached an important juncture of your life.'

'I met a man called Fox.'

'Oh, I had a fox in my tea cup,' said Madame Vera. 'I knew there must be a reason.'

'He and I talked of forming a political party.'

'You're going to do it,' she said. 'Wait. I'll turn up the cards. That will tell us a bit more.' She took the pack. 'Yes. You'll be in a very prominent position. I see you serving the multitude, Mr Pearman.'

'Am I going to lead the party?' asked Vincent tremulously.

'If you don't contradict your signs. That's the problem.'

Vincent put his hand over hers as it picked up a card. 'You must help me. I need you. This is too big to do alone.'

Madame Vera stood up. She was a tall woman and Vincent experienced a dwindling sensation sitting below her on the folding chair. He was very conscious of her power to help him.

'I tell you what,' said Madame Vera gaily. 'I'm going to make a nice cup of tea. And we'll have another look at the cards afterwards.' She slapped the pack of cards back on to the mantelpiece. There was an advertisement for Players cigarettes on the back of each card. 'I might have to invoke guidance, Mr Pearman, I've got an intuition the other world will be able to help. But my throat's too dry to think.'

He waited for her to come back with the tea, pedantically irritated with the stupid phrase, angry that someone so obviously his inferior should be so necessary. 'Would you believe it?' cried Madame Vera shrilly. 'There's another fox's head in my cup.'

'Do you believe in destiny, Miss Glass?' asked Vincent, wetting his thumb on the nicotine coloured sponge in front of him and counting pound notes.

She put her head at an angle and considered. 'I'm never sure what it means, really. Though I always say my destiny is looking after mother.'

'I do,' said Vincent. 'I believe some people can't escape responsibility, are destined to lead. And others are destined to suffer because they obstruct what is right.'

'I don't think anyone should suffer,' answered Miss Glass, pressing her lips together at the end of the sentence. 'Very quiet this morning, isn't it, even for a Monday?'

'That's where you're wrong,' said Vincent fiercely, ignoring the

last observation. He kept his voice low so that the girls in the partition behind him shouldn't hear. 'If something has to be done it's
no good being sentimental. Sometimes to achieve an end one must
be quite ruthless. For example, Miss Glass . . .' his voice was so
quiet she moved closer to him . . . 'all the West Indians who are
here, not only taking away the jobs from able British workers, but
marrying our girls and corrupting the race.'

'I think if people are really in love it doesn't matter,' said Miss
Glass, smiling.

'Well, I want to kick them off the buses,' Vincent hissed. 'I
won't get on a bus if there's a black conductor, and you should do
the same. If you accept them, you're encouraging the government
to allow them in. Let them stay in their own countries, not come
here, polluting our life.'

'I'm sure you're wrong,' Miss Glass said hotly. 'They're human
beings like we are.'

The door opened and a woman came in to draw her weekly
house-keeping money. Vincent could hardly contain himself to
make his usual polite conversational exchange, he was so anxious
to retort to Miss Glass. The woman counted the notes slowly and
put them into her purse. As the door swung shut Vincent turned
towards Miss Glass.

'Don't you see how these impurities drag the country down?
Don't you want England to be strong? Well, it won't be strong if
it's sapped by foreign matter. If germs get into your system, Miss
Glass, you're weakened, aren't you? Well, England's the body, and
all these non-aryans are its disease.'

Mr Fowler came out of his office on his way to the café across
the road to have his morning coffee. He held the door open for
Mrs Burgess to come into the bank.

'I never knew you thought like this,' said Miss Glass. She smiled
at Mrs Burgess. 'Good morning. Quite chilly outside, isn't it?' She
reached across the counter to take a cheque.

By Thursday Vincent's ardour was less violent. He felt depressed
and flat. There had been no word from Fox, no letter in reply to
the long one he had written after he had returned on Saturday

night. He had posted it on his way to Madame Vera on Sunday afternoon, and even allowing for delays at the sorting offices, Fox must have received it on Tuesday. In the country, talking to Fox, it had seemed so feasible, so comparatively simple. But in London, alone with no contacts except his mother, Madame Vera and Miss Glass, it seemed an impossible dream.

On Friday morning there was still no letter. He didn't feel like breakfast and arrived too early at the bank. The door was locked and he stood on the pavement, cold and upset. Madame Vera had told him that Friday was a key day, but the only planned activity was the routine evening with his mother. He couldn't remember being so loath to see her, or so solitary, or to have endured such a feeling of anti-climax.

'Good morning Mr Pearman,' It was Pamela, the machine operator with the spots. 'Are we locked out?' She stamped her feet on the dry pavement as though snow was clinging to her shoes. A watery spring sun was suddenly revealed between two clouds which a moment ago, amoeba-like, had been one. 'Do you think it's going to be sunny?'

'I've no idea,' said Vincent.

'If it keeps fine I'm going to play tennis at the week-end.' She picked a spot unconsciously. 'You don't belong to the tennis club, do you?' The spot bled.

'No.' To his relief Vincent saw the chief cashier stepping off a bus.

'Are you locked out?' asked the chief cashier, approaching with his key at the ready. He was a plump man with a softly curling moustache, so soft that Pamela said she thought he had never shaved it because there wasn't the trace of a bristle. It was this kind of chatter that Vincent suffered when he and Pamela walked home together, Pamela's unimportant ideas not only about the staff at the bank but about film actors and popular singers and the more glamorous examples of royalty.

The chief cashier opened the door and they trooped in, the chief cashier first because of his seniority, then Pamela since Vincent had been taught by his mother always to let a woman go before him, and lastly Vincent. He saw Miss Glass hurrying along the pave-

ment, breathless, carrying the string shopping bag in which she
brought her sandwiches. When she went home the shopping bag
was always full of food that her mother might fancy for supper. Mrs
Glass was an invalid and her capricious appetite sometimes reduced
Miss Glass to tears. Vincent felt stifled by Miss Glass's domestic triv-
ialities and Pamela's boggling admiration of celebrities.

Miss Glass panted into the bank.

'Good morning all.'

'Good morning Miss Glass.'

'Good morning Beryl' (from the chief cashier).

'Good morning everyone.' Mr Fowler came through the door,
smiling under his brown pork-pie hat.

'Good morning Mr Fowler. Sunshine today.'

'One swallow, as they say, Miss Glass.'

'Hallo Pam.' It was two of the girls, Joyce and Merle.

'Did you go to the pictures then?'

'I didn't see you.'

'I went with Keith. Were you upstairs?'

'No. It was full upstairs.'

'I'll dictate some letters when you're ready Joyce.' Mr Fowler,
divested of his coat and hat, put a stop to the girls' conversation.

Joyce took off her coat with its nylon fur trimming and gave it
to Merle. 'Hang it up for me, there's a dear.'

'Got a lot to tell you about last night Pam,' said Joyce giggling
as she snatched up her shorthand pad and rushed into the office.
Vincent could see her head shadowed behind the frosted glass and
hear Mr Fowler's voice – 'I am writing to tell you, for your information, that the overdraft on your account has now reached . . .'

Vincent made an effort to absorb himself in his routine work.

Mr Fowler came out of his office, frowning. 'Mr Pearman?'

'Yes?' Vincent looked up from his books.

'There's a personal call for you. You'll have to take it in my
room.'

As Vincent edged behind Miss Glass's girdled bottom to where
the counter lifted up to make a gate, Mr Fowler gave a loud sigh
and walked back into his office.

Vincent followed and picked up the telephone receiver which was lying on a large green blotter.

'Mr Vincent Pearman?'

'Yes.'

'I have a personal call for you.'

He heard Fox's voice. 'Pearman, I've had a hell of a time getting hold of you. I've rung all your local banks.'

Mr Fowler was standing beside his desk, tapping his fingers on the blotter and looking out of the window while he listened to what Vincent was saying.

'Sorry about that,' said Vincent.

'I've managed to get in touch with most of my group. I thought you might like to come down. I've arranged a hike tomorrow.'

'Thank you for letting me know.' Vincent tried to make himself sound brisk and business-like to deceive Mr Fowler.

'I'll get you a room at a hotel. The house will be pretty full. Let me know your train and I'll see Fayers meets you.'

'I'll phone you back in my lunch hour.' Vincent put down the receiver and apologised to Mr Fowler.

'It's all right this once. Mr Pearman. As long as it doesn't become a habit.'

Vincent went back to his position, biting his lip with excitement. A queue had formed in front of Miss Glass, but as Vincent returned a few people made a new line in front of him. Fox obviously intended his group to be the core of the Party, that was why he wanted them to meet him, their leader. A cold thought occurred to him. Suppose Fox had a potential leader in his group that he wanted to introduce to Vincent. He paid out twelve pounds ten to a woman in a hat decorated with speckled feathers. If Fox had a leader in mind, what did he plan for Vincent? But Vincent didn't want a role behind the scenes, he wanted to lead, and Madame Vera had said he could lead. When he had talked to Fox last weekend he had been taken by surprise at his own oratory.

He had his lunch break at twelve. He and Miss Glass took alternate weeks for the early lunch which they both preferred. At one o'clock the café was full and although Miss Glass brought her own sandwiches and only had a cup of coffee, she had to wait in the queue just the same.

Vincent ate his lunch very quickly and then walked up the road to the post-office to telephone Fox. It was a long procedure. First he had to have change from the post-office clerk, and then wait for a free telephone. The kiosk smelt terribly of stale smoke and there was a piece of cake lying in the dust on the floor. He telephoned the station to find out the train times, then he rang his mother to tell her he wouldn't be seeing her. She sounded so upset that he compromised and promised to drop in for half an hour – half an hour *only* – directly after work, but she wasn't to make a fuss when he left. Next he telephoned the enquiries for Fox's number, and finally he spoke to Fox.

'My train arrives at ten past ten.'

'I'll get Fayers to bring you here. He can wait and take you back to the hotel afterwards.'

'I thought I might go straight to the hotel, it will be late.'

'No time to talk in the morning. We leave at half past seven. You'd better get them to give you an early call.'

'You mean you want me to hike too?' Vincent was longing to get out of the phone box away from the germs and the particles of food in the receiver. He opened the door a little way to let in some air.

'Of course. Do you good. Get your muscles working again.'

'I don't know that I'm up to it.'

'Bring some stout shoes,' said Fox firmly, 'in case I can't get hold of some spare boots.'

'Where are you going?' asked Mrs Pearman plaintively. 'I didn't know you had friends in the country.'

'There's no reason why you should,' said Vincent.

'I'm not trying to pry darling, I'm only interested. I'm *glad* you've made some new friends. I've always thought you spend too much time on your own.'

'I'm bored by people for their own sake. I prefer to be by myself unless I'm really interested.'

'Then I'm glad you've found some interesting friends,' said Mrs

Pearman. 'Come along and have your tea. I know you haven't much time.'

'I'll just have a cup of tea,' said Vincent going into the dining-room.

'I've made a chocolate cake,' Mrs Pearman pointed to the table. It sat in the centre of the table closely resembling Mr Fowler's pork-pie hat. Beside it was a plate of cream-filled biscuits and another of paste sandwiches. 'Liver paste, darling,' said Mrs Pearman.

'No thank you mother, I really can't eat anything. It's all too rich. Besides you know chocolate cake makes me wheeze.'

Mrs Pearman looked at him anxiously. 'Do you feel wheezy now?'

'No, I'm perfectly well. I've simply come to the conclusion that all this kind of thing . . .' he indicated the table . . . 'is unhealthy.'

'Something *is* the matter,' she interrupted. 'Is your digestion a bit dicky?'

'Oh mother,' he said irritably, 'can't I have a cup of tea and nothing else, if that's what I want. I'm not getting enough exercise and I'm eating the wrong foods. I want to cut down on the starch, and as a matter of fact I'm going for a hike this week-end.'

'I always think if you enjoy what you eat, then it does you good. Have a tiny slice of cake, Vincent. I made it specially for you.'

'You've made too many cakes specially for me,' he answered. 'You didn't really give my upbringing proper thought. You just indulged me to make it easy for yourself. It's mothers like you who make the men today so unmanly – mother's boys. I didn't leave home soon enough. You've only got to look at those physically and mentally flabby youths without a decent patriotic thought between them to know that their mothers fed them on chocolate cake.'

'I only did what I thought was best,' said Mrs Pearman meekly, pouring the tea.

'I won't be in, in the morning,' said Vincent to Miss Glass from a station telephone kiosk. 'I think I've got 'flu. Will you explain?' He hoped she couldn't hear the noise of trains and wagons and voices that were almost blotting out her replies.

'Well?' asked Fox, letting him in, 'have you thought any more about it?'

Fayers climbed out of the driver's seat and into the back. 'I'll doze while I'm waiting. Will you be long, Colonel?'

'Oh, half an hour, I suppose.' Fox took Vincent's coat and hung it on the coat stand. Last week it had hung there alone, but tonight there were several other coats and raincoats hooked on top of one another.

'The boys are asleep,' said Fox, as Vincent followed him into the living-room and sat down. Fox seemed tremendously excited.

Vincent said, 'I've made some notes towards our manifesto.'

Fox stood in front of the mantelpiece. There was no fire tonight. 'To be honest all week I was half-hearted, it seemed too monumental a task. But when the boys arrived tonight I had the feeling that we could go ahead, because they have adopted my principles already, they are our hard core on which to build the flesh.'

'I thought the same thing,' said Vincent. 'In fact core was the very word I used.'

Fox took a big torch, cased in black rubber, from the mantelpiece. 'Would you like to see them?'

'Yes, I would.' Vincent stood up and together they walked upstairs.

Fox paused outside the room which had been his mother's, then opened the door softly. Vincent was first aware of the freezing night air which came in through the wide open window. The bed had been pushed up against the wall and three boys were lying in sleeping bags on the floor. Their haversacks and clothes were in a pile in the corner. Fox's torch shone in turn on each sleeping face. 'Ronnie Finch,' he said. In spite of the light the boy didn't move or screw his eyes. Vincent could see that he wore glasses, by the red mark across the bridge of his nose. 'David Walker, Charles Jessop.' He let the torch light rest on this last boy, the light exactly encircling the round face, and making it white. 'He's still at school,' said Fox. 'Seventeen, the son of a local magistrate, and I would say a born leader, games captain and senior prefect. Most of the others are carried along, but this one has the right qualities.'

The boy moved and said sharply, 'Turn that bloody torch off.'

Fox pushed the switch with his thumb and the room was lit only by the quarter moon. He turned and led the way on to the landing and quietly shut the door.

'You think he might make a leader?' asked Vincent, not wanting to sound anxious. The boy had everything in his favour, all the assets which Vincent didn't possess. Because of his background, Jessop was born to lead.

'Not yet of course,' said Fox, 'a kid of seventeen isn't likely to command much following. But later, when we need to hand over to a younger man.' He opened another door and Vincent looked in. The furniture in the room was covered by dustsheets, and several boys lay on the floor, like the others, in sleeping bags zipped up to their chins. One was snoring.

'Where did you meet them all?' asked Vincent. Fox put his finger to his lips as the snorer jerked and turned on to his side. He tiptoed back on to the landing. Vincent suddenly thought of Mrs Darling tiptoeing out of the nursery on the night Peter Pan was to take the children away. She had tiptoed out like this, holding up one finger for silence. Mrs Pearman always cried at this particular scene, knowing the heartache to come. She cried at the end too, when the children came back.

Fox shut the door. 'We'd better get some sleep too. Don't over-eat at breakfast, have something light. I'll expect you at about seven fifteen.'

'Where did you find these boys?' asked Vincent again. It seemed so wonderful to have formed a group like this.

'Oh, I advertised locally. And I suggested to one or two head-masters that healthy outdoor activities, properly organised, might keep some of the older boys away from coffee bars and clubs. They were quite keen. Not everyone could manage this week-end, of course. We have a fuller membership during the holidays.'

Vincent opened the front door and the light from the hall illu-minated the car, waking Fayers. He jumped out and held the door for Vincent, then climbed into the front. Vincent called good night to Fox, who remained standing, silhouetted on the step, until the car turned out of the drive.

The hotel was next to the station. It was an Edwardian house, with a plastered front painted cream. A panel of glass above the front door bore the words Fernhurst Family Hotel. An RAC badge and a bed-and-breakfast sign hung at the side of the porch. Fayers parked outside, took Vincent's attaché case out of the boot and walked ahead up the steps to the front door.

'The wife has gone to bed, Sir. But you'll have your breakfast at six sharp. The colonel told me you'd want to be at his place soon after seven.'

'Thank you.' Vincent followed Fayers past the dining-room where half a dozen breakfast tables with white cloths were set with knives, forks and plastic cruets.

His room was on the first floor and had curtains with a floral design and a washbasin. The water was very hot and everything looked clean. When Fayers had left him, Vincent felt the mattress and looked out of the window. Below was a square of garden, and beyond the railway station. A train shrieked past, rattling the window. He drew the curtain and out of habit crossed to the door and locked it. When he was in bed he propped the pillow against the plastic leather headboard, and holding the papers towards the small light on the bedtable, began once again to read his manifesto. Half an hour later, inspired, he turned out the light and went to sleep.

He ate his breakfast in the dining-room, alone except for Mrs Fayers. She was grey haired and gauntly thin. Her chin met her neck in turkey-like tendrons, and when she smiled she showed the shell-pink artificial gums of her false teeth. She served Vincent with cornflakes and a boiled egg. 'The colonel said you wouldn't want anything fried.' At seven Fayers appeared and Vincent drank the dregs of his tea and went out to the car. At a quarter past he was in the hall of Fox's house being introduced to the boys. They all wore hiking boots and shorts, Fox's being military issue, wide khaki ones which stopped just above his knees. Jessop was in leder-hosen. He was taller than the others, very handsome with a straight nose and blue eyes. Two of the others wore scout uniforms and hats. They were hoisting their knapsacks on to their shoulders and Vincent felt out of place in his sports jacket and flannel trousers. He wished he hadn't put on a tie, but tucked a scarf into the neck of his shirt as Fox had done.

'Here are your boots,' said Fox. Vincent sat down on the stairs and unlaced his well-polished shoes. The boots looked enormous, like army boots. Because of his asthma he had been unfit for military service – to his mother's relief – and his feet had never been subjected to such huge and heavy protection. When he put them on he felt clumsy and almost numbed as if he had club feet. He stood up and walked across the hall. The boots made a loud noise and in his mind he could hear them all marching, crunching down on the surface of the road like a regiment.

Fox had spread out a map on the floor and they all crouched round it as he pointed out the route.

'We'll be back by six. Then when we've eaten we'll have a bit of a pow-wow. Pearman here and I have a few ideas to put to you.' He folded up the map. 'Okay everyone, shall we go?'

Vincent felt strange walking in his hiking boots. The boys swung off down the drive and he followed with Fox, very conscious that he had made no impression on them, that he had scarcely even spoken. He felt physically inferior and he would have liked to have made a mental impact to counteract it. Even Fox, nearly twenty years his senior, even the boy with boils on his neck, were more upright and fit.

They turned out of the drive and along the lane, walking in twos and threes, talking and whistling, their knapsacks jogging up and down.

'We're going through some glorious countryside,' said Fox.

'What do we do about lunch?' asked Vincent.

'We've got sandwiches and fruit,' Fox said, 'I've taken enough for you, I didn't think you'd want a knapsack.'

The road became a track between hawthorn hedges. Puddles had evaporated, leaving cracked and shiny patches; the mud had dried into hard ridges which broke down into powdery dust beneath Vincent's boots. He found it a pleasant sensation, like putting his hands into the starched pockets of his cotton jacket. He was beginning to feel warm and wished he had thought of bringing it. Normally he wore it only on the hottest summer days. It was khaki coloured and had one or two tiny moth-holes.

The track turned left into a field, a stile divided them. The boys jumped over and Vincent tried to do the same, but as he landed on a lump of turf his ankle bent inwards painfully. No one saw him and he straightened up at once.

'You'll meet the older members tonight,' said Fox, striding along beside him, 'they couldn't come this morning.'

'Who are they?' Vincent asked.

'There's one schoolmaster, another ex-army chap, a shop-keeper.'

The two boys at the front, Jessop and Ronnie Finch, the one with glasses, began to sing and the others joined in. Fox smiled at Vincent and sang as well.

'Of Hector and Lysander and such great names as these.' The rhythm helped Vincent to walk faster. He sang very softly, inhibited, it was a long time since he had sung in public. They had now crossed the field. The ground was bumpy, his ankle still hurt, and to his horror he could feel his breathing becoming asthmatic. He knew that before they had gone much further he would have difficulty in preventing his wheezes becoming audible. The lane that led from the field – no stile this time but a big wooden gate, bleached almost white and fastened by an iron bolt – was bordered by woods on one side and more fields on the other. It was uphill. Vincent began to feel tired and more and more breathless. He glanced at his watch and saw that they had been walking for almost two hours. The boys were singing one song after another. Some he had learned at school, others he had heard but didn't know the words, in any case he had no breath for singing.

'We'll stop when we get to the top of the hill,' said Fox. It rose steeply, turned a bend and could be seen, still inclining, across the fields.

'Underneath the lamplight by the barrack gate,' sang the boys.

Vincent put one heavy foot in front of the other automatically, his legs aching, his lungs constricted. He thought if he stopped, even for a second, he would never be able to start walking again.

'My Lilli of the lamplight, my own Lilli Marlene,' sang Fox

loudly, just in front of him. Vincent suddenly remembered a similar discomfort, when his headmaster had, on a whim, sent the whole school out on a run across Hampstead Heath. It was on a spring day, like today, and the urge for exercise for his boys had smitten the headmaster, in the arbitrary way ideas always struck him. Fire drill, air-raid drill, an hour's hymn singing, a visit to bomb sites, all these had been ordered at a moment's notice to the surprise and bewilderment of boys and staff alike. The run across the Heath had been hell. Vincent had been last, stumbling, almost sobbing as he panted across the uneven ground, while the headmaster rode alongside on his bicycle, exhorting him. In those days he hadn't an inhaler; he longed to use it now, to break up the phlegm that had formed and was making the breath bubble in his throat. He could feel the inhaler in his pocket bumping against his thigh, but it needed more courage to use it than to stumble on. Then at last they were at the top, with a panoramic view below, and stopping Vincent felt he was on the point of fainting. Every pulse in his body seemed to be jumping, his blood pounding in his veins. He gasped like a goldfish. The boys flung themselves down on the grass verge, some lay back with their hands under their heads and others put their heads down on their knees. After a few moments they pulled off their knapsacks and took out apples and oranges and bread and cheese. Fox held out an apple to Vincent. 'Want one?'

He shook his head, he couldn't speak.

Jessop bit into an apple. Juice ran down his chin and he wiped it off with the back of his other hand.

Vincent felt ashamed, miserable, humiliated and ill. His ankle hurt. His feet hurt. His shoulders were hunched in his efforts to breathe.

'It's tough if you're not used to it,' said Jessop, throwing his apple core across the road into the opposite hedge. Its impact was such that it disappeared like a bullet into the barrier of leaves. He stood up and his thighs and knees beneath the short grey lederhosen, looked immensely strong. Thick blond hairs covered them from the knees down to short socks. Because they were so close Vincent could see freckles under the hairs. Jessop's legs represented everything that he was not, athletic, young, blond.

'Come on you lazy bastards,' said Jessop, 'let's go.'

'I don't think I can go any further,' Vincent said to Fox with difficulty. 'I'll rest a bit longer and then make my own way back.'

'I'll telephone to Fayers from the next village if you like,' Fox suggested. 'He can take you back.'

'Oh would you,' wheezed Vincent gratefully. 'I really am rather exhausted.'

'You look pretty done in,' said the boy with the blazing neck boil that had bobbed at Vincent's eye level all morning.

'Only too happy to oblige,' said Jessop. 'I'll go on ahead, shall I colonel? What's the number?'

Fox told him and he nodded, repeated it, and walked off. Ronnie Finch stood up and followed, catching him up at the brow of the hill.

'See you tonight then,' said Fox. He put on his haversack and the boys did the same. Vincent longed for them to be gone so that he could use his inhaler.

He watched in relief as they walked away with their astounding energy, and when they were all out of sight he knelt up on the grass and took out his inhaler. He unwound the long coil of thin rubber tube from the glass siphon and pumped and pumped. Gradually his breathing became calmer. He lay back waiting for Fayers.

He must change his name. He must have a name they could respect, just as they must respect him. Tonight he must blot out this weak image. Whatever else happened he must assert himself, surprise them. He might not be able to walk for miles, but he could stir their emotions, excite them to another kind of action. The name suddenly occurred to him, one of those flashes that come without effort. He would call himself Wright. It was simple, short, indicative. It could be rhymed of course, but it rhymed with good words, might, and fight and light. Fight for Right with Wright. He looked up at the sky, it was mid-day and the sun was directly above him. He shut his eyes against it and patterns moved over his eyelids, blue vein-like ravelled designs, spotted with red and gold. Gradually his body was returning to normal, the aches were subsiding, he no longer gasped. Yes, tonight he would fire them with enthusiasm. Slowly he went over the points in his mani-

festo; a vow to do everything in the power of the Party to make
England an independent nation; to rid it of non-aryan blood and
prevent marriages between Jews and Christians, blacks and whites;
to free the country from corrupt business-men; to try at all times
to instil the Party principles into the youth of the country; to
stamp out all forms of decadence in so called popular culture, and
to foster national art and music and literature; to encourage pure
British women to breed from aryan men; to re-establish the British
Empire in all its former strength and glory; to support such move-
ments as apartheid and other allied organisations.

While he lay there, phrasing and rephrasing, he heard Fayers's
car come slowly up the hill to take him back.

Chapter 4

'You couldn't quite make it then, Sir,' said Fayers, driving down the hill which had been so agonising to climb. Vincent lay back on the soft brown leather, his feet slowly emerging from their anaesthetised condition and beginning to ache, just as if an injection of cocaine was losing its effect.

'I'm not in training,' he snapped. He didn't want to talk about it, but Fayers insisted.

'The colonel's pretty strong. He's tougher than a lot of younger men. He can walk them off their feet, I've seen him.'

'I'm glad you were free anyway,' said Vincent, 'because it would have taken me a long time to walk back.' He spoke with a forced smile.

'The Colonel always has little jobs for me when he's got his boys down. He keeps me on call for the day. I've got to pick up Mr Patterson later, off the London train, and it wouldn't surprise me if he phoned again, like he did for you.'

All Vincent wanted was to take off his boots and sticky clothes and lie in a hot bath. It was still early, not yet one o'clock. Perhaps he could have some sandwiches and coffee in his room. He even had time for a sleep before the hikers returned.

'Will you be able to run me back to the colonel's house about six o'clock?' he asked Fayers.

'Mr Patterson's train gets in at five, Sir,' Fayers said without taking his eyes off the road. His neck was very red and thick with several deep lines that looked seeded with dirt, although Vincent was sure this was a visual illusion. Fayers gave the impression of being fanatically clean. 'Would you have any objection riding along with him to save me the double journey?'

'No, I don't mind.' They had reached the hotel. 'Who is Mr Patterson, Fayers?'

'A school-teacher friend of the colonel's, an Australian gentleman.' Fayers held open the door for Vincent. 'Shall I tell the wife you'll be in for lunch?'

Vincent asked if he might have sandwiches in his room. The steps up to the front door were cleaned white with hearthstone and his boots left big black imprints.

'Of course you can, Sir,' said Fayers.

Vincent went quietly upstairs past the dining-room. There was a fatty smell of cooked lamb and he could see Mrs Fayers in a striped overall clearing plates. He caught a glimpse of a suet pudding crowned with white grease on the sideboard. The lino-leum at the top of the stairs shone with polish. His room smelt fresh and was very tidy, his brushes were arranged on the dressing-table and his dressing-gown had been put away in the wardrobe. He shut the door, sank down on the bed and took off his boots. His socks smelt and the soles were dirty. Vincent was fastidious about his cleanliness. He dropped the boots down on to the floor and the impact shook off a powder of dry mud or dung. He peeled off his socks and let them fall on to the boots. Mrs Fayers knocked at the door and came in and asked what he would like in his sand-wiches, revealing her plastic gums on the word cheese. Anything would do, Vincent told her, ham or cheese or egg, whatever she had. When she returned with a tray she left the door open and a few seconds later came back with a brush and dustpan and swept up the mess his boots had made. Then to his embarrassment she picked up the boots and the socks and went out with them.

As soon as she had gone Vincent locked the door and undressed, and put on his dressing-gown which was camel hair with a green silk cord edging the lapels and looping into a design on the pocket. He washed his hands twice before he sat down on the dressing-table chair and ate his sandwiches.

When he had finished eating he brushed all the crumbs off the front of his dressing-gown, took his washing things and towel and went along the corridor to have a bath. A notice hung over it saying that a bath cost a shilling extra and would he leave it as he would like to find it. A tin of vim and a cloth were on the window-sill for the purpose, and a further notice, Please Leave the Bath-room Clean, was tucked into the corner of the mirror. The geyser lit with an explosive blast, and the first rush of water from the tap brought with it a tiny shower of rust particles which reminded Vincent of a bottle of Danziger Goldwasser his mother had once received as a gift from a more travelled friend, and had never opened. He let the rust drain away, and replaced the plug, and the bath filled. He climbed in and let it fill round him. When he had been a little boy he used to see his parents in the bath but they always spread flannels over their genitals and Vincent, copying them as a child, had retained the habit and now carefully floated a flannel over his groin. It was a pink flannel, and it rested on the surface of the water for some minutes until it slowly submerged and settled gently on his thighs. He had never seen his parents naked, they had always been censored by flannels, his father with just one, his mother with a second clinging to her breasts.

He sat in the bath, his head resting against the curved enamel, consciously relaxing. He was so tired he made no effort to get out until the water was lukewarm and his finger tips were white and crinkly. Back in the bedroom he lay on the bed and fell asleep, not waking until Mrs Fayers knocked at the door with his tea. She came in and he pulled himself up on to his elbow.

'I hope I've brought you enough.' She held the tray under his nose. There was some buttered toast, now cold, into which the butter had disappeared, two half slices of bread and butter and a fairy cake in a paper case.

'That looks very nice.'

'You were tired, weren't you?' she said, pouring him a cup of tea and bringing it over to the bedside table. He saw that his boots were back, cleaned. 'Not used to all that walking, I expect.'

'I work in a bank,' said Vincent, 'I don't have the opportunity to go for walks.'

'I've got a niece in the bank,' said Mrs Fayers. She stood with her hand on the doorknob. 'You haven't known the colonel long then?'

'No, only a week or so.'

'Don't think I'm prying. But all the colonel's friends stay here. We get to know them.'

'I expect I shall be coming down quite often now,' Vincent answered.

'He's been ever so good to us,' Mrs Fayers said. 'He lent us the money to start this place after the war. Goodness knows what we'd have done otherwise. And he sends all his friends. Mr Patterson's staying tonight as well.'

Vincent bit into the cold toast, trying not to show his surprise.

'This is Mr Patterson,' said Fayers, opening the door. The man climbed in. He was small boned and small featured, with sandy hair. He wore a grey flannel suit.

'Hallo there Pearman,' he said, with a strong Australian accent. 'I know all about you.'

Vincent felt there was a conspiracy from which he was excluded. First there had been the revelation about the hotel, unimportant really, no reason for Fox to have told him, and yet he felt excluded from a secret. Fayers and Fox were closer than their behaviour indicated. And now Patterson knew about him, obviously from Fox, while he knew nothing at all about Patterson. It galled him.

They sat in silence as Fayers drove them out of the station.

'Have you been in England long?' Vincent asked, feeling he must make conversation.

'Too bloody long,' said Patterson looking out of the window. In profile his blunt nose scarcely protruded beyond the contour of the cheek. He made no effort to talk pleasantly. Vincent felt he was being snubbed, the whole day had been an indignity, from his failure on the hike – not merely in walking but in making contact with the boys – to this disinterest on the part of Patterson.

'There's the colonel,' said Fayers, sounding his horn. They had turned a bend and in front of them, spread out across the lane were the hikers ambling home, Jessop still at the head, Fox at the rear, but no one flagging. At the noise of the engine they stood to one side and smiled and waved as the car drove past.

'I hope the house isn't bloody locked,' said Patterson.

The back door was open and Vincent and Patterson went in together, across the kitchen. Vincent hadn't seen the kitchen before, it was painted green and impeccably tidy, not a cup or a tin or a piece of food visible. The cooker was an old gas one, discoloured but clean, and the sink was chipped but scrubbed.

'It's an obsession, this endless scouring and scrubbing,' said Patterson. 'Did you know he's up at five every morning doing the housework. He doesn't trust his charwoman to clean properly. She's only allowed to do the washing and brush the dog.'

'You're a teacher, aren't you?' asked Vincent, as they crossed the hall to the sitting-room.

'In one of your primitive institutions,' said Patterson. The dog flew out of the room yapping at their legs. Vincent patted it.

'You know me boy. Quiet now.'

'Oh, shut up, will you,' shouted Patterson.

He went ahead of Vincent into the sitting-room and sat down on one of the armchairs. The warm, hairy dent in the cushion of the other indicated that the dog had slept there most of the day.

'Where do you teach?' asked Vincent.

'In a charming slum. I've got a class full of nigger kids.' He yawned and looked round the room. 'I wonder where he's hidden the liquor.'

'He doesn't drink,' said Vincent.

'But he likes to stock up for his boys. Our Jessop enjoys a spot of whisky when he's let out of school.'

'How did you meet him?' Vincent asked. 'Are you a collector too?'

'I'm strictly a one suitcase man,' said Patterson. 'What's your impression of the little museum upstairs?'

'Very comprehensive.' Vincent was thinking again about Fayers and Fox. 'Did you know the colonel financed the hotel?'

'Fayers was his batman all through the war. He could afford the gesture.' He pointed to a group photograph, postcard size, which hung beside the desk, framed in passe partout. Vincent went over and looked at it. He saw Fox in the centre looking younger, but otherwise the same. Then he found Fayers, almost unrecognisable, slim and handsome. They wore shorts and berets and Fox had a scarf at his neck, so that except for the beret he had been dressed the same this morning.

'Here they are,' said Patterson, as the front door opened and the sound of boots and voices could be heard in the hall. He went out to greet them and Vincent listened to the exchange of familiar

greetings and wished he knew them well too. After a moment he
followed Patterson and stood leaning against the lintel of the door.
The big hall was not big enough for the huddle of figures, limbs
extended, elbows jutting, as boots were unlaced and packed knapsacks dropped to the floor. There was a strong smell of sweat, of
heated bodies, a sense of healthy tiredness.

'Go and get cleaned up,' Fox shouted above the noise. 'Then
we'll have some grub.' He smiled at Vincent over the heads of the
boys as he climbed the stairs.

Patterson had edged across to Jessop. They might have belonged
to different species, thought Vincent. Jessop was almost six feet
tall, blond, pink-faced from the exertions of the day, his skin still
soft although of course he shaved, but probably not every day. He
would always be one of those men who never needed a second
shave. But Patterson had a hard, tough, greyish skin, and he was
small, five foot six, with thin hands and nicotine-stained middle
fingers and nails. He was talking intently to Jessop, who was
listening, smiling.

One by one the boys went upstairs, and Vincent heard their
footsteps overhead, taps running, voices calling. Fox came down
again, changed now into flannels and check shirt and asked Vincent
to give him a hand with the supper. Together they went into the
kitchen and Fox fried sausages and eggs in an enormous frying pan
while Vincent buttered slices of bread from cut loaves. The boys
came down to the kitchen wearing fresh clothes and with their hair
watered and combed. They knew the routine, took plates from the
cupboard over to Fox, who doled out sausages and eggs straight
from the pan. They took the buttered bread faster than Vincent
could spread it. 'Bloody hungry,' they said. 'Starving.' Then they
carried their plates into the living-room where Patterson was
pouring out the beer. Jessop had a transistor radio, about the size
of a packet of twenty cigarettes, which he stood beside him on the
floor and fiddled with the dial until he found Luxembourg.

'Well?' asked Patterson, 'Did you have a good day?'

'Ghastly row,' said Fox to Jessop, bringing in his own and
Vincent's supper. 'Can't stand this modern music, can you?'

'I don't like it,' answered Vincent, cutting into a sausage that was packed tight into its skin and slithered on the plate. He was holding the plate in one hand, the fork in the other. He sat down on the floor beside Jessop and Fox, and neatly cut a section of the sausage.

The doorbell rang, and Fox went out to answer it, returning a few minutes later with a stout, reddish-faced man in his fifties, wearing what Vincent called to himself working-class best, a blue suit with wide pin-stripes, wide lapels, wide trouser legs, the kind of suit that came into the bank sometimes just as they were closing on the local half day. Vincent placed it, a tradesman, self-employed. Fox brought the man over to Vincent, and he stood up quickly, not wanting the embarrassment of an introduction while he crouched over a sausage on the floor.

'I want you to meet Jim Dobson,' said Fox. They shook hands. Patterson poured a glass of beer and handed it to him. Dobson took it, smiling round at the boys, who knew him. He sat down on one of the armchairs and began to talk to the boys nearest to him about the cup final. Vincent sat down again, listening to the conversation. Dobson seemed to be of low intelligence, a male Miss Glass, amiable, friendly, Vincent wondered just what the tie-up was with Fox. Did he collect Nazi relics, was he an outdoor enthusiast, an admirer of boys, just another ex-army colleague?

'I'll give you a game of darts when you've finished,' said Dobson to the boy beside him, who was wiping his plate with bread. Soon everyone had finished eating, and taking the plates into the kitchen, each washed his own, dried it and put it away, while Fox supervised, his shirt sleeves rolled up, a drying-up cloth tucked into the top of his trousers. Once the boys had gone he took a mop and swabbed the floor, wiped over the stove and the sink, washed his hands up to the elbows with detergent, buttoned down his cuffs and went back to the sitting-room. Patterson was smoking, his legs tucked up under him on the chair. Dobson and several boys had gone to play darts upstairs, Jessop was reading a copy of a physique magazine and another boy was sitting on the floor staring into space.

'I'll get out the bagatelle board,' Fox said. He took a folding table from behind the curtains, and opened it up.

'I'll get it,' said Jessop, throwing down the magazine. He went out, bringing back an old bagatelle board which he placed carefully on the table. Patterson and the other boy stood up and the five of them gathered round the table to play. Jessop won the first game and Vincent thought he seemed unduly pleased. When he lost three successive games he became bored and irritated, and wandered out of the room. Dobson came downstairs, with a couple of boys, looking for more beer.

'What's the time?' Fox asked Patterson.

'Half past nine.'

'Ready?' Fox said to Vincent.

'You mean to talk?'

Fox nodded. 'Whenever you like,' said Vincent.

Fox put the bagatelle board away and moved the table to the fireplace end of the room. Then he carried in two chairs from the kitchen and placed them behind it.

'I'd like some water,' said Vincent. Fox fetched a glass and a glass jug of water and put them on the table, then he went to the foot of the stairs and called out. 'Come on down boys, we're going to have a bit of talk.'

The boys came down, and sat on the floor in rows, facing the table, with Patterson and Dobson in the two armchairs at the back. Fox motioned Vincent to sit behind the table, but remained standing himself. There was a slight movement as one or two boys lit cigarettes, shifted their legs and made themselves comfortable.

'Everyone settled?' said Fox. He waited for a few seconds more before he began. 'Pearman and I have been having a discussion or two, and have come to some conclusions which I think you'll find interesting. I'm not a speaker, so I'm going to leave the explanations to him. Afterwards you can put your questions. Okay Pearman, it's all yours.'

Vincent stood up and surveyed them. He experienced a sensation that was almost physical, a curious thrill that they were all men, giving the meeting a far greater seriousness than if women – women like his mother and Miss Glass and Pamela – were sitting there. Quietly, without much expression in his voice, he began to speak.

'Most of you I only met today,' he said. 'One or two of you I have known a little longer. I know none of you well. I am having, therefore, to make some basic assumptions but I have a feeling they are not wrong.' Jessop looked round for an ashtray, half stood and stretched out for it. Vincent waited while he knocked the ash off his cigarette. 'The first assumption is that we are all patriots, that our country is important to us, that in some way we feel deep inside us we have a duty, a shared duty to the land of our birth. I know, obviously, that the majority of you get great pleasure from walking through the countryside – I would too, if I had your youth and stamina. I venture to say however, that whether or not my legs are strong enough to carry me up the steepest hill or over large distances, no one . . .' He shouted the word no one and banged his hand on the table, and everyone started and looked at him . . . 'No one loves it more deeply, feels it a part of his own blood and bones and flesh than I do.'

He had their complete attention. His voice was lower again. 'I must admit however to a sense of shame.' The word shame was practically a whisper. 'Not, as you may think, because I cannot keep up the brisk pace you set on a march – that is a mere physical thing, splendid though it is in youth – and by a little training, by steady exercise, effort, I will soon be striding along with you.' He glanced at Fox. Fox was looking down at his hands. He didn't want the boys to adulate Fox because of his physical prowess. 'No. The realisation of where my failure lies is in the apathy with which I have looked on a succession of governments, at a succession of ministers and politicians frittering away the strength of the country for a whole variety of reasons. And what of the people? What do they do except to grumble on each budget day, to try and work less hours for more money, to bet on the pools and fill the bingo halls. And the youth? What of them? With their clothes and records, their scooters and' his eyes met Jessop's, 'their transistor radios.' Jessop looked away. 'I'm not saying that you should not have these things, that people shouldn't enjoy themselves. What I am saying is that these must not be an end in themselves as they are at present – the symbols of greed and self-indulgence,' his voice rose. 'But you don't need me to tell you this. I am sure that every one of you must at sometime or another have thought about it, and perhaps like me, felt guilty.'

The door opened and Fayers tiptoed in and stood at the back beside Dobson's chair, they were not unalike in appearance, both big heavy men with unrefined features, weathered complexions.

'What I am hoping,' said Vincent fervently, 'is that we here, we few, can band together to make the nucleus of a group, a movement, a party, which if it does nothing else will move the British people to an awareness of the depths to which they have sunk, of the greatness they are throwing away, of the tradition and heritage which they are so carelessly denying. Let there be no mistake. The task is monumental. The whole structure of our society is worm-eaten with selfishness, rotten with laziness. We are like a great overfed animal fattening itself to be the prey of other more wily creatures. And clinging to the back of this creature, sucking and feeding on its flesh, are a host of parasites; drifters, layabouts, profiteers, immigrants. Everywhere the situation is reflected in the fits and starts of a feeble economy; the get-rich-quick tycoons squatting over money-bags; transport a tangled and inefficient web which will take years to unravel; a culture based on pop art. And everywhere, everywhere, an apathy which stifles action, on the one hand the Conservatives proposing a wild free-for-all which has largely resulted in this very situation, on the other the Labourites with their watered-down Communism, that black spider threatening to poison us all. What is the answer?' He banged the table again. 'WE ARE. We must have strength and unity. We must have purpose and responsibility. We must be strong and self-sufficient and fight to bring back the greatness of our country.'

He stopped and poured out a glass of water and drank it all. Everyone moved their positions, no one spoke, yet he could see they were affected. Quietly he started to speak again.

'I see I've already been speaking for some time, but there is much more I want to say. Let me put it to you. Do you want me to go on?'

'We do,' said Fox at his side. 'We do indeed.'

'Go on. Go on,' said the boys on the floor.

'Very well,' Vincent felt a glow of success. 'I have prepared a manifesto of fifteen points which I feel must be the vertebrae of our movement.' He recited them slowly, sensing their response. 'These are the points we must accept, there may be others which we can add later. Now I come to the practical matters – electing a committee, fund-raising, recruitment.'

A boy in the second row began to speak. 'Mr Pearman, I just want to ask . . .'

Vincent held up both hands, his speech unhalting. 'Please. Questions later.' He outlined his plans, the headquarters here in Fox's house, a London cell, gradually cells in every town as the movement grew, a uniform, an insignia. 'I've designed one,' he said. 'I thought we might have a white ground with a centrally placed green disc representing the world. And over this disc, reaching out to the edges of the flag, the red cross of Saint George.' The next meeting, he suggested, should be the following Sunday, its aim to arrange the first public meeting. 'We must practise discipline of body and mind,' he finished up, 'we must be physically strong and mentally ruthless, we have a tremendous task before us.'

He sat down. For a few seconds there was silence and then the applause broke out and continued until Fox stood up and thanked him.

'You have inspired us all. To thank you for talking is inadequate. I know that everyone here is with me when I unhesitatingly propose you as leader of our Party.'

'I second that,' said Jessop standing.

'Are there any other nominations?' There was silence. 'Then I proclaim Vincent Pearman leader of the Party.'

'Wright,' said Vincent. 'I have changed my name to Wright. From now on I am to be known as Vincent Wright.'

'What shall we call the Party?' asked Dobson.

'Britain First,' answered Vincent. 'I've thought about this a lot. The sheer simplicity of Britain First has won me over other alternatives. Now I would like to propose Colonel Fox as secretary and Deputy Leader.'

Patterson seconded him. Dobson was elected treasurer. Fox declared the meeting closed, and Vincent asked Fayers to run him back to the hotel. He left with Patterson, and the boys were still talking excitedly, drinking more beer. Already he could visualise them in some kind of uniform, the armband insignia encircling those muscular biceps.

Chapter 5

VINCENT'S moods veered from confidence to despondency. He couldn't remember any other time in his life when he had experienced such intense emotions. The despondent periods occurred when he was alone in his flat. Then he was sure that he and Fox and a handful of youths couldn't possibly be the beginnings of a great national party. It seemed a mad fantasy that the country was ready for their kind of politics. What about the affluent middle classes, vast areas of them, did they care that Jews ran the entertainment industry, the clothing industry, owned most of the shops? Did they resent the Negroes who swept the streets outside their houses or drove them on the tube trains? It was unlikely. He kept a journal and attempted pages of a close analysis of the social scene. He made a survey of areas which might rise to his support either because there was an influx of West Indians or Greek Cypriots, or because they were already established Tory belts where Jews were denied membership of golf-clubs, and where the private schools didn't allow even a quota.

The times when he felt most confident were during the working day, when he was able to talk to Miss Glass. As he expressed himself in words the whole idea seemed possible, and when Miss Glass responded with an offended remark about British tolerance, he was able to answer that tolerance had brought Britain to where she was today, to being a third-rate nation. But what he wanted was real discussion, not Miss Glass's feeble 'Oh Mr Pearman, we're all the same under the skin.'

One night he couldn't sleep. He hadn't heard from Fox, or from Patterson who had promised to keep in touch, or Jessop who had indicated that if he could stir up interest at school he would let Vincent know. Had the idea died already? He got out of bed in frantic despair, dressed in the clothes which he had placed on the chair for tomorrow, and without a tie took the lift to the ground floor. The lift clattered and rattled making noises that were lost in the general day-time commotion. As he walked down the street he looked guiltily at the rows of unlit windows.

It was colder than he had realised, the bright full moon seemed to intensify the chill air. He passed several lovers pressed up against walls, one pair actually seemed to be in the throes of intercourse. Further along he met a lone dog pursuing a course, nose to the ground, and two policemen peering into the doorways of closed shops.

Madame Vera had not gone to bed, but once she had let him in she kept him waiting in the front room so that the session began with a row and he was convinced she was withholding some piece of vital information out of pique.

'You're not telling me everything. I know.'

'You've upset my psyche. Shouting at me like that. The aura just goes.'

'You weren't in bed. You didn't have to keep me hanging about for quarter of an hour. *Quarter of an hour.* You're beginning to make a habit of it.'

After a lot of shrugging and sighing she said he was to contact someone whose name began with the letter W. He asked for an indication when the contact should be made and she said coldly he'd probably know himself. Since his last visit a pink glass vase full of plastic daffodils had replaced the electric fire, and a sheet of the *Daily Express* covered the empty grate. He stood up, felt in his pocket and paid her. He would have liked to have walked out without another word, but she might refuse to see him again.

He went to see Mr Fowler the next morning. It was half past twelve before he was free and when Vincent went into the room he was standing between his desk and the door wearing a camel-hair coat and his hat. Like a Jew, thought Vincent sharply, wearing his hat indoors.

'What is it?' snapped Mr Fowler. 'I'm on my way to lunch.' He fiddled with his coat belt because the cloth was too thick for the buckle. 'There,' he said as he pulled it through with a sudden jerk. 'If what you want to say is going to take more than a few minutes

I'm afraid it will have to wait until this afternoon.'

'It won't take long,' said Vincent, 'I just want to tell you that I'm changing my name.'

'What on earth for?' said Mr Fowler, staring at him. His stomach rumbled. He spoke quickly, a fraction louder. 'What's wrong with your own name?'

'I don't like it.'

'Are you living with some woman?' Mr Fowler tried to look into his eyes.

'No I'm not.'

'No offence meant. I just wondered. Seems so very curious. Unorthodox, plain silly, if you don't mind my saying so.'

'I'm calling myself Wright,' said Vincent. 'I'd like my name-stand changed.'

Mr Fowler suddenly became annoyed. 'I don't know that the bank will accept it.'

'You accept it when a woman clerk marries.'

'I suppose there's no law.' Mr Fowler pulled on a pair of new-looking pigskin gloves, easing his fingers with a wriggling move-ment, each in turn. 'I don't understand you at all, personally. There's no inheritance question or anything like that is there?' Vincent shook his head. 'Then I'd like you to think about it well, Pearman and see if you can't change your mind.'

He left Vincent standing on the rucked Persian rug in the middle of the floor.

Vincent read the local paper over lunch. He ignored the impa-tient queue, and propped his paper against the water jug. Right at the foot of the page he saw a small paragraph headed Attack in Finchley. Underneath it said that George Winters and James Gary Wood had been fined for their attack on Michael Peter Gold outside a public house on the night of March 12th. The magistrate commented that only their previous good record prevented him from putting them on probation.

Vincent read it twice. There was no indication why the attack had been made, except that it had followed an argument in the bar. There was no implication that it had been for anti-semitic reasons.

But it was a possibility. Perhaps these two boys felt as he felt and in a moment of frustration had done the only thing they knew to make a gesture to society. If this was the case how grateful they would be to find an organisation which in a more logical way encouraged these very feelings.

'Here's your bill, dear,' said Doris the waitress. 'Sorry to hurry you but there's ever so many waiting today.'

He pushed threepence under the empty pudding plate and left, paying at the cash desk by the door. Was it James Gary Wood or George Winters whose presence had made itself known to Madame Vera? She said he would know when to make the contact, and he had a definite feeling that he should meet these two boys. He knew from the newspaper where they lived. He would go there tonight. There was no point in visiting them before evening. Evening was the best time to make the approach, because they could talk leisurely in a pub or a coffee bar. If he called now at a strange house, he would interrupt a mid-day meal, and his own time was limited. If he went directly the bank closed, then it was probably tea-time. In any case, it was late closing day in the West End and he had some shopping to do.

As soon as his work was finished he took the train to Oxford Circus and walked along to a government surplus store and stared in at the shirts and socks and anoraks displayed in the window. He was looking for a uniform. It had to be practical and smart, and it had to be cheap because to start with everyone must buy their own, although later he hoped there would be funds. He walked for some time, window-gazing. The conventional men's shops offered nothing. He went inside a large one to look at some khaki coloured trousers, but they weren't tough enough, or cheap enough, and khaki was the wrong colour, no point in resembling the British army. He found a men's boutique in a side road and saw in the window a grey denim jacket not unlike a workman's, with shoulder tabs and small brass military buttons. Beside it was a large photograph of two handsome young men on a beach. One was wearing the jacket with a pair of small shorts, the other with a pair of jeans. Vincent stopped and looked for some minutes, mentally putting first Jessop in the jacket and jeans, and then Fox and Patterson and himself. He went into the shop. Inside three boys were talking, wearing the kind of clothes Vincent thought of as decadent, too tight and too informal. They stopped talking as the bell rang and one boy rather reluctantly left the others and walked over to Vincent. He had the smallest mouth Vincent had even seen. It reminded him of a press-stud.

The stud popped open. 'Can I help you?' He elongated the word 'can'. Vincent's father had worked in a shop and Vincent had been brought up to expect a more servile attitude. He felt an intruder in this place.

'I'd like to see the grey jacket in the window.'

The boy took a drawer out of the cabinet behind him and put it down on the glass counter top. He took out three or four jackets in various colours. 'It comes in mauve, kingfisher and dirty pink as well.'

'I want grey,' said Vincent.

'Collar?'

'Fifteen.'

'Here you are. Want to try it?'

Vincent said he did and was shown into a small cubicle with yellow curtains. As he drew them the boy rejoined his friends.

Vincent took off his suit jacket and hung it carefully on a hook, then he tried on the grey one. As he fastened the buttons the new image grew in the glass. The high, closely buttoned collar, and the tabs on the shoulders gave him a more decisive appearance, an authoritative air. He decided to have his hair cut very short. He felt outside himself, seeing himself quite objectively, a man standing to attention in a grey uniform, a leader, obviously a leader. The yellow curtains made an imposing backcloth. He was on a platform draped with banners, speaking to his party. Then he thought, it's me, Vincent Pearman, born in Muswell Hill, Binky's friend. A tingling sensation began in his chest and leaped to his throat so violently it seemed as if it was a tangible object jumping about inside him. He had had this feeling at other times, it was more than excitement, he was fearful too because he believed he was destined and that his destiny was being carried out without his own will. He thought he saw himself, his corporal body, as well as his reflection in the glass. He had seen himself once before, sitting in Madame Vera's chair.

'How is it?' asked the boy, tweaking back the curtains and popping his head round. 'Oh, very smart.'

Vincent came out into the shop again, still wearing the jacket, seeing his reflection in the several looking glasses placed round the room.

'I'd like some grey cotton trousers.'

'Do you want a two-tone effect?' asked the boy, glancing at his friends who were still talking animatedly in the corner. 'Or a dead match?'

'I want it to match,' said Vincent. 'Exactly.'

'Gives a nice line,' answered the boy, flipping through a pile of cotton jeans. 'I quite agree. One doesn't want to be cut in half if one's on the short side. How's that?' He held up a pair.

Vincent returned to the cubicle and struggled out of his own trousers and into the jeans. He looked taller and leaner and ruthlessly efficient. He imagined a column of young men marching along a wide road, dressed in grey, arm bands on the jackets, and possibly boots, short black boots. The boy came in to him holding an orange sweater which looked to Vincent as if it had been crocheted, like the tablemats and dressing-table sets his mother made for bazaars.

'I don't know if you're interested? These have just come in.'

'I only want these. I wonder do you have a big supply?'

'We can always get them for you.'

'I might want something like forty sets. Perhaps more later.'

'Sounds fun,' said the boy. 'What's it for?'

'It's for a uniform,' Vincent answered as the boy put the clothes into a black and white bag. 'A new political movement.'

'They'll look dishy in these,' said the boy handing the bag over the counter. 'Might even join myself.' For a moment Vincent's heart soared, then he realised that the remark was merely flippant and he walked out of the shop, anxious to try the clothes on properly at home.

When he opened his front door he found two letters in the wire cage suspended under the letter box. One had been delivered by hand and was from his mother, the other posted and from Fox. Mrs Pearman said darling, why hadn't he come round this week, she was beginning to be worried but if he would only just pop in and say hallo her mind would be at rest. Fox asked him to telephone. Vincent read the letters in the hall and then, still holding the carrier bag, took them into the sitting-room and put them on the mantelpiece. He took the uniform out of the bag and spread it along the sofa, chose a record and put it on the turntable. As Wotan's joy at the sight of the completed Valhalla swelled within the ten feet by nine-and-a-half feet cream distempered walls, Vincent struggled out of his suit and into the uniform and walked about the room without seeing his reflection until the record ended. Then he went into the bedroom and stared at himself in the glass of the gently swinging wardrobe door. He thought of the knife and scabbard he had bought from Fox and in a state of great excitement pulled open the dressing-table drawer and snatched it from under the pile of handkerchiefs. He postured and snarled at the looking glass, and suddenly stopped the bellicose gesturing and smiled. He was behaving like a small boy playing at soldiers. He went back to the sitting-room to see the time. It was half past seven, and he decided to eat something at his mother's house and telephone Fox from there. Afterwards he would go to Finchley to find the boys and if they came up to expectations, were not merely thugs but had acted on a principle, then he had the beginnings of a London cell.

'What funny clothes, darling,' said Mrs Pearman tentatively after she had kissed him and closed the door.

Vincent said, 'I'm hungry, Mother, would you make me a sandwich while I phone?' He turned his back on her and dialled, irritated. He wanted to eat quickly and go.

'Of course.' She hurried happily into the kitchen and he heard the lid of the enamel bread bin clatter. 'I don't believe you're eating properly,' she called.

'Fox?' He kept his voice low.

'Things are moving here,' said Fox. 'We've scheduled a meeting for Saturday at six. We've managed to hire the church hall.'

'Aren't you being rather premature?' Vincent didn't like deci-sions to be made without him. Hadn't he been elected the leader?

'I don't think so. Dobson is advertising in the local press. We have to be out of the hall by seven. The weekly hop begins at half past.'

Through the open dining-room door Vincent glimpsed his truncated mother lurking at the hatch.

'You'll speak won't you?' Fox urged. 'We figured this was the best method to raise funds and stimulate interest at the same time. What do you think?'

'I think you may be premature,' said Vincent again, this time making a statement. 'In the meantime I'm on to something here.'

Mrs Pearman came into the hall with a pile of sandwiches on a plate. They were cut into little triangles without crusts. She pointed to the table with the telephone and mouthed 'Here?' He indicated the dining-room. 'I'll be down mid-afternoon on Saturday,' he said to Fox. He put down the receiver and followed his mother into the dining-room and ate the sandwiches while she watched.

'Enjoying them dear?'

'Delicious, mother.' He wondered whether he should tell her about his change of name and decided to wait. He foresaw her bewilderment followed by argument, which he didn't want to face at the moment.

Vincent went by underground to Finchley. People stared at his uniform but that excited him. Soon this uniform would mean something, when he wore it it would symbolise the principles of the Party, would instil a sense of fear or purpose or patriotism, just as, years ago, his father's home guard uniform had acted on him, arousing an emotional response.

In the breast pocket of his jacket he had the newspaper cutting, carefully folded. It gave the names of the boys and the street in which they lived, but not the numbers of the houses. He found the street easily. There was a public house on the corner and Vincent went in. He couldn't remember the last time he had been inside a pub, certainly not during the last five years. He thought it was probably at Butlins at Bognor Regis one Christmas, when his parents had arranged the family holiday in an effort to introduce Vincent to young people. They hadn't said so, but he knew. In fact his parents had gone out nightly to the olde tyme dancing while he had sat reading in his chalet. Before lunch each day his father virtually forced him into one of the bars. He had drunk shandy. Now, in spite of his vehement resolution to give up alcohol, he went over to the bar of the saloon and ordered one. His uniform imbued him with courage. He pretended he was a reporter and mentioned the *Daily Sketch* (Miss Glass's paper) then asked the publican, a tall man with grey hair that lay on his head like a piece of corrugated roofing, if he knew the addresses of the thugs who had beaten up Michael Peter Gold.

There was an immediate and thrilling response. This was the actual scene of the fight. The quarrel had begun in this bar. A man wearing a blazer with a double vent at the back and a handkerchief corner sticking out of the pocket above an unidentifiable crest answered excitedly. 'It's those beatniks at number ten, Windermere the house is called, Windermere, number ten. That's right, isn't it Mr Parker?' He appealed to the publican, who nodded.

'They played football in the garden the other night, had a searchlight at the window, you could see it for miles around, it was like during the war.'

'They're always playing ball,' said the wife of the man in the blazer. She had glasses and tight pink plastic beads. 'They go and ask Mrs Andrews – she lives next door – they go and ask her if they can go into her garden and fetch their ball. Grown men, they are, behaving like children, something terrible.'

'Children!' said the publican. 'It's orgies from what I hear.'

'There's ever so many of them,' said the woman to Vincent, her throat straining at the beads. 'Coming and going all the time, Mrs Andrews says she doesn't know who's living there and who isn't. It's Miss Hawkins' house really, but she's living with her sister at Southgate. She's had a stroke, the sister I mean, Miss Hawkins has gone to look after her.'

'All I can say is it would break her heart if she could see the place now,' said the man with the blazer heavily.

'We've never known anything like it,' the woman said, her voice raised, 'I said to Mrs Andrews, we might as well be living in the slums instead of a respectable road.'

'We all own our houses along here,' said the man. Vincent put down his empty glass.

'Thank you for your help.' He could barely keep his voice steady from his inward jubilation. He felt he was about to uncover the beginnings of his London cell, a group equal to Fox's group, but this one his own that he could mould right from the beginning.

'The *Daily Sketch*, is it?' asked the publican.

'That's right.'

'My name's Parker if you want a quote. I don't mind if you want to use my name.'

Vincent wanted to run up the road until he reached Windermere. He walked quickly, past the respectable neat houses, each of a slightly different design. Windermere had a gate like a ship's wheel and an oak front door. The upstairs windows were swinging open, the house had an air of desertion, the net curtains at the lower windows were dirty. The windows themselves were divided into very small panes and the ones either side of the front door were mullioned. He pushed open the gate and went up to the door and rang the bell. He didn't hear it ring and no one came. He thumped on the door with his fist. Inside a door slammed, and then the front door opened, quite slowly so that Vincent felt real suspense and until the boy was revealed to him, shortish, fair, handsome, several thoughts went through his mind. Who is going to be there? Are my premonitions going to be proved phoney? I know it's the beginning of something.

'What do you want?' said the boy.

'Are you George Winters or Peter Gary Wood?'

'Why?' asked the boy.

Vincent's voice was prim and pedantic. 'I want to talk to you. I think you'll be interested.'

'I doubt it,' said the boy.

Another boy came out of the kitchen, leaving the door open. Vincent saw an empty milk bottle and two tins of spaghetti on a table.

'Who is it?' said the second boy. He was big, heavily-built and bellicose. He had a middle-class accent.

'I don't know. Some insurance salesman or something.' Vincent thought if he didn't act quickly the door would be shut in his face.

'You stupid nit,' said the second boy to the first. 'He's probably after the rates.'

'Are you?' asked the first boy.

'No,' said Vincent. 'I'm leader of a new political party. I read about you in the paper. I think you'll be interested.'

'We've got to get them out,' said the second boy, and for a second Vincent thought he was referring to the government. 'I want to kip. They've been in bed all afternoon.'

'Come in,' said the fair boy. And Vincent was in the house.

'I'm going to smoke them out.'

'How can you?'

'It's Yates's idea. He's going to do it.' A third boy came out of the kitchen.

'When I'm ready,' he said, 'you run upstairs and shout fire. When I'm ready. I'll tell you when to do it.'

He went back into the kitchen and the boys and Vincent followed him. He stood at the sink screwing up pieces of newspaper and holding them under the tap.

'It won't work,' said the fair boy.

'What was the point of getting her over, if she goes and brings him?' said the heavily-built boy furiously. 'You should have made it clear on the phone.'

Yates had soaked all the newspaper now and was packing it into a frying pan. When it was full he took it over to the gas cooker which was brown with grease, lit a burner and put the pan over the flame. Blue smoke rose.

'Now!' shouted the boy. He seized the pan and rushed upstairs shouting 'Fire!' He flung open a door at the top of the stairs and held the pan at the opening, so that smoke issued into the room. The fair boy said to Vincent. 'Come on.' And Vincent found himself running up and down the stairs with the two boys, stamping and shouting and banging doors.

They stopped and stood in the hall looking at the half-open door at the top of the stairs.

'They just turned their backs,' said Yates. He looked about him in a frenzied way. 'I'm not going to let them get the better of me.'

Under a contemporary coat rack, white spindly metal hooks with red knobs, was a collection of empty bottles and cans and dirty glasses and cups, the relics of a party. He snatched up an empty pipkin tin, looked round wildly once again, then pulled a felt hat off a hook and began to stuff it into the tin.

'That's Reg's hat.'

'You're mad,' said the fair boy.

Yates had rushed back into the kitchen and was now damping the hat. He lit matches and pushed them into the can. The hat began to smoulder.

'This'll get him out,' he said. He seemed obsessed. 'You see. This'll move him.'

They followed him upstairs, more slowly this time. He held the tin between his jersey sleeves, like a pair of tongs. The smoke drifted backwards. It smelt disgusting. Vincent coughed. Yates opened the door wide and the others stood behind him. Vincent saw a boy and girl in bed. Yates walked into the room and set the pipkin down in the centre of the floor. The man leapt up, naked, picked up the tin and hurled it out of the open window on to the front path, then went back to bed.

'I wish you'd give us some peace,' said the girl. She looked about fifteen.

They retreated and the fair boy closed the door.

'She'll have to go soon,' he said comfortingly, 'her parents like her to be home by ten.'

They sat in the living-room waiting for the girl upstairs to leave with her lover. The fair boy – they had now introduced themselves, he was Gary Wood – had made instant coffee with milk that wasn't hot enough so that the coffee hadn't completely dissolved.

Brown flecks like freckles chased round in the whirlpool made by Vincent's spoon.

'Haven't we got any biscuits?' said Yates irritably.

'Always on about food, aren't you?' said the dark boy, George Winters.

It was so unlike anything Vincent had imagined. He had had various images, the two boys living separately with their parents in neat working-class homes, or in more affluent middle-class ones; either public school boys like Jessop, or what he still thought of as Teddy boy types. He looked around the room. It had been furnished by someone who had obviously cared about comfortable living. It wasn't Vincent's taste, he thought it too ornate, but he could see everything was expensive. The drawn curtains were brocade. They were lined, and had fringed pelmets and were pulled by a beige silk cord at the side. The carpet was quite new, thick and red, but there were crumbs on it and all round the edges by the cream painted skirting boards were rolls of grey fluff. An ashtray, a saucer and a plate were on the mantelpiece full of cigarette ends. There were cigarettes ends, a beer can and a crust in the grate.

'How long have you lived here?' he said.

'About two months.' Yates lit a cigarette, put his head back against the chair and shut his eyes.

'Nearly time to go,' said Winters grinning. 'They're cutting off the electricity next week.'

'And we've had a last demand for the rates,' said Yates, without opening his eyes.

'And the rent's due on the first of the month.'

'Do you just go without paying?' Vincent asked incredulously. The people in the pub had not exaggerated.

Winters nodded.

'Where do you go then?'

'Rent another place. Or kip with friends or something.'

'The police will catch up on you if you go on,' said Vincent.

'Oh, we don't give our right names,' said Wood.

They had no sense of moral obligation. They were undisciplined and irresponsible. Vincent had a sharp feeling of disappointment, almost of dread. He wanted to tell them about the Party, he wanted *them*, but they wouldn't want to know. The beating-up had probably been as casual as the way they lived here, a casual encounter resulting in casual violence. But it was a challenge, he must try. He stood up and said in a clear voice, slowly, 'Did you attack Michael Gold because he was a Jew?'

'No,' said Wood.

'We didn't but we might have,' said Winters. 'They're not my favourite people.'

'Why?' asked Yates.

Vincent stared at the brocade seat of the chair where he had sat. The pattern was obliterated by dirt, the material had been rubbed shiny. He raised his head and looked into Yates' grey eyes.

'I hate Jews,' he said. 'They've wormed their way like maggots into British business and culture.'

Yates flushed. 'I don't know. I've got a friend who's Jewish. She seems as English as I am.'

'Seems,' said Vincent. Yates had a conscience. But he was weak, he must be weak to live here with the others, he might respond to Vincent's rhetoric. 'Superficially. But not under the skin. Two, three generations here and there is a fairly slick veneer covering up those characteristics. Only under the skin it's there, just as it was in the grandparents who crawled in from some middle European ghetto. Hitler went back four generations in order to purify Germany.'

Yates didn't answer, but Winters said, 'People of your generation do bore one with Hitler. We weren't even born when the war ended. He means nothing to us. Nothing. We're not interested.' He stood up. 'They're out of bed. Listen.' There was the sound of movement in the room upstairs.

'They're coming down,' said Wood.

Hitler meant nothing. Hitler was just a name, a name like Nelson or Marlborough or Kaiser Wilhelm. What did Kaiser Wilhelm mean to him? Nothing, the first world war meant nothing. What did, or should, was the present. England today, that was the theme he must use, not Germany's past.

The girl put her head round the door.

'Good-bye everyone.' She had curly dark hair, a Semitic type.

'Where's your friend?' asked Winters sarcastically.

'He's here.'

The man appeared in the doorway. 'Sorry if we've kept you up.'

'Well, good night,' said the girl.

They didn't answer and the front door slammed.

'You may not be interested in Hitler,' said Vincent at once, before they could discuss the girl. 'But you're interested in your country, aren't you?'

'No,' said Wood, 'not in the least.'

Anger hit Vincent like a punch in the chest. This was exactly what he and Fox had discussed at their first meeting, this mood of apathy and amorality. These were Fox's 'shargars' brought up to date, gutless hedonists, living like a lot of ignorant peasants, doing a moonlight flit because they couldn't pay the bills and hadn't the courage to face up to the consequences; condoning and indulging in casual sexual intercourse. Should he walk out of the house, leave them to their cesspool of rotten living, forget them? But he didn't want to relinquish them so easily. They were young men without roots, and two of them at least had a sadistic streak which, properly funnelled, could be of use. He saw himself, dressed as he was now, walking along a street, walking along a country lane to Fox's house – he retained this image – with these three boys behind him, his bodyguard. He knew no amount of patriotic ranting could arouse them. He sat down again on the grubby chair and said, 'Do you want your rent paid?'

They all looked at him.

'Why?' asked Wood.

'I'll make a deal with you,' said Vincent. He could see that he had made an astute move and was pleased with himself. Not everyone responded in the same way, and if he was going to recruit members in the early days of forming the Party, then he had to adapt his appeal.

'Which side of the law?' said Winters.

'I'm never on the wrong side,' said Vincent sharply. They all laughed derisively.

'Yeah?'

'I'm forming a new political party,' said Vincent angrily.

'So you said,' Wood reminded him.

'So I said. And I want an office, a headquarters in London. I don't want to use my own flat. You let me have a room here and I'll pay your rent.'

'Is that all?' said Yates.

'No. I want a personal bodyguard.'

'Us?'

'That's right.'

'What sort of a party is it?' asked Winters, 'an anti-Jew party?'

'Yes.'

Winters shrugged. 'Okay. So what do we do?'

'Do you have jobs?' Vincent asked.

Wood smiled. 'We had them until the case came up.'

'What were they?'

'I was with a firm of music publishers,' said Wood.

'I was in a shop, packing department,' said Winters.

'I'm in a travel agency,' said Yates.

Excitement was fluttering in his stomach like a bird. 'Now,' he said, talking quickly, 'the first thing then is to get you your uniforms. And before I go tonight I want you to show me the room for my headquarters. I need you to come down to the country with me on Saturday afternoon. I hope you're free.'

'We're always free,' said Winters.

'Good. We'll put it in writing, of course, the deal.'

'Are you going to pay the rates too?'

'Yes, all right, this time. I'll pay it this time.'

'I'll give you the bills,' said Wood. He went over to the imitation Regency desk and took several papers that were weighted with a box of matches on the top. He brought them over to Vincent. 'You might as well have the electricity one too. We can't pay it, and you'll need light in your office, won't you?' They all grinned at one another.

They think I'm a crank, thought Vincent. They think they're taking me for a ride. They've got some surprises coming. He took the bills and put them in his pocket without looking at them.

Chapter 6

VINCENT took the boys down to the boutique in his lunch hour. He made them walk as he had planned, Yates a few paces ahead of him and Wood and Winters a yard behind. They walked along Regent Street and turned, at a command from Vincent, into a side street and halted outside the shop. Vincent was wearing a suit, the three boys were in jeans. He was aware that today, in the crowd of shoppers, the formation and the military bearing were unobserved. He longed for them all to be in uniform so the people would point them out. One day he and his bodyguard would be familiar figures everywhere in England.

The shop assistant was thrilled to equip them. He remembered Vincent and happily assembled the three boys in their grey jackets and jeans.

Vincent insisted that they kept the clothes on. They carried the shop's black and white carrier bags with their ordinary clothes inside. Vincent's lunch hour was almost over. He had to leave them at Oxford Circus and run down the escalator to catch a train. He turned his head as the stairs took him slowly away from them, and saw them going into the public lavatory. They were going to change, he thought. They felt fools dressed alike. Well, perhaps today they did. After all, although the Party had been formed, there had been no public meetings, no publicity. Later they would be proud to be seen in their uniforms, glad they had joined at the beginning, because if they served him faithfully he would promote them, give them a little power. They would feel happier too, when he was with them, dressed like them, just as he would relish the feeling of solidarity. Of course, he thought, he must make some difference between their uniform and his. On the train he toyed with ideas of insignia, pips, stripes, headgear, badges. He had reached no decision by the time he was back behind the counter, Miss Glass at his side. Her mother was ill, and while she worked she gave him details. 'Thick catarrh, Mr Pearman, and she says her throat feels like the piece of sandpaper at the bottom of budgie's cage. She managed a little soup last night, put it on a tray, you know, with a pretty cloth and a serviette, tempted her, you might say. Well, she had that, but wouldn't take a thing this morning. I've got the district nurse going in today, to give her a wash over.'

He nodded curtly, irritated and bored. Before the bank closed he went in to see Mr Fowler to confirm his decision about his name. Madame Vera had sent him a cutting from a Sunday paper, he knew from it that by merely calling himself Wright he could legally be known by the name. It wasn't necessary to change it by deed-poll, there was no expense incurred. Vincent had always felt Mr Fowler didn't like him and today he was more terse than usual, almost rude. He said he thought Vincent was being foolish, that it would confuse everyone, but reluctantly he had to comply with Vincent's extraordinary and to him ridiculous request. He didn't think, however, that he personally would be able to adapt himself to calling Vincent by any other name than Pearman. The interview was over, Vincent left triumphant for home.

He went to see Madame Vera on his way. Friction between them was smoothed. He had met not merely one W but two. She gave him a cup of tea and a cake. 'A milly fool,' she said, passing it to him on a flowered plate, 'cake of a hundred leaves.' He ate it with enjoyment. He felt very close to her. As he left he gave her an extra pound, 'Buy yourself a little present,' he said. He had never given any woman apart from his mother a present before. She waved and called good-bye from the doorstep but her voice was obliterated by the roar of lorries.

A note from Patterson was waiting in his letter basket. It asked Vincent to meet him on the platform on Saturday afternoon so that they could travel down together. He had spoken to Fox who was arranging for Fayers to pick them up, and Vincent gloated over the prospect of Patterson's surprise when he marched down the platform with his entourage.

After his abstemious supper of two boiled eggs and a glass of milk Vincent went to Finchley to inspect his office. Wood and

Yates were out, only Winters was there to greet him without enthusiasm, and Vincent was angry.

'I expected to find you all here,' he said sharply.

'You don't own us,' answered Winters. 'You've got your office and we've said we'll join your Party. But you haven't bought us.'

'Where have they gone?'

'None of your business, Mr Wright.' But during the evening he discovered that Yates was out with the girl who had been in Winters' bed.

His office was in an unused bedroom. He and Winters pushed the bed to the side of the room and carried out a dressing-table and wardrobe. Vincent made a survey of the other rooms and selected the living-room desk and two upright chairs, which they moved in. Vincent put one chair behind the desk and the other in front. It had been hot work carrying the desk upstairs. They had chipped the paint and had difficulty negotiating the corner. Winters sat down on the chair behind the desk.

'Christ, I'm exhausted.'

'That's my chair,' said Vincent.

Winters looked at him as if he were mad. Then he got up and shrugged. 'Okay.'

Vincent sat down at once and surveyed the room. It was small and painted white. The curtains were blue. There was a blue wastepaper basket and a London Cries picture of a lavender-seller on the wall by the door.

'Take the picture down,' he ordered Winters.

Winters gave him another long look and did as he was asked. 'I'll be out next time,' he said.

'No,' said Vincent, 'I'd rather you were here. If you choose at this juncture to be my personal assistant I'll see you're promoted.'

'We might just move, anyway,' said Winters. 'All right, you pay the bills, but we might decide we don't want them paid and just go.'

'Listen,' said Vincent, 'I think after Saturday you'll change your mind. At the moment you just think I'm dotty but I'll prove to you that I'm not, in fact I believe that by the end of the week you'll think I'm the sanest person you've ever met.'

'Yes?'

'You're a bright boy,' Vincent flattered him, lying. He thought Winters the least bright of the three. 'In a moment when I've finished talking you'll realise what the future holds for you if you play your cards right with me. You'll have position and money.'

Winters looked up sharply. 'Money? You think so?'

'Yes. England needs a leader, just as Germany needed one in the thirties. On the surface everything looks good, prosperity, welfare service, employment. But underneath it's rotten. Who are being employed? Niggers. Who by? Jews. For whose benefit? Their own, not the country's. Shall I tell you something?'

'Yes.'

'When I met you and the others I thought to myself, the weak, degraded products of a sick society.'

'You're joking.'

'Living off society, not contributing. Living immorally and illegally. Pretty despicable, I thought, unhealthy, irresponsible and mentally weak.'

Winters stood up. 'Look mate, if that's what you think, clear off.'

'I think that if someone suggests the right ideas you might get some principles.'

'Such as?'

'I believe you're patriotic at heart, worth something, but that you think it's smart to have this outer coating of disinterest. I like you. I want you in my Party. I think together we can help Britain.' As he spoke Vincent knew how important it was to enlist Winters. If he could convince this boy he could convince hundreds of others like him. There were hundreds like Winters, of every class, sitting in coffee bars, crowding the clubs, a great untapped source of political material, the ones who didn't care but who could be made to care. Don't care was made to care, by *my* oratory, said Vincent to himself.

'I don't think anything I might do will make much difference to Britain,' said Winters, grinning.

'That's where you're wrong.' Irritated by Winters' facetiousness Vincent leaned across the desk and gripped his arm. 'Look at it this way. One drop of rain doesn't even make a puddle, but if it goes on raining long enough there's a flood.'

'I get the picture,' said Winters after a pause. 'Okay, we'll string along for a bit and see how it goes. But it's not a legal sort of tie-up, is it? I mean, we can get out if we want to, can't we?'

'It's not binding in any way,' answered Vincent. He was exultant, but controlled his expression and voice so that Winters wouldn't know that he constituted a victory.

'That's all right then,' said Winters.

'How about making us a cup of coffee,' Vincent suggested.

As soon as the boy had left the room Vincent stood up from his desk and walked to the window, then turned and looked back at his desk. It needed papers, an index file of members, his own rough notes for a speech, to give one the sense that political business was being carried on. Eventually he would need a secretary. Should he have a man or a woman? He had an image of Miss Glass sitting on the opposite chair taking down his words in shorthand. And he must have his photograph taken. He would hang it there, instead of the lavender girl. He needed a photograph for the newspaper in any case.

As Winters placed a cup on the desk they heard the front door open and shut with a bang and voices in the hall.

'That's Yates back,' said Winters. Vincent hurried back to his desk, sat down and began to drink the coffee, burning his lips. He wished he had papers there, and a pen, so that he could look up when Yates came in.

Yates called out, 'Anyone there?' and Winters yelled back, 'Upstairs, mate.'

They came in together. The girl was wearing jeans and a short red jacket. Vincent had an intuitive feeling that Yates had returned deliberately to see him. He looked at Vincent and said, 'Oh, hallo Wright. I didn't know you'd be here.'

Vincent stiffened. How dared Yates speak to him like that, not even a mister. He must invent a title, quickly, something implying rank. It came in a flash. Of course they must call him Leader.

'This is Judy,' said Yates. He added defiantly, 'Judy Solomons.'

Vincent looked at Yates and then at the girl, dislike creeping like gooseflesh over his skin, a physical feeling of revulsion. What was the motive? To irritate him, to get him to insult the girl so that they had an excuse to kick him out? Was it a plan, thought up by Yates and Winters?

'She wants to join your Party,' said Yates. Winters smiled.

Then it was a kind of test. 'This is an anti-Jewish Party,' Vincent said levelly.

'I'm anti-Jewish,' said the girl.

'Don't you see,' said Yates, putting his arm round her, 'how much more you'll be able to get away with if you've actually got a Jew in the Party?'

Vincent chewed his lips, staring out of the window. Were they baiting him? Or was it genuine? Hitler scourged Germany of Jews, he went back generations to prise them out. But this wasn't Germany. He doubted that Jews would actually be shipped out of England. The most he could hope for, was a recognisation from the British people that Jews shouldn't be patronised or employed. Then they would emigrate of their own free will. They could all go to Israel, to their self-made ghetto. If he had this Jewish girl in his Party, actually denying her own people, and at the same time giving a cover to the Party motives, it might well be the cleverest move he could make. He could hear himself at a press conference, when a reporter attacked him for aping the Germany they had fought and defeated, 'We are not like the Nazis. We don't seek to exterminate Jews. In fact we have a Jewish member.'

'Are you an agent?' he said to her, looking into her eyes. 'Are you acting for a Zionist group?'

She shook her head. 'No. I just rather agree with what Bill's been telling me. About your Party, I mean. Of course I'm not completely anti-semitic. But I'm like a lot of the young generation – Jewish young generation, I mean. We don't want to be associated with the community, or typed. I don't want to meet "nice Jewish boys" all the time. I'm myself, and I'm an atheist.'

What would Fox say? Did it matter what Fox said? Vincent was the leader, and he had the power to convince Fox. At that moment he felt he could convince anyone of anything. Look how he'd won Winters over. Look at the way Yates had been persuaded. Look at the boys that week-end, how they'd sat there drinking in his words. He looked at Judy. A Jewish girl who renounced Jews. He thought of the effect of those communists who had rejected the party at the time of the Hungarian uprising. He remembered their confessions in the press. Those changed beliefs, those turncoats did a lot to aid the anti-communist cause. What would Judy do for them? If she dyed her hair and became blonde she would be making a positive rejection of her origins.

'What I want to do,' she said earnestly, 'is to help girls and boys of my generation to be integrated absolutely into the British culture, I can't bear the way it is now, all sticking together.'

She had got it quite wrong. But what did it matter? Her motives didn't matter to him. He could use her. She was Jewish trash and he could use her in whatever way he selected. He smiled at her.

'All right, Judy. But you'll have to dye your hair. You ought to be blonde.'

'And my eyebrows?'

'Those too.'

'Okay, I will.' She was little more than a prostitute, sleeping first with the man the other night and now, no doubt, with Yates.

'How old are you, Judy?'

'I shall be sixteen in October.'

He felt like God, manipulating her for his divine plan. What a glorious, irrefutable answer to those who would accuse him of unreasoned anti-semitism. Look at Judy here. What about Judy? If we hated Jews would we have Judy with us? Judy, Jew, Judaic Judy, Judy, Judas, the kiss of Judas, Juden raus. She couldn't have a more apposite name.

'I'll have my hair done tomorrow,' she said giggling. 'What on earth will they say at home?'

Patterson was waiting at the platform barrier, small, sharp and putty faced. They approached in rank, first Yates, then Vincent, then Winters and Wood, and a little way behind them, Judy. They were all in uniform, they marched with heads up and a brisk step. Patterson glimpsed them behind a trolley snaking through the crowds and loaded with mailbags. He looked again. Yates reached the barrier and halted, feet clamping together.

'Break rank,' ordered Vincent. They joined him. He went up to Patterson and nodded. 'Hallo, Patterson. All set for an exciting week-end?' And he raised his fist and brought it across his forehead in salute.

'Good Lord!' said Patterson, satisfyingly bewildered. 'What on earth are these?'

'I don't let grass grow under my feet,' answered Vincent, smiling.

Patterson looked at Judy. Her jeans were tight and she had her jacket collar turned up. Her blonde hair was short and boyish and recently set.

'And who is this sexacious number?' asked Patterson, his eyes lingering at crotch level.

'Party member number four, London cell,' said Vincent.

Patterson shrugged, 'Sorry and all that matey, but I don't get it. Isn't it a little early to start recruiting?'

The front of the train appeared, foreshortened at the end of the platform, then slowly pulled alongside extending like an expandable paper chain. Patterson grabbed a door handle and walked beside the train until it stopped, then he opened the door and stepped up into the carriage, shoved his small case under the seat and sat down in a corner.

The others climbed in after him and put their duffle bags and cases on the rack. Winters and Wood sat in the seats beside Patterson, Yates and Judy opposite. They held hands at once. Vincent thought, Yates is contaminating himself, just as the camp guards did when they had affairs with Jewesses. He sat down next to Wood and Patterson leaned across the two boys.

'I spoke to Fox last night. He didn't say anything about all this.'

'He doesn't know,' said Vincent smugly.

'Don't you think he ought to know?' asked Patterson, 'after all, the whole thing is his idea. It's his Party isn't it?' He lit a cigarette.

Judy and Yates stared across the carriage at Vincent. Wood smirked. Rage began just below Vincent's diaphragm, a marble of lead that spread up into his chest and throat. He stared at Patterson, and Patterson seemed to detach from the background of patterned railway upholstery and become disrelated from everything around him. He took a long inhalation of his cigarette and then blew the smoke out in Vincent's direction. As Vincent opened his mouth to speak he tasted the smoke on his tongue. He stood up, snatched the cigarette from Patterson and hurled it into the corridor, rushed after it and stamped on it, then turned and faced them from the doorway.

'It's my Party. My Party. I'm the leader, not Fox. Fox is a dreamer, I'm the one who acts. I formed the Party. It's my idea. I was elected. I don't have to consult Fox. Or you. Or any of the other hangers on.' He leant over and took hold of Patterson's lapels. 'I'm the leader. Fox did nothing until he met me. Me, me, me! I'm the one who decides.' He let go of the lapels and went and sat down again in the corner, his face still burning and a pulse throbbing at the base of his neck.

Patterson took out his cigarette packet and lit another. Judy said in a high voice, 'Oh, we're moving.' The train left the station slowly then gathered speed. Vincent thought, I shouldn't have done that. Then; yes I should. I was right. I must put down dissenters from the beginning. What a stupid pathetic dim little Australian twit he is, trying to be British. What does he know about England?

Fayers had parked the car among the other taxis in the station yard. It occurred to Vincent as he crossed the yard that he had made no sleeping arrangements for Judy and the boys. No doubt Fox would find a space for them. Vincent didn't want to pay Fayers for hotel rooms if he could avoid it. To his delight the boys automatically took up their positions as bodyguard. Judy walked behind with Patterson, and he carried her airways bag as well as his own attaché case.

Fayers gave no indication of the surprise Vincent knew he must have felt. He stood beside his highly polished car and opened the back door.

'I hope you won't find it too much of a squash, sir,' he said to Vincent. He took their luggage and put it in the boot. 'I'll sort this out after I've taken you to the colonel's. He's anxious to see you.'

Vincent had stepped into the car first, but Patterson waited until everyone was in the back, Judy on Yates's knee, before sitting beside Fayers. Vincent was irritated with himself. He should have sat in the front, in the more dignified position. In future he would go straight to the front of the car, unless there were no other passengers. Then it would be more suitable for him to ride alone in the back. He didn't like physical contact and felt disgusted by the closeness of Judy and Yates by his side. They were very close and Yates's right thigh pressed alongside his left like its pair. Judy's foot dug into his calf. He sat rigid, listening to Patterson quizzing Fayers on the day's plans. Jessop, it seemed, had mustered five new boys, and they had arrived last night with the other members of Fox's group. A coach had been hired to take them all to the meeting tonight. Dobson had put an advertisement into the local paper and had managed to distribute a dozen posters to shops and private houses. Fayers pointed out one in a cottage window as they drove along the lane leading to the house. The poster was obviously hand-done but quite arresting. It had the word SATISFIED? in red, across the top and underneath WHAT CAN WE DO FOR BRITAIN? The car had passed before Vincent had time to read the small writing at the bottom which presumably gave the time and place of the meeting. Not bad, not bad, thought Vincent. But it was too haphazard. From now on they must have a proper campaign, a recognisable sign, like the swastika, for every poster, leaflet or appeal.

The trees had budded since his last visit. They were now in full leaf and partly hid the house from the lane. When Fayers turned the car into the drive and the house was revealed Wood said, 'Blimey, it looks like a prison.'

'No, a school,' said Yates, 'just like my prep-school, no curtains and red brick.'

'There aren't any curtains, are there?' said Judy, easing herself in preparation for levering her body off Yates's lap. Her elbow stuck into Vincent's chest for a painful moment.

'It is a school,' Winters said incredulously. 'Look!' Several fully grown boys wearing what was, without doubt, a school uniform, walked round the corner of the house and in at the open front door.

Fayers sounded the hooter and the dog yapped and Fox came out on to the step. Because he had been the first into the car, Vincent was the last to come out. Patterson had greeted Fox and walked straight into the house, but Yates, Wood, Winters and Judy stood awkwardly waiting for Vincent to take command of the situation. He put his feet on to the gravel, stood up and shook Fox by the hand. Then he turned to them and said, 'At ease.' They shuffled. 'Colonel, these are members of the newly formed London cell. You'll observe I have equipped them with a basic uniform. I'd like to propose it as the official uniform at our next committee meeting.'

'Very nice,' said Fox, 'very neat. Well, come in all of you and have a cup of tea.'

Fox had disappeared while they drank the tea that stood ready in two large brown metal teapots. There were fifteen boys in the house already as well as Dobson, Patterson and Fayers. Patterson sat in a corner with Jessop, talking quietly but intensely. Vincent glanced at them several times, momentarily obsessed with desire to know what they were saying. The coach arrived at five, and the driver came in for a cup of tea too. Fox came downstairs again, dressed in a War Department surplus khaki uniform, stick in hand. He looked immensely strong and military, and Vincent felt his own uniform was overshadowed. He called his group over to him so that they commanded attention merely because they were all dressed alike. Fox beckoned Vincent, Patterson and Dobson and suggested they talk for a few minutes before leaving for the meeting. They went upstairs to Fox's bedroom and sat on his hard low bed.

'Have you prepared your speech?' Fox asked Vincent.

Vincent smiled. 'Up to a point. I prefer to extemporise, I like to gauge atmosphere and adapt myself.' He stood up so that he could look down on Patterson and Dobson on the bed. Fox was already standing, leaning against his record player. 'May I make a suggestion?' Vincent said.

'Go ahead.'

'We mustn't be amateur. No more hand-painted posters.'

'Funds?' said Dobson.

'We must try and raise some tonight. Everyone must have a uniform. We can't have people wearing what they like, it looks messy, undisciplined.' Vincent glanced pointedly at Fox. 'We want to make a list of members tonight, advise everyone here to buy the clothes.'

'I agree,' said Fox. 'But I think we must smarten it up a bit, shining boots, polished belts.'

'Why not wait and see how things go,' said Patterson, 'I don't want to pay for a uniform I'm not going to wear. The British Government isn't that generous to the teaching profession.'

'No,' said Vincent. 'Right from the beginning we must be a professional party. We aren't a collection of people, we are one body.'

'Hear hear,' muttered Dobson.

'I think we should go,' suggested Fox. 'We don't want to be late.'

As they walked downstairs Vincent saw them as the Party executive, four men in iron control of a countrywide network. They walked briskly into the living-room where the boys and Judy were waiting. She was glowing and animated, surrounded by young men. They don't know she's Jewish, thought Vincent with a flush of secret enjoyment.

They climbed into the coach and it drove off down the narrow roads. Jessop started to sing Green Grow the Rushes-o, and everyone, except Vincent, joined in enthusiastically. They sang the Foggy Foggy Dew, Cockles and Mussels and one he didn't know about a student with a beard on a train. The word rollicking came into his mind. They were rollicking, the coach bouncing along, everyone swaying and singing and shouting. The coach slowed down at the outskirts of the small country town, passed Fayers's hotel and drove through the main streets to a small Norman church. The church hall was a kind of nissen hut, prefabricated with a tin roof, and another of Dobson's posters was displayed outside. The Vicar heard the coach and came out of the hall to greet them, smiling a welcome. He shook Fox by the hand and Fox introduced Vincent.

'Our speaker,' said the Vicar, beaming at Vincent. 'I told the colonel that I may give you a paragraph in our parish magazine. It's quite influential you know. The Colonel tells me you want to stir up patriotic feeling, and I'm right behind you. Loving one's country is part of loving God, don't you think?'

'Possibly,' Vincent answered shortly. He nodded to the Vicar and went over to Wood. 'I want you three on the platform with me. And Judy.' Judy was the worm on the hook, they'd go for a blonde. They'd be in sympathy when they saw Judy up there, be prepared to listen, to 'string along' as Winters put it. And just like a worm Judy had no idea that she was being used as bait and that when he caught the fish he didn't care whether or not she was eaten alive.

The hall seated about sixty people. Vincent stood in the aisle directing the boys into seats. They filled the front two rows. He stationed Jessop at the door and another boy just inside. The Vicar tiptoed in and took a seat at the back. Vincent went up on to the small platform, and Dobson pinned another of their posters over one for the Women's Institute advertising a sale of cakes. Vincent waited until he had gone down the steps into the hall, then he stood Wood and Winters either side of the speaker's table, and Yates centrally behind. He placed Judy on the right. There were three wooden chairs with round seats at the back of the platform, and he invited Fox, Patterson and Dobson to sit on them. Patterson said he'd prefer to stay in the audience but Fox persuaded him and the three of them joined Vincent on the platform.

'Shall I introduce you?' asked Fox.

'No,' said Vincent. 'We don't want a boring preamble, I'll go straight into it.'

A few people began to arrive, several middle-aged women who Vincent thought probably attended every church function, two men, then a handful of local louts with long hair and spotty faces and badly cared for but fashionable clothes. They created a deliberate disturbance, showing off before they had even sat down.

'What's all this then?' one called out. 'Look at those poufs up there.'

'They got a dolly with them. 'Allo darlin'.' They all whistled. Jessop went up to them.

'Shut up and sit down. No one's come here to listen to you.' His middle-class accent delighted them.

'Aoh, naouh, of carse yew 'aven't.'

They sat down near the back. The Vicar went up to them. 'This is a serious meeting, if you don't want to behave you'd better leave.'

They replied rudely, but subsided, until one of their girl-friends arrived and sat with them. They shouted out several obscene and pointless remarks for her enjoyment. Vincent stood up and banged on the table loudly for half a minute. Another woman came in and looked round for the Vicar and sat by him, and two more men wandered in through the door and were directed by Jessop to seats near the front. He turned towards Fox and mouthed 'I'll start.'

Dobson leaned forward and whispered, 'Wait a moment longer. I'm sure some others are coming. I sent a circular round the members of the local tradesmen's guild.'

Vincent was impressed by Dobson's thoroughness and initiative. They belied his first impression that Dobson was stupid. He waited another five minutes and several more people came into the hall. He glanced at Dobson who nodded. He stood up. The low talking subsided and everyone looked at him.

'I feel excited,' said Vincent. 'This is the first public meeting of a new movement that I hope will sweep the country. I think it's going to, because not only is it what I believe the country needs but is also the kind of stirring and vigorous movement which stimulates the imagination and awakens patriotism. Patriotism! A lot of people would say it is an out-dated word.'

'And they're dead right there,' shouted one of the local boys. Wood leaped up and went over to him, pushing past the people in the row. He said something, and indicated the front seats, where Fox's boys sat. Then he went back to his own place. The boy who had shouted grinned at his friends but remained silent.

'Patriotism,' said Vincent. 'Pride, power. I'm humiliated by the country today. I've heard people citing past glories, military and artistic. I don't care what we did in the trenches in 1914, or what Shakespeare wrote in the seventeenth century, whether we pushed back the ships of the Spanish Armada or gritted our

teeth during the Battle of Britain. I'm concerned for the present
and for the future. I want a future for England that makes past
achievements seem paltry.' He knew that Fox and Patterson and
Dobson were waiting for him to start decrying the Negroes and
Jews as he had done in his previous speech in Fox's house. But
he had a strong feeling that today this would be wrong, would
stop the Party growing beyond this miserable church hall. One of
the women sitting beside the Vicar was scribbling away in shorthand, he guessed she was a reporter from the local paper. These
people were like his parents, respectable trades people who were
mentally blocked by clichés, who needed a gradual persuasion, a
re-education. If he spoke too strongly they would react like Miss
Glass reacted, out of habit. What he was saying now would have
better appeal, more concrete results. What he wanted tonight was
money.

'I have a feeling,' he said, 'that what is happening tonight in this
hall is going to be very significant. In the months to come people
all over England are going to look to this parish, this church hall,
and say, "That's where it started." Every venture begins in some
room or another, there are always the first members of every
movement. I'll be frank with you. I want your support. I want your
membership in whatever capacity you feel able to join. Some of
you perhaps, because you are young, will join in a pioneer spirit,
enjoy the activities, the comradeship. Others, older, will be able to
donate something to help us carry out our aims.'

Except for the little group of local boys everyone seemed to be
listening intently.

'I'm not offering you a social club so that young people can
make friends. It isn't a boy scout movement or like any existing
political party. Who would want to be like any existing political
party? What have we got but watered-down communism on the
one hand and a bunch of obsolete tories clinging to the nineteenth
century on the other, as left-over as a dog's dinner. I want to build
a party which is the nation, a nation which is the party. I want
our youth to be strong in mind and body, I want their elders to be
cleansed of all the muddle-headed clichés that they have absorbed
from the woolly-minded politicians who have been in power since

the war. We must build a nation that is proud to be independent and is strong because of that independence. Yet we must never forget that the individual makes up the whole.'

'What 'ole? Arse 'ole?' called out the heckling boy. Wood stood up, glaring. Vincent motioned him to sit down again. He didn't want an interruption that would detract from what he was saying.

'What whole? Have you not heard of the whole man? The man who is physically strong and brave, has a true heart, a clear head and a keen mind? I want to see England alive with such pure men, I want the misfits and the intruders to slink away because they can't compete with the race we can produce. I want a resurgence of national pride, and I want us, us here tonight in this hall in a small but very British country town to be the forerunners, the leaders of a movement that will fire the enthusiasm, that latent patriotism of the whole country. What do you say? Ask me anything you like.'

The Vicar stood up. 'I am a little perturbed that you haven't mentioned God in all this. What is needed is a return to the essence of Christianity, a rejection of material values.'

'I didn't mention God,' said Vincent, 'because I am not qualified to talk on religious matters. That's your concern. I'm here to discuss political questions.'

The Vicar sat down again, nodding but obviously not satisfied.

'What I have deliberately left till last,' said Vincent, 'is the name of the Party. We are called the Britain First Party, and I'm sure you'll agree we couldn't have a more appropriate name.' He was deliberately drawing the audience into a conversational mood, making them feel they were now discussing something of mutual interest and gain.

'Do we get paid for joinin'?' asked one of the heckling boys.

'I can't pay anyone now,' answered Vincent. 'We haven't any money. When we raise some it will have to go first of all on mundane items like stationery and flags and advertising. But later I want everyone to be paid, just as soldiers are paid. I'd like to pay you. Now I have to ask for support and trust and your own sense of obligation to your country.'

'But we'll be paid later if we joins now, then?' said the boy.

'Without doubt,' said Vincent.

The scribbling lady stood up and spoke in a high clear voice with meticulous diction.

'I represent the *Gazette*. I want to ask you how you plan to spread your movement, what are your next steps?'

'That depends on the money we raise tonight,' said Vincent.

'How do you envisage the Party growing?'

'I already have the beginnings of a London section,' said Vincent. 'Under my leadership Colonel Fox has a sizeable group here. Eventually we hope to have sections in every major town in Britain.'

'May I come along with a photographer tomorrow?' asked the lady.

'By all means. I shall be at Colonel Fox's house most of the day.'

The lady sat down. One of Dobson's tradesmen stood up. 'What I'd like to ask is what you mean by raising funds? Do you expect people to give you money, like a charity?'

'No,' said Vincent, 'because we are not a charity. We are an investment. An investment for the future. I don't want anyone to give a penny if he isn't convinced. But if you can afford to write a cheque, or make a covenant or even put your hand in your pocket for half a crown because you *believe*, we shall receive your donation gratefully.' He felt he must add something to endorse his conviction. 'I am paying for all the uniforms at present out of my own pocket. I'm glad to use my savings for a cause I believe in.' He had saved for years, he had three thousand pounds in the bank, he drew nothing all the years he had lived at home, his mother wouldn't take a penny. 'I also pay for the rent of the London headquarters. I am absolutely convinced that within two years at the outside the Party will be rich enough to pay me back should I want repayment. If you feel you want to make a loan, I'll legalize it.'

The Vicar stood again and came to the front of the hall. Vincent looked down on to his fluffy crown. It was white and the remnants of his hair looked like the bits of feather that floated out of his eiderdown when he made his bed.

'I'm afraid I shall have to end this most stimulating meeting. Stimulating was one of Mr Wright's own words tonight, and it was an apt one. Unfortunately we have to clear the hall to make

it ready for the dance and I can see our band waiting just outside
the door to take their places on the platform. You can come in,' he
shouted through cupped hands. Four men entered carrying instruments. One heaved a drum up on to the platform beside Vincent
and rolled it into place.

'Thank you for allowing us to use your hall,' said Vincent. 'It's
given me great encouragement to listen to your questions, you're
probably longing to ask more. As you heard me say to the lady
from the *Gazette*, I'll be at Colonel Fox's house most of tomorrow.
If any of you want to know anything further come along. If you
are already with us in,' he was going to say spirit but met the
Vicar's eye, 'your hearts, I'm sure the Vicar will allow us a few
more minutes while I take your names and enrol you as members,
or accept your cheques.' He said this with a smile as though he
might be joking.

The band men had taken off their mackintoshes and revealed
blue lurex jackets which glittered as they set up their instruments. A
large placard, Buddy Willis and the Music-makers, was suspended
where Dobson had hung his poster.

'Before we are finally deposed,' Vincent said, his voice raised to
keep the attention of his audience who were beginning to stand
and put on their coats, 'I want you to know that when you join the
Britain First Party you will be joining a very fine group of young
men. Stand up, boys.' Fox's boys stood up to attention in the two
front rows. 'They are in the forefront of the nation's youth. They
are the vanguard, our spearhead.' He stood to attention and after
a pause he raised his arm and placed his fist decisively against his
forehead.

To his joy Fox's boys responded. In unison they raised their right
arms and clenched their right fists to their brows. Vincent thought,
this is holy communion.

Chapter 7

'I THINK,' said Vincent, 'that if we're going to receive the lady from the press, we should keep your curios out of sight. All we need at this point is to be labelled a neo-Nazi party.'

He and Fox were sitting on the terrace at the back of the house in the early morning sun. They held tin mugs of tea. It was very quiet and sheltered in the garden. In the house Judy and the boys were finishing the breakfast Fox had cooked for them, pounds of sausages, tea poured from the canteen-size teapots, thick bread. Patterson was having a second meal in the kitchen. Fayers had called him early, and had waited on him and Vincent as they sat facing across a small table in the otherwise empty dining-room. Newly-shaved, with a cut on his neck that had bled on to his collar, Patterson's skin seemed as devoid of hair roots as if he suffered from alopoecia. They didn't speak during the meal, except for Patterson to say 'Has my neck stopped bleeding?' Fayers had driven them to the house and departed again by nine o'clock.

'How do you think it went?' asked Fox.

'I think the response was good, very good. I felt overwhelmed when the boys returned my salute.'

'I think it went well too,' said Fox. 'Now we have to wait and *see* just who was moved enough to join.'

'I'm not worried if they don't. We can get members. The point is that we have held a public meeting, it's going to be reported in the local paper. It's a beginning.'

'A church hall putsch?' asked Fox, smiling.

'I don't know yet how convinced they were.'

'My boys were, you should have been here last night. We sat up until one o'clock talking. It was like a night before an attack, that sense of unity, an "all in this together" closeness. And a firm belief that what they were doing was right.'

'*That's* the feeling I can generate. I can make them believe, give them a purpose.'

Fox put his empty tea mug down on to the ground. 'I'm sorry you had to bring a girl down here,' he said abruptly, stemming Vincent's self-praise.

'I had a reason,' answered Vincent.

'Women are all wrong in this sort of game.'

'It's the twentieth century,' said Vincent. 'We can't keep women out. But don't worry. I'm not a communist. I won't give them key jobs. They can do the clerical stuff, secretarial work, that kind of thing.'

'Last night the mood we've captured here before was quite lost. When there are just men one has a wonderful comradeship, a special brand of British humour, and a real rallying spirit. She spoilt it. I could tell that some of the boys wanted to lay her, they were distracted, it wasn't the same.'

'Did anyone lay her?' asked Vincent curiously.

'I put her in a room on her own. I don't know whether she stayed in it.'

'She's a tart,' said Vincent, 'a Jewish tart.' He enjoyed delivering such a shattering surprise.

'My God!' said Fox.

'She's our foil,' said Vincent casually. 'How can we be like the Nazis if we have a Jew in the Party? We can't be *un*discriminating, but *dis*criminating. We only dislike the bad Jews. Get it?'

'I don't know,' said Fox doubtfully, 'I think it's too subtle, it will put people off.'

'We have to be subtle. You're a soldier, you like things to be straightforward. I don't think we can be at this stage. It's why I didn't parade the main racial issues last night at the meeting. But if you're right, if it does deter people from joining, then we'll just dispense with her.'

Breakfast was over and some of the boys wandered out into the garden and sat on the grass. It was very pleasant for Vincent, with the sun on the trees and the boys at his feet. Together they discussed a projected meeting in London, perhaps after they had had their uniforms fitted. Gradually everyone came out of the house and they talked and joked and laughed, then became serious again.

'We must recruit as many people as we can,' said Vincent. 'At the moment we'll concentrate here and in London, there's no point in trying to spread ourselves until we have consolidated something worthwhile.'

'We can send the word round the school,' said Jessop. 'Once we go back with a uniform they'll want to join.'

'We might even start a sort of initiation group among the young kids.'

'Why not,' said Vincent excitedly. 'A Britain First youth movement, why not get them in at fourteen, fifteen.'

'They fought in the German army at that age,' said Fox quietly.

'Exactly. That's the time to begin our teaching.'

'I can do the same at my school if you like,' said Judy.

Vincent hadn't realised she was still at school.

'Actually my parents think I'm staying with a school-friend this week-end.'

'Leave it alone,' said Fox. 'We don't want girls, especially schoolgirls.'

'No,' answered Vincent. 'We want anyone we can get. We can reject later when we have a strong membership.'

'Teenage girls aren't going to give us the right image.'

'Girls have parents, friends, one conversion is worth at least four more.'

'I agree with the Colonel,' shouted Patterson, suddenly leaping up from the grass. 'You're trying to make us appear ridiculous.'

'Allow me to be the best judge of my own Party.'

'It's *all* our Party.'

'You're not in a position to express opinion.'

'I'm part of the committee. I agree with Colonel Fox. We don't want schoolgirls.'

'We want members.'

Fox stood up, on the point of answering. He seemed to be angry with Patterson, not Vincent, but before he could speak Dobson came through the house with a man Vincent recognised from the meeting.

'Good morning all,' said Dobson.

'Get some chairs,' said Fox to Jessop.

Jessop went straight into the house and returned with two chairs, and Dobson introduced the man to Vincent, and they all sat down. The man was red-faced, tall, and with a military bearing that matched Fox's. He had a white goatee beard that was immaculately trimmed, and when he spoke he played with it. His name was Geoffrey Delage, he was retired, and it transpired after five minutes' conversation that he was rich and wished to help with the Party funds. He was prepared, he said, to make a covenant for a thousand pounds a year. Dobson had shown him a copy of the proposed manifesto, he liked the ideas it expressed, they were his own sentiments. He had very little family, he wanted to use his money for the good of others, he donated to several charities and could afford another. This appealed to him.

'Ghastly common people Jews,' he said, 'they're buying up all the decent property round here, driving about in their Jaguars, using the amenities of the place. I've lived here for thirty years and I never thought I'd be surrounded by a lot of East-End wide boys. They're up at the golf club, their children actually hunt, they'll soon be running the place.' He accepted a cup of coffee from Judy, and Vincent enjoyed the irony of the situation. He despised Judy, not only for her origins but for her lack of loyalty to her own race. He wouldn't give a candle for her loyalty to the Party. She heard Delage's comments. No doubt she even agreed with him.

Sudden overclouding and heavy rain brought the meeting to an end. Everyone ran into the house, and the boys split up, playing darts or billiards or cards, or listening to Fox's records. Dobson and Delage left after a few minutes, Delage promising to see his accountant on Monday and to finalise his gift with Dobson next week. Vincent had a wild dream in which he banked the Party's funds at his own branch, opening a second account. But he knew that his activities must be kept from Mr Fowler, that smug bourgeois with his modern detached house in Friern Barnet and his Jewish friends. He liked Jews because they brought money into the bank. It sickened Vincent. Why, then, didn't he leave his job now? He contemplated it but some tenet of his upbringing clung and he didn't want to relinquish a steady occupation. Not yet, at any rate, until the Party was accepted as a real alternative to other forms of government. While he could manage to duplicate his positions as cashier and leader he would go on doing it. Would the bank sack him if his Party activities were discovered? It was likely. He realised he had been premature in insisting on the changed name-stand. He should have kept both identities until a final, glorious revelation that Vincent Pearman and Vincent Wright were the same man. That wouldn't have been possible, though, because his photograph would soon be in the papers, and Miss Glass – without doubt it would be Miss Glass – would spot it and bring it into the bank, agog. The situation nagged him as he conducted a brief interview with the woman reporter, and had his photograph taken and made arrangements with Fox to bring the boys to London at their half term. They would have a public meeting in Hyde Park, all in uniform. When he left after lunch in Fayers' car, with Patterson, Judy and his own three boys, he didn't feel as cheerful as he thought he should, with the money from Delage and the success of the week-end. Directly the train reached London he left the others, saying good-bye on the platform and taking a taxi to Madame Vera's house.

To his surprise it was not Madame Vera who opened the door but a stout lady in a navy blue blazer and panama hat. Madame Vera was standing in the hall, similarly dressed, with a cream flannel skirt that wrinkled and convoluted round her hips like tripe. She showed him into the front room with a social laugh, and he discovered three more ladies in the armchairs.

'I thought you'd be on your own,' he said shortly.

They wagged fingers at Madame Vera.

'It's my bowling Sunday,' said Madame Vera. 'We've been at the club practising, we've got a match with the Maidenhead ladies next week.'

'May I see you privately? It's important.'

They oohed and aahed again and Madame Vera shepherded them bleating into the kitchen. Still in her panama hat she sat at the table and took his hand.

'I have a sense of foreboding,' said Vincent.

'There's trouble. I see you serving the public, you're in a shop, no, it must be the bank. There's money there.'

'That's the bank then.'

'You can avoid it.'

'The trouble?'

'Yes. I see a letter too, an important letter.'

He paid her and went home, still uneasy, In his flat he pressed his uniform and prepared his clothes for the morning, bathed and went to bed. He lay stiff and still on the tightly tucked undersheet. He hated rucked sheets, an untidy bed. The princess and the pea his mother used to say laughingly when she made his bed. What was the trouble Madame Vera saw? How could he avoid it?

It was the Party of course. Mr Fowler would ask him to resign. He visualised the scene in the office, Fowler behind his desk patting the smooth green blotter as he told Vincent that his behaviour wasn't in keeping with bank policy. But if, thought Vincent, in some way I am exonerated before he finds out about the Party, then it will be doubly difficult for him to dismiss me. If I'm proved a perfect cashier he'll think twice before he asks me to go, because he'll have made a mistake already in doubting my abilities.

The idea, when it struck him, when it suddenly flew out of a vague undergrowth of thought like a bright bird, it overwhelmed him with its brilliance. He would write several anonymous letters to various personnel at the bank, accusing himself of forging the books. In an atmosphere of suspicion his books would be checked and found to be accurate and perfect. They would have to apologise, shake his hand, ask forgiveness. When other accusations were made against him, this time about the Party, it would be a long time before any action was taken. Long enough for the Party to become established on the political scene.

He turned on the light and swung his legs out of the covers. He went into the living-room for his writing paper, found a blue biro pen and, sitting at his small oak bureau wrote four letters in block capitals, holding the pen in his left hand. Fingerprints! He tore up the letters and went back to the bedroom for a pair of gloves and then wrote four more. He put them in envelopes and addressed two to Mr Fowler and one each to Miss Glass and the chief cashier. Then he went into the kitchen and tore up the rest of the writing pad, piled it in the sink and burnt it, washing the black ashes down the plughole. He hid one letter to Mr Fowler for posting later in the week and pulling his clothes over his pyjamas ran down the flights of stairs to the street. He took one of the last buses about two miles along the main road, bought stamps from a stamp machine outside a post office, posted the letters, still wearing gloves, dropped the biro pen in the gutter and walked back to his flat elated.

Lying in bed again he realised that his feeling of gloom was quite dispelled and he endured a surge of gratitude to Madame Vera that left him as exhausted as if he'd had an orgasm. Looking forward to the reaction to his letters he fell asleep.

No one said anything although he knew at least one letter had arrived on Tuesday by the early morning post. He had seen Merle carry in the mail to Mr Fowler's office and had recognised his own envelopes. Perhaps in the exigencies of sorting the other three were still waiting to be delivered. Miss Glass received no personal mail and was still absorbed, conversationally, with her mother's illness. Her mother had refused to let the district nurse wash her feet. Miss Glass had to do it when she returned home in the evenings. 'I think she's ashamed of them,' Miss Glass revealed. 'Her toenails are horney, and she's got bunions. She doesn't want nurse to know, that's my opinion, because nurse said the first time she came what lovely skin mother had for her age, like marble she said it was.'

Vincent wanted to ask Miss Glass to do some typing for him. She earned what she called 'spending money' by copy typing in the evenings. He wondered if she still managed to work at home now that her mother demanded so much of her time, instead of helping, as she had done before the illness. Then supper had been waiting for Miss Glass when she returned home.

'Oh, Miss Glass,' he called, as she left for her morning coffee break, 'can you spare me a moment?' She retraced her steps. 'It occurred to me you might not have time for your typing . . .'

'But I do, Mr Pearman. One has to keep up one's interests, one can't let everything go.'

'In that case would you do a little duplicating for me?'

'I haven't got a proper machine for duplicating.'

'Of course, I know that.' She knew he knew it. 'I need some carbon copies that's all. I don't want any favours, your proper prices please.'

She said she'd be delighted, and hurried off before her quarter of an hour was truncated further. He decided to bring the copy for her tomorrow. He was anxious to have it done, a letter to be sent to every member advising the time of the next meeting and a handout to be given away at the meeting itself, setting out the Party aims, and including the most dramatic items of the manifesto.

The mid-morning post arrived and Vincent thought he spotted another envelope. Mr Fowler gave no indication that he had received it, and continued to ignore Vincent whenever it was possible, as he had done since the request for the new name-stand. This had not yet arrived and no one else in the bank had been informed. Vincent wondered if Mr Fowler was deliberately suppressing it.

The chief cashier had several letters and Vincent thought he looked sharply in his direction twice before lunch. Miss Glass's letter came in the afternoon and she showed it to him at once.

'Oh, Mr Pearman, just look at this.' He read it with simulated horror. 'It's a poison pen, isn't it?' she said. 'Who ever could cast aspersions on you, we all know how hard you work.'

'I should take it into the office,' said Vincent. 'Mr Fowler may wish to take the matter to the police.' To his relief Miss Glass immediately agreed and within seconds was tapping indignantly on the glass panel of Mr Fowler's door. She came out with the disappointingly reassuring news that he intended to do nothing about it.

A more straightforward letter was in Vincent's letter basket when he unlocked the front door of his flat after work. It was from Jessop, asking if he might come up for the day on Saturday because he had an idea he wished to discuss with Vincent. Vincent was surprised at his own feeling of triumph. Jessop, Fox's most cherished member, had approached him and not Fox. He wrote a reply at once saying he would expect Jessop for lunch, and spent the rest of the evening composing and rewriting both the circular letter and the hand-out. Miss Glass's services were adequate for the time being but Vincent could see that shortly he would need a full-time secretary, working in the office in Windermere. He made daily notes on the things to be done, and which he had no time to do. He wanted his armband design translated into actual armbands; he wanted to complete the uniform in other ways but had no opportunity to look round the shops. There were boots, caps, shirts still to be chosen. He didn't want to delegate the authority but realised he would have to. He wanted printed letterheads, incorporating the Party insignia, but needed to discuss it with a printer, even employ a proper designer, before he commissioned an order. He contemplated asking Miss Glass to leave her job at the bank and work for him. He didn't doubt that she would, he was sure she had a secret admiration and respect for him. In the meantime he had sent Judy on one or two errands after school; she had gone down to the boutique and told the boy there to make sure there were adequate stocks. She was also compiling a file index, at the moment housed in a small maroon cardboard box with a flap lid. She had found two new members herself, one a schoolgirl from her class and the other her mother's Irish maid. The three boys were also recruiting from the various clubs and pubs they used. They reported success in that quite a number of people had agreed to come to the Hyde Park meeting, but had only one ardent convert, a man in his forties who was out of work because he suffered from epileptic fits. He had only had two in the last two years, he told Yates, but they had both occurred at work. The first one had been overlooked but the second resulted in dismissal. He had worked as a packer in a toy factory, the owners of which were Jewish. Yates had met him in an Oxford Street Lyons.

Vincent decided that Windermere must be used as a social centre for members for an hour or so each evening. Without a meeting place he felt new members might lose the interest that had been fanned up by the boys. When he arrived at the house on Wednesday evening he met the three new recruits, Wednesday being the maid's night off. He made a point of changing into his uniform every night now, and Wood, Winters and Yates did the same. Judy was not always able to, since her parents objected, and some evenings she did not come out at all because of her homework.

On Wednesday evening Vincent posted the second letter to Mr Fowler, it was more damaging and more specific in its charges and Vincent was certain that it must make Mr Fowler check up on the books. He couldn't overlook it, some germ of suspicion must be in his mind. Vincent had seen the letter to the chief cashier lying on the managerial desk, they must have discussed it, soon he would be questioned.

On Thursday Miss Glass brought in the typing she had done for him and handed it to him in a big buff envelope without comment. He paid her, and she put the money carefully into a red plastic combined wallet and purse. The charge was one pound nine and six.

'I expect there'll be some more next week,' Vincent said.

'I'm sorry, but I don't wish to do any more,' said Miss Glass, not looking at him.

'Not enough time?' asked Vincent sympathetically.

'I've plenty of time, but I don't like what you're doing, Mr Pearman. Whoever this Mr Wright is I think you should leave him alone, not get mixed up.'

'You ought to hear him speak,' said Vincent.

'I don't want to, thank you. It's just like the Nazis, don't think you're pulling wool over my eyes. We've fought two wars to rid us of that evil.'

'One war, actually, Miss Glass. And it's a matter of opinion just what was evil.'

'All that killing and camps.'

'The Britain First Party doesn't kill or have camps.'

'I don't want to argue. I just don't wish to type any more.' She tightened her mouth, and clipped her handbag shut.

'It's people like you, Miss Glass,' said Vincent, 'that are bogging Britain down with your nineteen forties mentality. You'll be telling me to eat carrots soon, so that I can see in the dark.'

So that he should see if his ledgers had been searched he put a hair across the closed pages of the one he had specified in the last letter, trapping the ends under the hard covers. He had spent five minutes in the lavatory trying to pull out the right length hair from the crown of his head. It was astonishingly difficult and painful, and his hairs were all too short. Eventually he took one out of a comb the girls had left on the shelf over the washbasin, and had the problem of carrying it back to his ledger, not knowing, because it was too fine to feel, whether it was still in his hand. He had to hold his hand loosely, since it would look strange if he walked with a tightly closed fist. He wound the hair round his middle finger and let it fall on to his palm. It wasn't a thing he could put into a pocket or wrap in a handkerchief. When he had finally placed it in position he felt pleased at his subtlety over the whole manoeuvring of his plan.

He had arranged to telephone Patterson during the week, to see if he had recruited any new members. As a schoolmaster Patterson had to be careful, especially since, in his position, he was able to imbue the young with Party ideals and his job was therefore valuable. Vincent made one of his brief visits to his mother and telephoned from her house to Patterson's digs. Because Patterson lived and taught in a negro-populated area he had had a good response. His landlady and her husband, who refused to take coloured lodgers, had wanted to give Patterson their signatures as proof of their enthusiasm.

'We must get membership cards,' said Patterson.

The landlord of the local pub also wanted to join because his white customers now went elsewhere. Several other people, who felt that the immigrants had taken the homes they might have had themselves also asked for membership.

'They'd do anything to get the blacks out,' Patterson said, 'kill their own mothers if they had too, the feeling is really high.'

The matter of membership cards was of prime urgency. During his next lunch hour Vincent ordered them from the stationer next door to the bank. There was a three week waiting period for orders, but Vincent made the stationer telephone the printers while he was there, and the waiting was reduced to ten days. When he returned from lunch the hair had fallen out of the ledger.

Vincent heard Jessop come up the noisy lift. He waited just inside his front door, listening, and knew it was Jessop when the gates clanged back on his floor. It was only a few steps from the lift to the door, and in seconds there was a long, firm ring on his bell. Vincent stood quite still in the hall so that Jessop should not know he was eager for the visit. He had been waiting anxiously since eleven o'clock, first at the window, then in the hall, and once even peering through the letterbox when he thought he heard someone walking about on the landing outside.

When he opened the door and they stood facing, Vincent saluted and almost simultaneously Jessop saluted back, then came in and took off his raincoat which Vincent hung on a hook in the hall cupboard. Together they went into the sitting-room.

'Sit down,' said Vincent, sitting down himself.

Jessop sat on the sofa, and lit a cigarette. 'I'm not in training today.' He smiled charmingly.

Vincent gave him the news of the new recruits and Jessop added another one, the janitor's daughter who served in the tuck shop.

'She'd believe anything I told her,' he said, 'I wouldn't say it's an intellectual conversion, but she may be useful. We all have her, but the sun shines out of me. I'm quite important in the school you know.'

Vincent recalled that he was head boy.

Over lunch Jessop told Vincent his ideas. Fox, he said, would think it corrupt, and in a way it was. But if they wanted to pull in young people they had to use the right aids, it was no use hoping that they would appeal on policy alone. Just as highly ethical products were advertised in a way that might be considered immoral, so the Britain First Party might rouse members who would otherwise not respond at all. No one would deny that some advertised medicines were efficacious, yet one might decry the method used in a commercial. What he suggested was that a pop group might be used to sing some Party songs, they might even bring out a record, give the Party a really contemporary pull to the teenage market.

'Market is hardly the word I'd use,' said Vincent, giving Jessop a piece of the treacle tart his mother had made him take home on Thursday.

'Well, it's not the right word,' said Jessop. 'Yet in a way it is. It doesn't matter how we get them, so long as they're convinced later. They're so bloody apathetic these days, you've got to have a hard sell.'

In the afternoon Vincent took him to Windermere, and the three boys discussed the idea with them. They thought it was marvellous. Judy, arriving breathless from a visit to her grandmother, said it was a brilliant suggestion. What group could they have? Should they approach an existing one, a popular one, or form a new one out of the members? How about Jessop's school? Was there one there?

'There is,' said Jessop, 'but they're not much good.'

'There's enough talent around,' said Yates. 'You've only got to go to the coffee bars or pubs. Hundreds of aspiring kids with their guitars and drums. It shouldn't be difficult to find a good group.'

They decided to make a round that evening. Yates and Wood made a list of the most likely places, while Vincent, Jessop and Winters toured the local shops for suitable boots. Jessop felt that ordinary motor cycle boots with zips at the back were the most practical and smart. Winters tried them on, since he was wearing the uniform, and Vincent bought them for him straightaway, and a pair each for himself and Jessop. 'We'll send the others down,' he said, as they walked back to Windermere along the tree-lined road. The boots made a firm tread, a definite noise where shoes were silent. The uniform was now almost complete. Judy's father was having the armbands manufactured for her in his dress factory. He was under the misapprehension that they were for a secret society at her school. Vincent thought there was a supreme irony in this, he liked the idea of that prosperous Jewish family being undermined by the daughter of the house and the trusted maid, and the head of the family actually providing the insignia in total ignorance.

The other boys and Judy bought their boots, and Vincent lined them up in the hall of Windermere and inspected them. It was an exciting moment. Somehow the boots made an enormous difference to the effect, made the uniform authoritative, more purposeful. Over supper they planned their route round the pubs and clubs, and Judy and Yates took a taxi round to her house to collect her father's car for the evening. He lent it to Judy's boy friends when they took her out, said there would be no excuse for her to stay late, his car had a homing instinct. They parked it outside Windermere, and then, with Vincent in the front seat and the four others in the back, Yates drove the Jaguar saloon down to Mile End, their first stop.

The pub was called the Lord Nelson, they could hear the best music through the closed windows of the car. Boys and girls stood on the pavement, going backwards and forwards through the swing doors. Motorbikes, scooters and cars were parked in the sidestreet and the alley behind the pub. Yates made sure all the car doors were locked and then they pushed their way through the packed bar to where the group were playing on a small platform. There were four boys, rather scruffy and dirty-looking, with untidy long hair, playing and jerking and singing the number that was currently number one on the hit parade. They had two amplifiers which magnified and distorted, and Vincent had never experienced such claustrophobia as he did now from the noise, smoke, jammed bodies and smell of beer. An hermaphroditic creature minced through the crowd with an upheld tray, like a maid in a farce. Four pairs of girls danced close to the platform. They had sharp bird features, long beads, thin legs and elaborate hair. Everyone, except Vincent and the hermaphrodite, was young.

'Come on,' said Yates, 'let's go.'

They shoved their way out again and Vincent sank down in the car with relief.

'Wasn't it heavenly,' said Judy rapturously.

They drove further into the East End, where the group they had come to see was part of a series of turns. A blonde woman was singing seductively as they went in. Vincent had no idea it was a man until Winters told him, and he then could barely believe it, although he thought he could detect a darkness on the chin and upper lip beneath the heavy powder. The next turn was also a man dressed as a woman, and this one, in a tight green dress with red hair reaching to her shoulders and theatrical eye make-up, told a number of blue jokes before singing a Marlene Dietrich number.

The group which followed consisted of five boys. Vincent thought they seemed better than the ones in the last pub, but Yates said, 'Much too camp.' And they left before the song was finished.

They went next to a club in Hackney, which was in a darkened room, lit only with red bulbs. The group here, which sung blues, had a young negro trumpeter, which ruled it out as far as the Party was concerned. Three more clubs, in Finchley, Swiss Cottage and Charing Cross Road, and a final pub in Fulham, just before closing time, completed the boys' list. To Vincent all the groups, except for the one with the negro, sounded alike. His own preference was for the one in Swiss Cottage, because the members had short hair and a smarter appearance. They wore black shirts which gave a suggestion of Hitler Youth. But the boys were adamant about their unsuitability. 'Anyone can have his hair cut and put on a black shirt,' said Jessop.

'Two years out of date,' said Wood.

They told Vincent that the four boys from the Lord Nelson were the right ones to attract the young people they wanted for the Party. This group could make the charts, they said, with the right handling. The others never would, were too derivative.

'All right,' said Vincent, 'I take your word for it. Get hold of them for me. I'll see them at the office any evening you can arrange it.'

It was half past eleven when Yates dropped Vincent and Jessop outside Queens Mansions. Vincent had expected Jessop to go back to school, or home for the rest of the week-end. Now he hurriedly made up a bed on the couch, and while they drank a cup of tea he played Jessop the overture to Rienzi.

'I prefer that to the Colonel's Gilbert and Sullivan,' Jessop said. 'I can't understand why he goes for it. But this really stirs you up. It's great stuff.'

'I feel,' said Vincent carefully, 'that you are closer in outlook to me. I may not be able to take you on cross-country hikes, but I can lead you in more important ways. I believe you have something of that spark.'

Jessop grinned. 'I know so. I've always been a monitor, patrol leader, prefect, now head boy, ever since I've started school. Even at kindergarten I led the class into prayers. Richard Jessop lead, Miss Dingle would say, every morning.'

'How are you getting on with the Britain First Youth idea?'

'Quite well. I'm afraid I'm neglecting my work a bit, I'm supposed to be going up to Cambridge next year. The old man will be furious if I don't get the required A levels, but I find the Party absorbs me. We've had several meetings, the boys I took to the Colonel's last week-end, and myself. We have some ideas I'd like to put to you one day. This thought about a pop group came from one of our meetings.'

'I'd no idea you were so organised.'

'Oh, you'd be surprised. I only wish I could get it going in other schools. Public schools produce the type of man you want, we know how to lead, have the right sort of background, upbringing. I've been trying to think of a way to get the movement going in say the top six or seven schools.'

'And the younger boys?'

'I've started weekly meetings in the hour they have after prep. I take along a bag of buns from the tuck shop, it's put the member-ship up no end, the word got round. I should say by the end of term I'll have something like twenty boys. They're a bit flat-tered I'm interested in them, a lot of them have crushes on me. Normally I discourage it but I don't mind using their adoration for this purpose.'

Of course they adore him, thought Vincent, tall, handsome, dominating. He remembered the PT instructor from his school who was suddenly called up, leaving a gap that was never adequately filled during the rest of his school days, a series of elderly men over fighting age succeeding one another. Boys like to have a hero. Jessop was the kind to be worshipped.

They talked for a little longer and then Vincent said good night, leaving Jessop to read *Mein Kampf* by the electric fire.

Chapter 8

JESSOP left on Sunday at midday, and Vincent decided to spend the afternoon at Windermere, writing a rough speech for the meeting next week-end and organising the office in preparation for the stationery and membership cards which would be ready during the week. To his great surprise Patterson was there, drinking coffee in the living-room with Wood and Winters and the member who had epileptic fits. Patterson had bought a uniform, but hadn't, of course, acquired the boots. Vincent thought how stupid his tan laced-up shoes and hand-knitted socks looked. He was annoyed to find Patterson in the house, he resented the way in which Patterson always conducted long private conversations with one or another of the boys.

'I hear Jessop's been with you,' he said, as Vincent came in.

'Yes. I think he found the week-end interesting.'

Patterson didn't answer, and Vincent thought, he'll report that straight back to Fox.

'I've brought along my list of members,' Patterson said. 'I thought you'd like it, so that you can file them. I've got twenty-three.'

'Pretty good, isn't it?' said Winters.

'Excellent.'

'Also I wondered if you would have time to come over one evening, and conduct an informal meeting. I think it will ensure they turn up for the Hyde Park gathering. You know, so far I've been the only proof that there is a Party. No membership cards, no armbands. That's why I rushed along yesterday to get this gear. But it's not enough.' He seemed to imply that Vincent was inefficient because the armbands and cards were not ready. 'You asked us all to recruit, but it's pretty tough going when there's nothing to back one up.'

'I can probably manage an hour or two,' said Vincent coldly.

'What about Tuesday, then?'

'All right.'

'Can you pick me up from school at four?'

'I may not be able to be with you as early as that.'

'If you'll forgive me saying so,' said Patterson, 'if you're leading the Party you've got to be available.'

'Why do you want me so early?'

'I want to introduce you to one or two members who can play an important part in local recruitment. And I thought you might like to see just what a racially mixed area looks like close at hand.'

'I'd be interested to have a look round,' said Vincent.

'Exactly. It's no use being all hypothetical, you have to know the problems personally. Otherwise you'll find yourself in a bit of a spot when the heckling starts.'

In a way Vincent was grateful to Patterson because he was being helpful, only his help was given with such veiled sneering Vincent would have liked to refuse it. Nevertheless Patterson had been extremely successful in his recruitment, and it would be pointless to snub him, at any rate at this juncture. Patterson was the type to walk out on the Party altogether if Vincent really riled him, taking other members with him.

Although Vincent was stimulated and excited by the growth of the Party he felt tired. His work at the bank demanded concentration and he had had no time to relax at home. Even when he tried to listen to a record or read a newspaper, he thought about the Party and all he must do during the next weeks. Every tiny detail of organisation had to be worked out and at times he felt he was at the centre of a tightly wound ball of wool from which he must free himself. It was a visual image. The ball of wool was Air Force blue and lay on his mother's red patterned carpet. The ball jerked as she knitted, and became smaller. As he straightened out the problems of planning it was like the knitting growing and the wool diminishing. The knitting his mother was doing was a balaclava helmet, dredged from memory, strange that it should come back to him now, he had forgotten it absolutely until the idea of the ball of wool struck him. The helmet had been for a cousin in the Balloon

Barrage who had now emigrated to the United States, and sent yearly calendars with pictures of the New England autumn.

On Sunday evening, having finished all he had to do at Windermere, he decided to go to his mother's house and spend a few hours there. He suddenly felt in need of an armchair in front of a fire, the television meandering on in a corner, a sandwich brought to him on a tray and a cushion plumped behind his back. All the things he despised and rejected were at that moment desirable. To his frustration his Uncle and Aunt were there, his Aunt planted in the chair he coveted, the television off and a conversation about members of his family in progress. They were pleased to see him, his mother proud to demonstrate that although no longer living at home, he still popped in whenever he could. He kissed his mother and Aunt, sat on a hard chair and heard about June's confinement and Aunt Mavis's ungrateful daughter-in-law.

'When are you going to surprise us, Vincent?' said his Aunt.

'Vincent's never bothered about girls,' said his mother for him. 'He's too wrapped up.'

'He always was thoughtful,' replied his Aunt, nodding. 'The clever one of the family.'

Vincent endured it for half an hour and then left.

'I've got a feeling he's hurrying away because he's got someone special to see,' said his Aunt coyly. Mrs Pearman's face froze. Vincent reassured her.

He walked home aware that he was irritable and overwrought, made himself a cup of Horlicks and went to bed. He fell asleep more quickly than he had expected and dreamed that his mother was going to marry Patterson. He shouted at his mother and she cried. He told her she was marrying a Fascist, and she at once brought out a plate of tongue sandwiches which she said she had made especially for him. He awoke and it was only half past twelve. He didn't fall asleep again until after four.

Mr Fowler asked him to come into his office. Vincent closed his till and repressed a smile, assumed a puzzled expression and knocked on the door.

Mr Fowler was embarrassed. He looked at the papers on his

desk, at the clock, the calendar on the wall, out of the window. No doubt, he said, Vincent was aware of the anonymous letters which had been sent to bank personnel. He himself was the recipient of two. He felt it only fair to tell Vincent that although he didn't believe that Vincent had in any way defaulted at his job, he had to satisfy himself that the letters were libellous. He was examining Vincent's books dating back over the last four years. This would take time, he was sorry to have to tell Vincent anything so unpleasant but he couldn't do anything behind the back of an entrusted employee. He could go back to work now.

It had worked like a charm. Miss Glass looked at him with blatant nosiness as he stood beside her but he ignored her. She must have guessed, he thought. Probably she was enjoying it, she and her mother probably pulled him to pieces metaphorically every evening. Was he a crook or wasn't he? Would he be dismissed? Would they call in the police? Vincent paid out small cheque after small cheque, and enjoyed keeping the queue waiting as a tradesman paid in last week's takings. He was tired but last night's despondency had gone. He would go to bed early and have a good night's sleep, and be alert and vigorous, ready to address Patterson's recruits tomorrow.

★   ★   ★

He said he had to go to the doctor and Mr Fowler nodded sympathetically, as if this had something to do with the allegations against him.

'I'm not sleeping too well,' Vincent added, taking the cue. He went by bus and then underground to Paddington, and sure he would get lost in spite of Patterson's directions, took a taxi from the station to the school.

It was a big, dark Victorian building with some shed-like extensions at the side, and on the right of the school was a site of shabby prefabricated houses. A board in the playground said Parton Street Primary School. Headmaster, Mr I. P. Jones. Vincent waited a few moments at the gate and then decided to go into the school. He met a girl coming down the stairs on her way to the outside lavatory and asked her where he might find Mr Patterson. The girl said he was in class four. Before he had climbed the stone stairs the bell rang, jangling along a corridor and back again. There was an immediate hubbub and Vincent was nearly swept downstairs again by a pushing crowd of children. He stood at one side, pressed against the glazed brick wall, until most of them had gone and then went on up to find Patterson. A woman teacher directed him to the classroom, and Vincent could see through the windows that gave on to the corridor that Patterson had not yet released his class. Patterson saw Vincent and called out that he should come in. Vincent opened the door and the forty children watched him, wondering who he was. They looked defiant and Vincent guessed that Patterson was keeping them in as a punishment, Patterson seemed elated. His cheeks were flushed. He continued to address the class as though Vincent was not there, although Vincent felt Patterson was very aware of his presence and putting on a show for him.

'I am keeping you all here,' said Patterson, 'because one boy has let the whole class down. He's a rude, insolent, impolite *pig*, the kind of boy this kind of school has to put up with because it can't choose its pupils. Derwent, come out here.' A pale, fat boy in tight jeans, plimsolls and a blue sweater with a hole in it came out to the front of the room. Patterson grabbed his arm and jerked him forward. 'I met Derwent in the street this morning, on the way to school. I said good morning to Derwent, but Derwent chose to ignore me. He was wearing a school cap but he didn't raise it. He didn't answer me. Where are your manners, Derwent?' He pulled the boy's arm. He didn't answer. 'You see, he doesn't speak to me. He doesn't think it necessary to speak to those superior to himself. I'm going to teach you a lesson, Derwent. Shall I send for the punishment book and cane?' A gasp went up from the class. 'No, I've got a better way of making bad mannered boys behave. Out into the playground everyone and wait for me.'

The children scraped their chairs back and went to the door, whispering at first and then talking normally.

'Shut up,' yelled Patterson. They clattered down the stairs, Patterson still grasping Derwent's arm, Vincent following.

'Go and get your cap, Derwent,' said Patterson. Each time he said the boy's name he spat it out as if it was a disgusting word. The boy came back holding his cap. The rest of the class were clustered round the door leading to the playground.

'Put your cap on,' ordered Patterson, and snatched the cap and banged it hard down on to the boy's head. 'This is a boy who can't raise his cap to a master,' said Patterson shrilly to his class. 'We're going to show him how to raise his cap, aren't we? He's going to walk round this playground twenty times and he's going to raise his cap to everything he sees. Go on, Derwent. Raise your cap.'

The boy, obviously close to tears, touched his cap.

'Raise it, I said raise it. Take if off and put it back on your thick skull. Now go on, walk, walk. Take your cap off. There's a tree. Take your cap off to the tree, Derwent.'

The rest of the class stood silently.

'We must cheer him on, mustn't we?' said Patterson. 'Let's cheer when he raises his cap, shall we? There's the toilets, Derwent, raise your cap.'

Derwent lifted his cap in silence.

'I said cheer. Cheer when I tell you to or I'll have the whole lot of you walking round after Derwent.'

The class muttered, then under Patterson's orders, raised the sound to a cheer. Patterson exhorted them as the boy progressed round and round the playground, raising his cap at the solitary tree, the lavatory building, the netball posts, the prefabricated buildings, the gate through which he must have longed to run home.

At last he had made the twentieth circuit.

'Come here,' Patterson commanded. 'Now raise your cap to me.' Derwent did. 'And don't forget in future.' He gave him a blow on the head which made him stumble, and then turned back into the school. 'Good night,' he said to the class.

'Good night Mr Patterson,' they chorused. Subdued they walked across the asphalt and out of the gate.

Patterson laughed as he led the way upstairs. 'Won't make that mistake again, will he? What did you think of my psychology?' His hands trembled as he opened the staff-room door. He's unstable, thought Vincent, he's hysterical. Patterson collected his books and raincoat and together they left the school. 'We get the dregs round here,' said Patterson, 'the lowest lousiest children in the district.'

Children were playing on the pavements of the side streets through which they walked, little girls with rusty prams, small boys with carts, other girls with skipping ropes. More than half the children were negro.

'Filthy, isn't it?' said Patterson. The front doors of the four- and five-storey houses were open revealing unpainted passages, more prams parked inside. People looked out of windows or stood on steps. A well-dressed negro girl in her twenties came along the pavement and had to stand to one side to avoid them.

'I'm not giving way to any nigger,' said Patterson.

'It's a disgrace to the country,' said Vincent. 'The government had no right to let them in. They should follow the Australian policy, no black immigrants; segregate the schools for those they have got, like you do with the aborigines.'

'Derwent deserved what he got,' said Patterson, 'but if he'd been black I'd have beaten the guts out of him.'

His digs were close to the Portobello Road. They walked along past the antique shops and arcades until they came to the turning.

'It's a bit better here,' said Patterson, 'although there's nowhere decent for what I can pay.'

The house, similar to those in all the terraces they had passed, was in a better state of repair, and the hall was papered with a design in red and grey. There was a carpet on the stairs. Patterson led the way to his room on the first floor, large with a moulded cornice and ornate fireplace, now blocked and fitted with a small gas fire. A box with the meter stood inside the grate, where there was also a gas ring. The walls were papered with the same red and grey. There was a paisley bedspread. Patterson's slippers were at the side of the bed and his slightly soiled black silk dressing-gown hung behind the door. He had a new television set on thin black metal legs.

'Hired,' he said to Vincent. 'If I can't find some tart to screw at night I watch it.'

Vincent recoiled. Patterson was showing himself to be more and more unpleasant, the pathological display in the playground, the vain boast just now in an attempt to imply he was a sexual success when Vincent was sure that he was a failure. He had seen how Patterson shadowed Judy, while Judy treated him as if he were her own school teacher in fact, certainly not as a possible lover. And Judy wasn't fussy. He can't be relied upon, thought Vincent, he would abuse privilege.

The meeting went well. Patterson's landlady, slovenly and venomous, her more easy-going husband who said that all blackies weren't that bad, the local publican who seemed genial until roused by the subject of immigration, half a dozen women who were the landlady's friends, all seemed stirred and promised to turn up at Hyde Park. Vincent asked them all to bring at least two friends.

'I want a solid mass of support,' he said. 'I want people to notice us and say, "These aren't the usual Hyde Park cranks. This looks important." I'll have the armbands for you, and the membership cards. If there are any reporters around tell them why you're there. Tell the passers-by, tell the policemen, make sure they know what the Britain First Party is. If you feel you can afford the uniform, this is where you can buy it, if you want to see how things go before you commit yourselves that far, just wear an armband. But be there. Support me. Support Britain. Put Britain first.'

The morning of the Hyde Park Rally, as Vincent thought of it, was bright and crisp, the air was clear, it was the first real summer day of the year. Vincent met Fox and the boys at the station. Jessop had recruited a few more and, without counting, Vincent thought there were at least thirty. Dobson and Delage were on the train too, and Fayers was driving up later on, Fox said, with Mrs Fayers. A friend was looking after the hotel. Vincent thought he recognised one or two people from the first meeting, but wasn't certain.

Judy's father had promised her that the armbands would be ready today and she was going to take them up to Windermere. He had collected the membership cards during the week and Winters had been detailed to fill them in. Members had been asked, if possible, to foregather at Windermere.

Patterson had telephoned early to say he would meet them in Hyde Park with his party of recruits. He had added the fathers of several of his class who objected to their children being taught with foreigners. Held back, was the phrase they used about their own children's education. He had called at the homes of the parents he felt would sympathise. It was a risk, he said, because an approach to the wrong type, some communist for instance, would mean a chance of dismissal, but fortunately he had met only with immediate and heartwarming support.

Yates, driving Judy's father's car, took Vincent, Fox, Dobson and Delage to the Park. Judy chose to come with the boys, by underground. In one way Vincent would have liked to be with them, it would be the first public appearance of a uniformed contingent, he would have liked to see the reactions in the carriage and on the platform. But he decided that his position as leader demanded that he travelled in grander circumstances.

The boys were under instruction to march to the meeting place. Fox had rehearsed them in the back garden of Windermere, and they looked forceful and menacing, four abreast, Jessop tall, blond and unmistakably of his social class at the front.

Vincent arrived first and together with the other members of the committee decided on the position for the meeting. Other speakers were already deep in tirade; a small woman with grey plaits and a cloak who claimed to have had a personal vision of Christ; a large man denouncing blood sports; a young student with a Middle-European accent demanding unilateral banning of the Bomb. Vincent stood as far away from them as he could. Yates had put a chair in the capacious boot of the car, which he carried about until Vincent selected the exact spot for him to put it down. He didn't climb on it, but walked round it several times, closely surrounded by the other four. He saw himself as a leader surrounded by henchmen. Patterson and his supporting unit appeared from the subway under the road. Vincent saw them and saluted. Patterson responded. Behind him the middle-aged landladies in coats and hats and the few suited men raised their arms and placed their fists on their brows. Only Patterson was in uniform. Jessop, also appeared from the subway, leading his battalion.

The contingents merged and Vincent climbed up on to his chair. He spoke passionately and eloquently and his audience cheered him. A crowd drawn from other speakers swelled almost to the edges of the area. The scattering of grey uniforms caught the attention of car drivers and passengers on the buses as they passed. Vincent saw in a kind of dream state the pale blobs of the staring faces as they passed him. He was uplifted, in a state of inspiration. He felt the hearts of the listening people beat in unison, that he dictated the speed of the pulse.

'I know,' he said, 'that I am not speaking in a vacuum. I know that you are waiting to free Britain, that you have been waiting like bubbles that rise in a pan at that instant before boiling point. I am the flame under that pan. The flame is high now. You have waited for me to come as your leader. I welcome you with a bursting heart because you are the salt of the earth, true Britons, the most loyal and brave and proud and strong of men. You are right to want your fertile country for yourselves and your children. You don't want this human scum lapping round you, blocking progress, flooding your homes and schools and businesses. You wouldn't take an unwholesome stranger into your family, would you? Why should you? Yet aren't we one family, we British? Why should we open our homeland to those who defile it, sap it, and misuse it for themselves? Our children in our British schools sit side by side with alien brats who can't even speak our beautiful language, who believe in primitive Gods and have very very different values to ourselves. Let them build up their own civilisation in their own countries *if they can*. I have been accused of intolerance by our Communist friends, but I say, where does one draw the line that marks tolerance from intolerance. Is it intolerant to want the best for our own children? Do you think it right that some foreigner should have a hospital bed while Englishmen wait in a queue? You may be able to queue behind a negro in a fish queue, and not come to harm. But why should you queue behind him for a place in hospital? Should you wait on a housing list while intruders sail into our harbours and take the very homes our labourers have built for us? Should a British trained teacher devote time to instructing an African child to speak English, or should that time be spent in teaching an English child to read?'

Two policemen had now joined the crowd and were watching

intently for trouble, ready to break up any arguments that might develop. Vincent saw them.

'If the government agrees to an immigration plan for the black races, why aren't they in Parliament? Why aren't they in the police force? Because the government knows the people wouldn't stand for it.'

'What about the hospitals?' someone yelled.

'And the buses?'

'I suggest that some of our own unemployed could give you the answer,' retorted Vincent. 'How about some grants so that British women might train as nurses? What about higher wages? It's a cause, not an effect. Kick them out and we'd manage all right. The hospitals wouldn't close. Transport wouldn't come to a standstill.'

'We finished 'Itler once,' a man shouted. 'If you keep on I'll do it again.'

' 'E's a Nazi.'

'Pipe down Jew-baiter.'

Wood and Winters and two other boys leaped at the hecklers and there was a violent scuffle. The policemen pulled them apart. Other policemen arrived, and broke up the crowd. Vincent climbed off the chair and called to Jessop to assemble the boys and leave. A man came up to him.

'I'm a free-lance journalist. I'd like to phone a story through to the evening papers. What is the name of your party?'

'The Britain First Party.'

'And your name?'

'Wright. I am the leader.'

'An apt name, you seem pretty far right to me.'

'You can say,' said Vincent curtly, 'that we have considerable support. There's been a big response at our meetings in the Home counties, and in certain London areas.'

'Where are your headquarters?'

'In North London,' said Vincent. 'That is as much as I wish to divulge.'

'Frightened of getting some fireworks through the letterbox?'

A policeman came up. 'Move off, please. You're causing a disturbance.'

'You'll wish you never said that one day,' called out a member of Patterson's group.

Vincent said to Yates, 'Start the car.'

Wood, Winters and Yates escorted him to the car, where Fox, Delage and Dobson were waiting anxiously on the back seat. Vincent saw Fayers's car for the first time, parked just behind them, with Mr and Mrs Fayers in the front seats, he in his chauffeur's uniform and his wife in a pale blue costume with a fur stole. Yates drove away slowly and Fayers pulled out after him.

'You were really in form,' said Delage warmly as they cruised along the Bayswater Road.

There was nothing in the first or second editions of the papers but in the third edition there was a small paragraph on an inside page. It was headed Nazi Disturbance in Park, and said that a speaker calling himself the leader of an extreme right wing party provoked heckling and some fighting among spectators at Speakers' Corner in Hyde Park. It didn't mention either the name of the party or its leader. Vincent, who had sent for the papers from Windermere, was furious. He made Judy look up the telephone numbers of the leading dailies, and rang them in turn, giving an account of the meeting, and a glowing description of the support. When asked for his name he gave Fox's. He told the news-desks that many party members were in London and that they should keep an eye open for the uniform, which he described. The telephoning completed, Vincent called Jessop to the office and instructed him to send the boys to the West End, in groups of four or five. 'Make sure you're seen in prominent places,' he said, 'Piccadilly and Trafalgar Square, avoid punch-ups, but try and let people know who you are, I want to give an impression that there are considerably more of you than there really are.'

Judy had borrowed the car for the day, and Yates drove him to Madame Vera. She promised to chart his next moves with minute care. 'Don't keep secrets from those close to you,' she said as he left, 'it could cause harm.'

'I haven't any secrets,' said Vincent.

Yates drove him back and they passed Judy and Jessop walking towards the house. Perhaps that's what she meant thought Vincent, perhaps I should tell Jessop that Judy's Jewish.

'Could you spare me a few moments, Mr Pearman,' said Mr Fowler on Monday morning.

'Certainly.' Vincent followed him into the office.

'I want to tell you,' said Mr Fowler, 'that we have examined your books and there is not one error.' He held out his hand and averted his eyes, then with a show of willpower forced them back to meet Vincent's. 'Personally I never doubted your integrity, and I'm sure you understand that we could not do otherwise than we did. Nevertheless I want to apologise to you for any unhappiness that the situation accorded.' He held out his hand. Vincent took it. Mr Fowler applied pressure and withdrew quickly. 'I know you will not bear a grudge.'

'Not at all,' said Vincent.

'Your new name-stand should be here later today.'

'Thank you.'

'I won't keep you from your work any longer, Mr Pearman.'

'Thank you.'

Vincent closed the door quietly behind him. Miss Glass looked up.

'Was it about the letters?'

'Yes. There was of course no shred of evidence that the allegations were correct.'

'I knew that. Does he know who sent those letters?'

'No.'

'He said the police have them.'

Vincent was surprised but not worried. 'They couldn't find out! No one who's likely to send them would make any stupid errors.' In any case there was surely no law in attempting to libel oneself.

'Do you want the early lunch?'

'That's very kind of you, Miss Glass.' She must have believed the letters, this could only be an atonement.

He had bought copies of all the papers he had telephoned, and over lunch he scanned every page. There were two small reports, one in the *Sketch* and one in *The Times*. Both mentioned his name. Mr Fowler read the *Telegraph* but Miss Glass took the *Sketch*. However she didn't know about his changed name and by tomorrow, when the new name stand arrived, she would have forgotten the paragraph, even if she had read it. He decided to keep the new stand for the time being and retain Pearman for his private life, until it was impossible to have a private life any longer. Before leaving at the end of the day he told Mr Fowler that he hadn't decided about the change of name after all, and Mr Fowler shook his hand for the second time.

'I think you're being wise,' he said. 'Only confuse people.'

Miss Glass caught him up at the bus stop. She waved the folded paper.

'Is this the Mr Wright I did your typing for?'

Vincent reread the item.

'It may be, Miss Glass. I wouldn't know.'

'It won't catch on here,' she said, hailing a bus.

Vincent took the buttons and the belt and the dagger out of his chest of drawers, and put the handkerchiefs that had concealed them in a neat pile. Then he closed the drawer and wrapped the objects in the sheet of newspaper that was laying ready on the bed. He bound the ends with sticky tape, and pressed the parcel into the rubbish bucket in the kitchen, emptied the contents of the sink-tidy on the top, then picking up the bucket by the handle carried it out of the flat and down in the lift to the basement where the main dustbins were. The usual practice was for the porter to empty the rubbish from the bins that the tenants put outside the doors of their flats each night. He was in the basement when Vincent emerged from the lift.

'Bit of an overflow today,' said Vincent, tipping his bucket over the heap of rotting refuse and watching the parcel disappear under the potato peelings and wet tea leaves he had tipped on top of it. It looked now, like an old newspaper, or one of those packages his mother made of the scraps from the dinner plates.

As he rode up in the lift, the empty bucket swinging from his hand, he suddenly remembered the school kitchen one morning in nineteen thirty eight or nine. He had gone to fetch the milk straws, the job of the week's monitor, and the German cook who had left soon after, had been peeling potatoes over a bucket, listening to the wireless. Her name was Elli. The children called her Belly. When he went in for the straws she was laughing, and as he left tears had been running down her face. She had been terribly excited. He had been nervous and remembered telling his mother that evening. She said comfortingly that all foreigners were excitable, and probably the cook missed her home. It dawned on Vincent, as the lift stopped at his floor, that Elli had been listening to Hitler. Perhaps, if she was still alive, one day in Germany she would tune in to him.

Chapter 9

'I BELIEVE,' said Fox, opening the window, 'that the answer is large-scale manoeuvres.' It had been raining and the windows ran with water. The air in the room, strong from Dobson's pipe smoke, was refreshed by the smell of wet earth and grass. From where he was sitting Vincent could see a blackbird already on the lawn pulling at a worm. The worm looked elastic in its desperate stretch for life. The blackbird jerked it out of the ground and hopped off across the grass before setting it down and pecking bits out of it.

'Don't you think manoeuvres are a bit military?' asked Dobson. 'It might give the wrong impression.'

'I don't think so. A show of strength and purpose could only give the right impression. That we mean business.'

'On the contrary,' said Vincent slowly, 'I think the very word manoeuvres will antagonise people. Let's call it field craft or tracking.' He had instigated the meeting to discuss a way of bringing the Party to the attention of the press. He had been disappointed by the three insignificant lines sandwiched between items on an inside page that the Hyde Park meeting had produced.

'Call it what you like,' said Fox eagerly. 'The people who matter will know we mean action. I thought we might do something in the school holidays, two or three days in the New Forest with daily exercises and emergency rations.'

'If we advertise it in the right way,' said Dobson, 'parents might send their boys from all over the country. We could phrase it in Outward Bound terms.'

'I reckon old soldiers will want to join,' said Fayers. 'Get away from their families for a bit, they miss the war. Look how they love that fortnight with the territorials.'

'We might even mention civil defence,' said Vincent.

'I am convinced,' said Fox fervently, 'that this is the kind of gesture we must make. We are not merely a political party, discussing policies round a conference table. We preach physical fitness and bodily strength, let's demonstrate it too with a hard core of members in peak condition, battle condition.'

'The papers will love it,' said Fayers, 'reporters will be round like dogs after a bitch.'

'I agree,' said Vincent, 'but we must be very careful in the way we handle them. If Fox feels he can organise it, then it might make the impact I want. But it mustn't go wrong, it mustn't become a jamboree, I don't want women in the tents at night or an inferior type of boy taking part. It has to be serious, controlled and impressive.'

'I'll handle it like a military campaign,' said Fox. 'I could let you have details in two weeks.'

'Very well. I don't think we need vote on it, we seem to be of one mind. By the way,' Vincent looked at Fox, 'I'd like you to give Jessop some real initiative tasks, I want to know how he reacts.'

'I can tell you that now,' said Fox. 'I could tell you every move he would make.'

Their eyes met. 'I may want him up in London the next few week-ends,' said Vincent coldly. 'In any case I don't want him to waste his time boy-scouting down here. I'm thinking of promoting him.'

'Basically Jessop is a soldier,' Fox answered. 'It would be a mistake to bog him down with administrative work. He's officer material.'

'I plan to make him my Youth Leader. I am arranging an office for him at headquarters.'

'His headquarters are here,' Fox snapped.

'I also want to discuss finances,' said Vincent after a pause. His voice was level but inwardly he was seething with anger at Fox's assumption that Jessop was his property, how dared he question authority over a Party member. Fox was a repressed pervert, all this worshipping fitness when the real god was a muscular body.

'How effective was the local appeal for money?' Vincent turned towards Dobson.

'We haven't finished talking about Jessop,' Fox said excitedly, his neck was mottled in the open collar of his khaki shirt.

'Was it successful?' said Vincent to Dobson, ignoring Fox.

'We raised almost a hundred pounds by door to door canvassing,' Dobson said, looking at Fox nervously. 'Mr Delage has spoken to a friend who might give a comparable amount to himself. The report in the *Gazette* was favourable, as you know. There have been letters from two youth clubs and an offer of a gymnasium at reduced terms.'

'What about Jessop,' shouted Fox, jumping to his feet.

'Jessop is a member of the Party,' said Vincent, 'and his allegiance is to the Party. He's not a tennis ball to be served from one side of the court to another. And I'm not either, so don't think you can bat me about to suit your cults and crushes.' He turned back to Dobson as if there had been no interruption. 'I want you to budget an amount for three days' manoeuvres during the holidays. You must work in close collaboration with Colonel Fox. I shall want a report by the fifteenth of the month. I now declare the meeting closed.'

'She won't go into hospital. The ambulance men came right in and stood at the end of her bed with red blankets and a chair on wheels. She simply went on listening to the morning service as if they weren't there.'

'Stubborn,' said Vincent without interest.

'That's the word for her, it really is. You'd think it wasn't for her own good the way she goes on. She needs to be properly looked after. I can't do it if I'm out all day.' Miss Glass's eyes were dull with anxiety. 'If I give up working here, what would we live on. Oh, it is a worry. You ought to see her bed sores, Mr Pearman, well, I wouldn't be exaggerating if I told you she's rubbed raw.'

On the word raw the side of the swing door marked 'Out' was flung inwards and Madame Vera hurried over to Vincent, leaned across the counter and whispered, 'I must have a word in private dear.' Miss Glass stared.

'Go across to the Toro,' he said softly, 'I have my coffee break in ten minutes. I'll meet you there.'

'Is that your lady friend,' asked Pamela smirking in the partition behind.

Vincent crossed the road apprehensively. The Toro coffee lounge was where he lunched every day. There was a tank of fish swimming in the window and he could see Madame Vera looking for him above the murky water.

He went in and sat down beside her. On the table was a bottle of tomato ketchup, a green metal ashtray and a bowl of brown sugar with a black hair in it. Doris, the waitress who had shed it, came over.

'Coffee?'

'I'll have a gateau too if I may,' said Madame Vera. She selected a wet rhum baba from the preferred tray.

'What do you want to see me for?' asked Vincent.

'I'm afraid it's bad news dear.'

He felt a pain in his chest, a tight constriction equidistant from either nipple, which was the way fear affected him.

'My sister's hubby's met with an accident. She can't cope alone. I've promised to go and stay for as long as she needs me.'

'I need you,' said Vincent, 'probably more than your sister. When are you coming back?'

'That's the point. I thought I'd look for a bungalow up there, or a nice flat. It's my home town, you know, I think I'd like to settle there. It's so noisy where I am now.'

'But what about me?' asked Vincent frantically. 'At this stage of my career I must have guidance, I daren't proceed alone.'

Madame Vera put her hand on his suit sleeve. 'You'll be all right,' she said comfortingly. 'I wouldn't make the move if I wasn't sure your future's bright.'

'Are you sure? You know I rely on you for my decisions. This is of national importance.'

Madame Vera sucked some cream off the prongs of her pastry fork, then withdrew it reflectively, leaving a faint pink veneer of lipstick dulling the shine of the oxidised silver.

'You are able to act alone,' she said, when she had swallowed. 'I say this with true knowledge. Your course is charted fair.'

Thank God, thought Vincent. But what of the daily happenings, those small problems he referred to her.

'What about the minor decisions?' he said.

Madame Vera put down her cup. 'Don't worry.' She picked up the last crumbs between her first finger and thumb. 'I'm off next Saturday actually,' she said. 'I'm sorry to have to break it to you like this, dear, I really am.'

'If I offered you more, would it make any difference?' Vincent suggested desperately.

She shook her head. 'It's very kind of you, I wish I could say, yes. But one's family comes first, doesn't it, and I can't let my sister down.'

'Well, give me your address,' said Vincent, 'so that I can write to you.' It would take longer but she could help him by post.

'That is a good idea. We don't have to lose touch altogether, do we?' Madame Vera wrote her sister's address on a paper napkin folded like a dart.

'I'll come and see you before you go.'

'That's right, we'll have a last session on Friday, and I can tell you if there are any last minute changes for the week-end.'

They left the Toro together, Madame Vera going to the grocer's shop next door for a cut loaf, and Vincent returning to the bank. Miss Glass was waiting with her hat on to go for her coffee, and as he went in she stepped out, like two figures in a weather house.

The last meeting with Madame Vera was tense. Most of the furniture had gone and they sat at the card table in an almost empty room. She seemed disinterested, he thought, preoccupied with the cleaning she had to do that night to leave the house ready for the landlord's inspection.

'He'll make me pay for anything that's spoilt,' she said. She had a little tin of paint to touch up the skirting and the doors.

'Damn the landlord,' Vincent shouted suddenly, and he hit the table with his fist so hard that a china clog jumped off the mantelpiece and cracked on the fender.

'He'll make me pay for that,' shrilled Madame Vera, snatching it up and examining it. 'Oh, I don't know whether to throw it away or hope for the best. He'll spot it, I know, he's like that, eyes everywhere.'

'I'll pay, I'll pay,' said Vincent impatiently. 'Look, here's some money.' He pushed a ten shilling note across the table.

'It's not that, is it?' said Madame Vera. 'It's the sentiment, not the cost.'

'Well, I'm sure he's not sentimental about the things he leaves in a rented house.'

'Don't judge, Mr Pearman. It happens his mother lived here before she passed over. This was his mother's.' She brandished the cracked clog.

'Look, I'm sorry,' said Vincent. 'Tell the landlord to write to me if he's not satisfied with ten shillings and I'll give him more. Just let's get on with my hand, shall we? After all, we won't have another opportunity.'

She read his hand, but couldn't turn up the cards because she'd packed them. He felt she wasn't really trying to reveal the future, it was too cursory and she said nothing new. He paid her and left before the half-hour was over, she clasped his hand and promised that all would go well with Fox's manoeuvres and his own rise to power, but already her eyes were skimming the hall for damage she might repair. He couldn't control the sense of foreboding as he rode home on the bus.

Dobson was anxious to increase the Party funds. He suggested to Vincent that any member who could afford it should donate a weekly sum. As soon as it proved unnecessary they would no longer be asked to do so. He anticipated that inside the year there would have been sufficient publicity to draw rich patrons.

Vincent had confidence in Dobson that now exceeded his trust in Fox. Not only was Dobson handling the finances with intelligence and competence, but he was recruiting successfully for the manoeuvres by putting advertisements in the personal and educational columns of carefully chosen local newspapers. The word manoeuvres was never used, but among themselves this was the way they referred to the three days now planned for the August Bank Holiday.

Vincent addressed a meeting of the boys at Fox's house during the final week-end of term. This was the last term for several of the boys before going up to university in the autumn. Whatever

they were going to do, Vincent said, they must use every opportunity to convert new members to the Party. The three days in
August were going to be testing. A great many people would probably turn up and try to take part without having any real convic-
tions. It was their job, as founder members, to retain the wheat and
discard the chaff.

The boys all wore their uniforms at these week-ends. Vincent
had decided against any distinguishing alteration to his own, he
now liked the idea of being the leader but at the same time remain-
ing one of the Party, quite undifferentiated from other members.
His determination grew from Fox's obvious anxiety to appear
superior to the boys. He still wore his khaki uniform, pretending
he had not yet found time to buy the Party clothes.

In spite of these feelings towards Fox, Vincent was impressed
by his plans for the manoeuvres. He had spent one day at Windermere examining the membership file – there were now two
hundred and eleven members – and selecting those suitable for the
three days at camp. He had then travelled to Dorset and obtained
permission from a local farmer to use his field for pitching tents.
The farmer agreed to be paid ten pounds a day, otherwise he said
it wasn't in his interest, because holiday makers liked to park their
caravans there for the night. There was an outside lavatory and
they could buy milk and eggs from the farm. The farm was in a
village half a mile from the sea. For several miles along the coast
there were extensive sand dunes, and it was here that Fox intended
the manoeuvres to take place. He drew a map and pinned it up
on the wall of his sitting-room. It included every detail of the
landscape, houses, bathing huts, breakwaters, scrubland, shops,
farms, ice-cream kiosks and car parks. He divided the area in two
with a thick black line, and shaded one half blue and the other
red.

'I shall divide the section of men into two,' he told Vincent,
'the reds and the blues. On the first day the reds will attack the
blue area and on the second day I shall detail the blues to take over
the red sector. On the third day I am planning an initiative drive
and an assault test.' He was going down to Dorset again before
the start of the manoeuvres in order to make a close survey of

the surrounding area, so that he could work out both tests and course. The initiative tests would be along the usual line of leaving a man in an unknown position and letting him make his way back to camp. The assault course he hoped to set up in forest land. He had spent some of the Party funds on wire ropes, barbed wire, barricades and digging implements. Dobson had found a carrier who was transporting them to the farm. The final drive for recruits was to be a series of advertisements in the personal columns of the national press. Less officially, Wood, Winters, Yates and Judy had a thousand sticker labels publicising the manoeuvres, giving anti-semitic, anti-negro propaganda and advertising the song which the group were going to record privately next week, in time for the summer holidays. They spent an entire week-end travelling by underground, sticking the labels on escalator walls and over advertisements on platforms. Dorset rally, August 1st, commuters read as they hurried to catch their trains; Britain First for Britons; Go go go for a White Christmas; Britain First, the Party with the pop ideas; Hear the Britain Firsts, the pop group with the purpose.

The song itself was causing some trouble. Yates had had no difficulty in signing up the group, or getting them to agree to changing their name from The Sparrers to the Britain Firsts. The leader of the group, who was also the vocalist, said he thought groups were on the way out, and they'd never make the big time anyway. Jessop and several other boys were attempting to write the number, and there was to be a session at Windermere to try out the best and decide which to use. The actual recording was going to be made in a studio in Paddington belonging to a friend of Judy's parents. The friend was charging only a nominal sum, because he had known Judy since she was a baby and often came to dinner on Friday nights. He had been led to believe that the group were Judy's friends, and had arranged for a hundred copies to be made on thin plastic, the kind of record which is given free for advertising. Judy had asked if she might have a few extra and he had agreed indulgently. She rang the company and ordered a thousand more. The title was to be non-committal because Jessop and the group had assured Vincent that the kind of patriotic slogan he wanted would discourage young people from listening to it. The group

had promised to include it every time they performed at the pub.
Jessop had written a blues which began :

> The nigger done gone live in my land
> And taken my job away
> The Jew-boss, he leads me by the hand
> And make the profits pay.

Another boy had composed a less melancholy rhythm but with
similar sentiments of complaint:

> I got the wrong livin'
> In the right place
> I'm tired of givin'
> To the wrong race
> I want the kids next door
> White as the snow
> And a just law
> To make the black folks go.

But the choice for the record had a compulsive, swingy beat, and
had been written by a fourteen-year-old boy from Jessop's school,
an enthusiastic member of the under-sixteen section. It was called
Get With the New Way, and the instrumentalists chanted while
the vocalist sang the lyric. The underlying chant was:

> Kids! Get with the new way
> Man! Get with the good way
> The good good good way
> The way we want it
> And not the way we got it.

The first verse, which Vincent particularly liked, began:

> Get with the new way of living good
> Jew boy we don't need you and never could
> My baby don't want a black lover man
> So get back to the shack quick as you can
> Before we send you away from here.

'This has the right mood,' he said. 'It's positive, determined, and full of vigour. I'd like the press to know it was written by a schoolboy.'

As soon as the title was decided, Vincent ordered more sticker labels saying simply Get With the New Way, sensational record by the Britain Firsts. On the day copies were available Judy and the boys were going to paste the stickers up in the underground, and free records were going to be distributed outside certain stations; Leicester Square, Earls Court and Edgware and others yet to be selected. It depended on the response, but Judy had tentatively arranged with the company for a re-issue of five thousand, this time at the Party's expense. Once the contact had been established she didn't feel she needed to approach her father's friend and had ordered direct.

'Her business contacts are useful,' said Vincent to Jessop. 'We've done pretty well with the armbands and the records.'

'She's been useful too,' said Jessop. 'At least half the boys have had her one week-end or another.'

'I had doubts about accepting her membership but I think I made the right move.'

'Why doubts?' asked Jessop.

Vincent had had no intention of revealing Judy's Semitic origins. He wasn't certain that other people would share his certainty that she was a weapon for them to use if accused of Nazi sympathies. But as he faced Jessop at a table in a Chinese restaurant close to the recording studio he suddenly remembered that Madame Vera had told him it would be dangerous to keep secrets.

'Because,' said Vincent, looking directly into Jessop's eyes, 'she is a Jewess.'

Jessop whistled between his teeth. 'I just don't get it.' He shook his head twice. 'I should have guessed really, with the Jag and her father in the rag trade, we've got boys like that at school. But I can't see why she wanted to join.'

'She's anti-semitic.'

'They often are,' said Jessop. 'The ones at school never mention it, and go to chapel and all the rest, they try bloody hard to assimilate.'

'Without success, even with dyed blonde hair,' said Vincent.

'Has she? It never occurred to me. I'd like to make a suggestion to you.'

'Go ahead.' Vincent cupped his hand round the small bowl of urine-coloured tea.

'Well, I think you've made a mistake. She's been useful and got us some things on the cheap, but I think the time has come to drop her.'

'My main reason,' said Vincent, 'was to use her as a cover for anti-semitic propaganda. I believe many people still reject our views because they are sentimental about Belsen. If we produce a Jewish member we can't possibly be equated with that kind of fascist.'

'It wouldn't wash,' said Jessop. 'Honestly, no one would accept it. They'd just despise Judy as a turncoat. They wouldn't swallow us as a selective anti-semitic party. Besides, I think that would be wrong. We mustn't be afraid to stand up for what we believe. We don't want to whitewash ourselves. I think Judy could do immense harm to the Party. I'd like to see her out of it.'

'Perhaps you're right.'

'When you took her membership you did the right thing at that particular point of Party development. You might have needed her early on. But now is the time to sack her. Believe me. By making a bold decision and letting the public know you'll get plenty of converts, more than you'll get by holding her up as an example. And you'll get the type we want, Jew-haters, not the kind who is afraid to go all out.'

'Very well,' said Vincent. 'We'll let the record deal go through, and then I'll leave it to you to dismiss her from the Party. As Youth Leader I think it is your job and not mine.'

'Okay,' Jessop said smiling. 'Leave it to me. I rather like the idea of watching her enjoying herself for the next few days, doing all our work, and knowing she's on the way out.'

Dobson put the advertisements in the national press during the last week in July. He also advised the news desks that the advertisements were there. The publicity however did not stem from this source, but from some local Dorset lads who claimed that they were going to rout the fascists who intended to camp and carry out exercises in their village. 'We're warning them to keep out,' one had been reported as saying. First a local paper and then the *Daily Mirror* ran the story condemning the Party.

'Just what we want,' said Vincent. 'Lots of news space.'

'If they want a fight,' Fox promised, 'we'll give them one.'

Vincent was mentioned by name in two reports but although he waited at Windermere to be interviewed, no one telephoned or called. The records were delivered to the house and Vincent had copies sent to the papers which covered the story; a pictorial Sunday paper gave an interview to the Dorset boys, who said they had a shotgun and a supply of swedes and turnips which they intended hurling at intruders. The records were given away at the exits to the undergrounds on a Friday evening, and Judy confirmed the order for the second issue. Vincent slept at Windermere on a camp bed in case of last minute developments, and was aware of Wood, Winters and Yates bringing girls into the house at night, although they kept them out of Vincent's way. He asked Yates one morning if he had been mistaken in thinking he heard a girl's voice. 'Just some German au pair girl,' said Yates casually.

'We always have au pair girls when we're pushed for sex,' explained Winters. 'There's thousands of them all round here.'

'Sprinkled like confetti all over North London,' said Yates.

'Lots of Germans,' added Wood, 'all in Jewish homes.'

'They like to get Germans into their houses,' said Winters, 'to show they're the top-dogs now.'

'They speak German anyway,' said Yates.

'Yiddish,' Wood corrected.

The London members were to leave for Dorset in one of three trains. Fox, who had come from Kent the night before, was travelling on the first, Patterson on the second and Vincent the third. Dobson was already there, to receive supplies and equipment.

Vincent slept badly the night before. He was tremendously nervous and excited and at four o'clock he had to use his inhaler because he felt an attack coming. Later he built up his pillows with a coat and took a pill, to make certain he would be well in the morning. The pill made him alert and his heart beat faster, and he only managed to doze for short periods. But he could breathe freely and the back-ache which was a symptom of his asthma receded until it no longer worried him. He drank the coffee that Yates brought him in his room, but could not eat. Then he dressed in his uniform and looked at himself in the reflection in the long mirror on the wardrobe door. He combed his hair carefully, pressing it into place with his fingers. Yates came into the room to collect the breakfast tray, and Vincent saw Yates behind him in the glass. His own appearance, which moments before had seemed powerful, immaculate and autocratic, was immediately spoilt because Yates in his uniform, was some nine inches taller. In that split instant, until Yates had moved out of sight, they were a comic pair, a very tall man, the stooge of the short one.

'Get out,' Vincent ordered Yates, 'I'm dressing.'

Yates picked up the tray. 'Sorry, but you said we were in a hurry this morning. Judy's washing up downstairs.' He went out, closing the door.

Vincent stared at himself. He was ready now. Yes, he looked splendid, but he must remember to stand away from tall members at public meetings. That meant Fox, Jessop, and Yates must all be placed at a distance. Patterson was his own height, Dobson only an inch taller, Winters and Wood taller, but not enough to reduce Vincent to ludicrous proportions. Hitler had been a short man. So had Stalin, Nelson and Napoleon. Stalin had surrounded himself by short men only, but that was stupid. If a man had value in the party, then he must not be excluded. He must just stand somewhere else in a room, or be seated on a platform, or the leader must be on a dais. Of course, that was the answer. At every public meeting Vincent would stand on a dais. Not only would it diminish the stature of loftier colleagues, but it would draw attention, focus all interest upon himself.

Downstairs Judy and the boys were waiting for him. It was ten o'clock. Fox had left at seven to be on the eight o'clock train. Patterson and his contingent had departed on the one that left London at nine – he had telephoned from the station, to say that he had the full quota of male recruits from his local area. Vincent was leaving Windermere at eleven to catch the midday express. For the next hour members taking part arrived at the house. These were mainly the boys from Jessop's school who lived in London and the ones that had been rustled up from the coffee-bars. The Britain Firsts came with their guitars, to embellish the evening sing-songs round the camp fires, that Fox was anxious should take place. There was nothing, he told Vincent, that could better establish a feeling of unity and solidarity than community singing in the hour before going to sleep. In anticipation he had duplicated song sheets on his own typewriter, although Vincent had doubts that the faint mauve carbon would be discernible in the dusk. The songs included Fox's favourites and, of course, the Party's own song, 'Get with the new way,' which would be sung whenever possible.

Fox was ready for the opposition in the village. Dobson had telephoned to say that the local boys had organised a meeting in the pub, but that he thought they had no idea of the numbers that were converging on the farm. The shotgun was a reality, nevertheless, and so were the turnips, stones and cudgel-like sticks locked in an outhouse near the camping site. This was being guarded by men and dogs, and unless there was an out and out fight for it, seemed unassailable. Two reporters from national newspapers had booked in at the pub.

Vincent had a sandwich lunch on the train. When he marched up to the camp the last remnants of a meal of stew, biscuits and cocoa were being cleared away, the boys queuing to wash their plastic bowls and beakers under a single running tap.

Fox marched up to meet Vincent, and there was general saluting and stamping to attention. Fox escorted Vincent round the field, giving him details of the guard duties he felt necessary and of the afternoon's exercise. They crouched in Fox's tent, peering at the map Fox stabbed with a pencil. When they emerged into the sunlight, each boy had been issued with a blue or red armband which he wore on the left arm for the Party armband was on the right. It reminded Vincent of the teams the gym master had organised on wet days, relay races and obstacle courses round the school hall. Fox blew a whistle, and everyone on the camp came running.

Fox called them to attention and shouted orders. They stood there in the sun, over a hundred men in ten rows deep, bareheaded, booted, dressed in grey denim, Vincent's recruits. His pride was so great he had tears in his eyes and he found he had to take long slow breaths. Fox was talking about him, in a minute he would speak to them himself. He remembered about the dais. He signalled to Patterson who was standing on the other side of Fox. Patterson came over. 'I want something to stand on,' Vincent whispered. Patterson hurried to tell Fayers, and they ran off together looking anxiously round the field. Then, blotting out Fox's words, Fayers backed his car in through the field gate and over the bumpy grass, and he and Patterson lifted Vincent on to the bonnet so that he could scramble up on to the roof. It was slippery and scalding to touch. It burnt his hands as he bent to steady himself, but when he finally stood and surveyed the camp the discomfort was negligible compared to his bursting happiness and feeling of achievement.

'This is our chance,' he shouted, 'to show our fellow country-men that we believe in our Party, that the people of Britain will rally to sound ideas and healthy living.' From his elevated posi-tion on the car roof he saw suddenly that about thirty youths had converged on the field and were on the point of leaping over the hedge armed with stones and three large mongrel dogs.

'The enemy,' he yelled. 'Look out, we are being attacked!'

Before Fox had time to give any orders, the youths burst into the fields hailing stones, while the dogs scrambled over the hedge in hysterical excitement, barking and snapping and running fren-ziedly among the scattering ranks of grey.

'No panic,' Fox bellowed. 'The reds block the gate.'

But no one heard him and the Britain First members and the village lads pitched into each other with gusto. The dogs ran about wildly, snapping at legs and jumping up in the air. The stones were hurled at random into the scrum and out again. Vincent sprang into the car and shut the door and locked it, and half-lying on the back seat watched the pandemonium with a thumping heart through the side window.

Fox tried to break up the fighting mass, blowing his whistle and tugging at any boy near to him. Fayers had waded in, punching hard. Dobson and Patterson had disappeared. Then Vincent saw them at the gate with two policemen, and seconds later the bell of a police car was heard ringing in the lane leading to the farm. The village boys and the dogs tore away through the hedge, and for the first time Vincent heard Fox's whistle and the flailing arms subsided like clockwork running down. He opened the car door and stepped out to meet the police.

'You see,' said the young policeman, in a Dorset accent, 'this marchin' about is very provokin' to the people that live here.'

'We are absolutely within our rights,' fumed Dobson. 'We are renting the field. Do you let the locals attack everyone who stays in the village?'

'Blowin' the whistle, and havin' parades is just exasserbatin' the situation,' said one of the policeman from the car.

'Well, I hope you find the louts,' snapped Vincent.

'I doubt that we'll find them,' said the young policeman, 'unless you can give me descriptions.' The older one grinned, and then controlled himself.

A man in grey flannels and open-necked checked shirt approached through the gate, and came up to Vincent. 'I wonder if I might have a word with you,' he said. 'I'm a reporter.'

'I'll see you in a few moments,' answered Vincent. He walked over to Fox who was standing by the rows of boys, a few yards away, listening. 'Blow your whistle,' Vincent snapped.

When the boys were standing to attention, Vincent faced them, his lips tight together. He surveyed them, up and down the lines in grim displeasure.

'I'll give you ten minutes to clean yourselves up,' he said, 'and then I'll see you back here.' He walked back to the reporter who had now been joined by another.

'We'd like a story,' said one. 'Would you tell us what happened?'

'I'd be delighted,' said Vincent. 'The situation should be brought to the public notice. We are down here to practise our field-craft, and were in fact just about to set out on an exercise devised by Colonel Fox, when we were attacked by thugs, outnumbering us two to one. They set their dogs on my boys, who were desperately

anxious not to become involved, but were forced to defend themselves.'

'They say you're a Nazi party,' said one of the reporters, 'may
we have your comment.'

'We are not a Nazi party,' answered Vincent. 'We are a pro-
British party, sickened by the moral decay of our country and
determined to do something about it. You can see by the lads here
that we are attracting the very best of British youth.'

'I've heard the record you put out,' said the first man. 'It sounds
pretty fascist to me.'

'It was written by a fourteen-year-old schoolboy,' Vincent said.
'We thought it worth listening to but don't necessarily consider it
to be an example of mature thought.'

'So the views in the song aren't your views?'

'My views aren't so simplified,' Vincent said.

'Will you tell us your views. Do you for instance want the Jews
out of Britain?'

'Yes, Mr Wright. And are you against immigrants coming here?'

'If they are taking homes and jobs from our own countrymen,'
Vincent said. 'And the Jews have their own country, haven't they,
given to them by a British government? I would add that these
views are those of more than half the nation, and I am a mouthpiece for many decent English families.'

'What will you do if the locals attack you again?'

'You must excuse me,' said Vincent, 'I have to attend a meeting.'
He half bowed and then walked briskly away and across the field
to Fox's tent. Fox was waiting for him.

'Call them over,' ordered Vincent. Fox blasted the whistle. The
boys came running and fell into their lines.

'Sit down,' said Vincent. He remained standing. 'Well? Are you
pleased with yourselves?' He paused. 'I'm not. I'm not pleased
with the way you comported yourselves when faced with an
attack. There was no discipline. You could have set those village
idiots by their heels in two minutes, but instead you entered into a
wild foray that was a disgrace to the Party. I have decided to form
a *corps d'élite* which will be highly trained to cope with such situ-
ations. Those chosen will wear some differentiating uniform, and

be our vanguard. Colonel Fox, no doubt you've had some thought on how to prevent a further attack.'

'Yes,' said Fox, 'I propose to have a permanent guard on the camp, which means jettisoning some of our plans for field exercises. I shall be lecturing on unarmed combat when this meeting is over.'

'Very well,' said Vincent. 'I have no more to say, except that you are not children scuffling in a playground, but men in the public gaze.' He saluted, Fox shouted for the boys to rise and salute back, and Vincent marched off to his tent. When they were absorbed in what Fox was saying he dropped on to all fours and quickly crawled inside.

The sun shone through the orange canvas and he lay back in the filtered light, pleased with the way the events had given the Party publicity and kudos, looking forward to the reports condemning the local boys as hooligans, and praising the restraint of the Party. He had handled the newspaper men well, he thought, Fox had been right in suggesting the manoeuvres. It was proving to be just the fillip they needed to put them in the news.

Patterson called through the tent flap.

'Are you asleep?'

'Of course I'm not asleep.'

'Some people have turned up, they've come by taxi from the station.'

'Reporters?'

Vincent began to come out.

'They say they want to take part in the exercise. They've brought their own tent.'

Vincent eased himself through the flap. Four men and a woman in hiking boots and khaki clothes were standing just inside the gate, looking round apprehensively. Vincent stalked over to them.

'I'm afraid this is not a public camping ground.'

'Oh we know that,' replied the woman. 'We're sympathisers. We've come to join in.'

'You should have applied properly,' said Vincent. 'We can't admit you now, this is a highly organised rally.'

'We've come from Birmingham,' said one of the men.

'We didn't know about applying earlier, we thought we just had to come. There are the others.' He pointed down the road.

Vincent turned, and saw a column of men, women and children, all with knapsacks, filing through the gate of the field. The men leading the advancing column stopped and to Vincent's astonishment gave the Party salute. Horrified by the disruption, he still felt a warmth towards them for their unexpected support. He returned it.

'You're the Leader, are you?' asked one of the men, detaching himself.

'I am. My name is Wright.'

'It's Mr Wright,' said the man excitedly to the people behind him.

'We had to come,' he said. 'You don't mind the kiddies, do you?'

Vincent saw that one child was being wheeled in a pushchair.

'As it's the Bank Holiday we thought we could kill two birds with one stone, give the kids some fresh air and help get the niggers out.'

'What you're doing is wonderful,' called one woman. 'We're all behind you on our estate.'

One man began to sing 'For he's a jolly good fellow', and they all joined in. Vincent looked at Patterson.

'How are you going to get rid of them?' Patterson said.

'Get rid of them?' replied Vincent, 'I'm not going to reject such loyal people who have travelled half-way across England to tell me how they feel.'

Fox and Fayers and Dobson had now come over and were listening in astonishment. The singing died away and the man at the front called for three cheers.

'What are you going to do?' asked Fox under cover of the cheering.

'I want you to make room for them,' answered Vincent.

'My God,' said Fox, 'Are you joking?'

'No. I am not.'

'The whole purpose of the manoeuvres will be lost. Look at them! Riff-Raff.'

'They are our spearhead in the Midlands,' said Vincent.

'I am engaged in training men to protect the camp,' said Fox. 'I haven't time for this lot. The villagers aren't likely to leave us alone after one skirmish.'

'That's true,' said Dobson. 'He'd better get on with it.'

'We'll cope with these,' said Patterson.

'You are welcome to the Party,' shouted Vincent. 'I cannot tell you how stirred I am to find that our movement can arouse such enthusiasm. But I cannot own to being surprised, you are, after all, British people.' He raised his voice so that it almost became a scream. His throat hurt and his eyes watered, but he went on. 'British people who do not want to see their beautiful countryside,' his arm indicated the field around them, 'despoiled and polluted by nigger filth and Jew filth.' He dropped his voice dramatically. 'You have come to me for leadership and I will give it to you.' His voice rose again hoarsely. 'Together we will rid this land of the blight that has settled on it.' There was a thin cheer. Vincent stood nodding at them, then he turned and said, 'Section Leaders Patterson and Dobson here will show you where to pitch your tents and give you something to eat and drink.'

'It means more supplies,' whispered Dobson. 'What we've got won't last three days if we're going to feed them.'

The child in the pushchair began to cry.

'Come on,' said Patterson, 'over here.' He led the way to the far side of the field which had been set aside for the daily physical training. A roll of coconut matting was propped against a tree.

'The food simply won't last out,' said Dobson. 'And we can't get any more. It's a Bank Holiday.'

'Then we won't stay three days,' retorted Vincent. 'The situation has changed.' He was beginning to feel exhausted. He had had little sleep last night and the day had been a strain. He had needed the rest in the tent and it had been disturbed by this extraordinary influx. He had sounded in control but he felt an inner panic, this carefully planned demonstration of military precision was suddenly haphazard and disorganised. He went over to Fox.

'Come in to my tent.'

'Wait while I dismiss the men.' Fox shouted some orders and followed Vincent back across the field.

'What do you think we ought to do?' he asked Fox.

'We must keep these civilians separate, and carry on the best we can. We mustn't lose sight of our objective.'

'Dobson says the food won't last three days.'

'Then they must find their own food.'

'They are immensely valuable to us,' Vincent said. 'It shows our support extends beyond the home counties.'

'Yes, that's true. But I don't want to lose this opportunity of training your *corps d'élite*.' Fox looked crafty.

He wants to play soldiers, thought Vincent, he thinks he can hoodwink me. Nevertheless, to relinquish their plans which had been publicised would be detrimental to the Party image.

'We shall have to rethink our position,' he said to Fox. 'And see if we can make alterations within our framework.'

But by nine o'clock, when the last train had left the station, a dozen more people had arrived at the Camp, including a militant woman in a trilby hat, a South African nurse and a man over seventy in a home guard khaki battledress, and carrying a tin helmet.

At a late night conference, Dobson, Fox, Patterson and Vincent decided that they must leave early on Monday morning, that the manoeuvres would have to be confined to one day, but at half strength, leaving a strong guard at the camp to deal with intruders, that Patterson would be in command of the newcomers, and take them on a hike and that while they were here the best must be selected as local leaders and told to keep in close touch.

Vincent slept badly again, unused to a sleeping-bag, and repelled by the sound of night animals close to the tent.

Breakfast was at seven. The new members, which was how Vincent thought of them, although Fox referred to them as civilians, had banded together and had lit a fire. They were surrounded by children, clothes, pots, pans, thermos flasks and scattered pieces of paper. Most of the men wore their trousers and vests, and the children were running about naked.

'They look like gipsies, don't they?' Judy said bringing Vincent's breakfast. 'I hope the reporters don't write about them.'

Fayers had gone into the village for the papers, and he brought them straight to Vincent who was sitting outside his tent eating.

Vincent turned the pages quickly. There were reports of yesterday's battle in an evening paper, which hadn't arrived until today, and in most of the Sunday ones. The reports were inclined to make a funny story out of the fight and one paper spoke of 'pseudo-military cavortings encouraged by a referee's whistle'. Headings varied from 'Free for all in field' to 'Neo-Nazis attacked'.

As soon as breakfast was over Patterson led the straggling hikers out of the field and Fox left his red team in control while he took the blues off for initiative tests. These were to include negotiating a river, finding food, making an undetectable hide-out and capturing an enemy post. Jessop, who was in charge of the camp guard, came over to Vincent and said, 'I haven't spoken to Judy yet. But if you like to keep out of sight tonight you might find it amusing to watch while I tell her.'

'What are you going to say?' said Vincent curiously.

'You'll see. I'll give you the tip off when to follow us.'

The hikers returned at twelve. Patterson had been supposed to keep them away from the camp all day, but they had complained of weariness and insisted on coming back. They cooked their own lunch with Dobson's supplies, and then slept in and out of their tents. There was no sign of the villagers, but the reporters came down to the field once or twice and Vincent saw them talking to one of the women. At half past six Fox marched in with the blue team, all ravenously hungry and two short. Dobson handed out meagre rations, and the boys ate them, grumbling. Dobson went up to the farm and came back with extra milk and eggs, and Fox saw that fires were lit and handed round his song-sheets. Vincent waited until the singing was under way and then he went over to Fox.

'What are you going to do about the two defecting men?'

'I'm worried,' said Fox, 'in case the local boys have captured them.'

'Exactly. So am I. You seem to have slipped up.'

'I'll send out a search-party.'

'And inform the police.'

But before Fox had asked for volunteers the two missing men came in through the gate, sunburned and intoxicated, having spent the day on Weymouth front and the evening in the village pub. Vincent was furious.

'Suppose they talked to reporters,' he said furiously to Fox, 'they're too drunk to know what they're saying. Do you think we'll be taken seriously again. You've made a complete mess of the week-end.'

'It wasn't my fault,' Fox retorted. 'They were supposed to be under cover. I didn't miss them.'

'Thank God we hadn't sent out the search-party or involved the law.'

'We hadn't, so there was no harm done, was there?'

'Unless they blurted out secrets.' Vincent walked away and Fox went back to the camp fire. The Britain Firsts had their guitars out and were swinging songs like It's a Long Way to Tipperary and Keep the Home Fires Burning. Fox shouted at them to play the bloody things properly, and the boys booed and said that was the way they liked them. Jessop came over to Vincent and said quietly, 'We're going for a midnight bathe. Come down after us.'

The boys were still singing and a new brew of cocoa was being handed round when Vincent saw Jessop and Judy walking away behind the tents. Jessop had his arm round Judy's waist, and as Vincent followed Jessop stopped and kissed her. Vincent was excited as he followed them along the dark road towards the sea. He wondered if Jessop was going to leave her on the beach to find her own way home, if he was going to beat her up or even drown her.

Once or twice as they walked Jessop looked back at Vincent. By the sand dunes he and Judy stopped and pulled off their boots, and when they were on the beach they took off all their clothes and ran into the sea. Vincent stood in the shadow of the dunes and watched them. The sea looked black and he could only just discern their heads above the water. After several minutes they raced back up the beach and fell on to the sand quite close to where Vincent was waiting. Jessop stood up but Judy lay there, panting and laughing. Silently two boys emerged from the dunes behind Judy and came right up to her before she saw them. When she did she tried to stand, but they seized her and held her down.

'Do you know what happens to Jewish girls who join Nazi parties?' said Jessop, standing over her. 'Especially to Jewish girls who let themselves be had by everyone in sight.'

Judy struggled and shouted at the boys to let her go.

'They're used,' said Jessop, 'and then they are kicked out of the Party and told that if they come anywhere near again they'll be burnt alive.'

Vincent stood absolutely still. For the first time in his life he was involved in acts of intercourse. Physically they were outside his comprehension and desire and when Judy cried as she stumbled about the beach looking for her clothes long after Jessop and the boys had gone, he was completely unmoved.

Chapter 10

DURING the night a sea mist had drifted up from the coast and light rain began to fall. Breakfast had been a failure, fires would not light and there was no more butter for the bread. The children were given milk and biscuits but there was not enough left for a hundred and twenty adults. As they took up the sodden tents the local boys returned and flung ineffectual firebrands into the field, which fizzled in the rain and were quickly stamped out. Fox had been preparing for an attack and called his trained force to give chase, but the villagers had thrown the flaming wood and fled and by the time Fox had organised his men and they had charged, shouting, through the gate, the enemy had disappeared into the mist.

Judy had spent the night in Patterson's tent and sat with him on the train. She ignored the boys who spoke to her and Vincent saw her turn away when Jessop walked along the swaying corridor of the coach. Vincent shared a compartment with her and Patterson, Fox and Dobson. He expected a discussion of Judy's assault, but Fox produced the newspaper cuttings with the reports of the week-end activities and began to analyse them.

'I am looking at them, Wright, in terms of the promotion of the Party image and any new membership drive we decide to make. All these reports show sympathy with the boys who attacked us, or dwell on what they consider amusing elements of the setting up of camp and subsequent exercises.'

'That's your fault,' said Vincent. 'I left the organising to you. The exercises flopped because you lost two of your men.'

'Don't question my leadership,' answered Fox, his eyes blazing. 'I have led men into military battles and brought them out victorious.'

'This was a peaceful operation planned to give us beneficial publicity. Your *leadership* didn't achieve its end, did it?'

'Your leadership allowed a hotch-potch of ill-dressed and inadequately equipped civilians to overrun the camp, eat our food and make us a laughing-stock.'

'You were incapable of adapting yourself to emergencies, Fox.' What was he suggesting? Was he trying to imply that Vincent was unfit to lead? How dare he? How dare he?

Yates pushed open the door of the compartment and said to Judy, 'Don't you feel well?'

'She's just tired,' Patterson said quickly.

Judy looked down at her lap. 'Oh, do go away,' she said.

At Waterloo, Patterson shepherded her solicitously into a taxi. Vincent said goodbye to Fox curtly, leaving him to make his way with Dobson to Victoria. The Windermere detachment travelled to Finchley by tube.

They were all tired and hungry and Winters scrambled some eggs and made coffee, and when they had eaten they took it in turns to bath before going to bed for the afternoon.

Vincent lay on his bed and stretched his toes which were still numb from wearing his damp boots. The ceiling was lined with a bumpy paper resembling baked beans. Vincent stared up and planned his *corps d'élite*. Jessop, of course, would lead it. Wood, Winters and Yates and perhaps another four or five carefully screened boys would be the nucleus from which he would form a nation-wide organisation. They would wear olive green shirts instead of grey, but the same grey jeans and green armbands. They would accompany Vincent wherever he went, stand behind him at every meeting, he would have to forget his misgivings about height, be flanked by the shorter boys and have the taller ones at the rear. He would send them to judo classes, and make them train at gymnasiums. This *corps* would be stronger than the bodyguard he had had until now, alert, tough and aggressive. They would deal with hecklers at public meetings and any situation that required hard handling.

Although he was tired and knew the boys would be sleeping, he went to the door of his room and shouted for them. They were irritable and complained they had been on the point of sleep.

'This is important,' said Vincent. They followed him into his room and sat on the bed and the floor.

'I must have a small nucleus I can trust utterly,' he said. 'You are the sinews of the Party, young and strong.' He explained his ideas about his *corps d'élite*, watching them carefully. In the new uniform, banded together, they would look powerful and menacing. Jessop was tall, fit and blond. Wood was fair too, and wiry. Yates and Winters were dark, Yates tall and muscular and Winters medium height and thick set. He could still lose some weight, thought Vincent. Only Jessop had good features, bright blue eyes, even teeth, straight nose, the Greek God type. His arrogance and the coarser thuggishness of the others made them a formidable group.

'I want you to stand,' he said, 'and place your hands on your hearts and swear an oath of allegiance to me.'

'Come off it,' said Yates indignantly. 'You can trust us.'

'I must have implicit trust,' said Vincent. 'Now, stand, all of you, and say after me . . .'

'Really . . .' Jessop began hotly.

'I must have absolute faith. Now, put your hands on your hearts.' They obeyed angrily. 'I swear by my honour and the love of my country . . .'

'I swear by my honour and the love of my country . . .' muttered the boys.

'. . . to be at all times loyal and faithful to my Leader and to serve him dutifully and without question.'

They repeated it, and Vincent nodded at them and smiled and told them they could go back to bed. When the telephone rang he let them sleep and went down to the sitting-room to answer it himself.

'Fox has asked me to ring you,' Patterson said. 'He wants to call a special meeting for the week-end, at his place.'

'I call the meetings,' said Vincent. 'Not Fox.'

'This is urgent. It's about Judy. She was assaulted.'

'That scarcely warrants a special meeting.'

'When you know the full facts you'll understand. The poor kid was in a bad state. She came to me for protection, she was very upset. I don't think she'll stay in the Party.'

'I'm sure we can manage without her,' said Vincent smiling, drumming his fingers against the dial.

'Then I can tell Fox you'll be down on Saturday?'

'Yes,' said Vincent, 'yes, I'll accept his summons. You might ask him to arrange a public meeting in the church hall to follow our session at the house. I'd like to consolidate the local support there.'

'Will do,' answered Patterson.

Jessop, Yates, Winters and Wood joined the YMCA so that they could use the gym and went daily to practice weightlifting and swimming in the pool. Yates had given up his job and Vincent was paying all three of them out of his own pocket, giving them two pounds pocket money each week and paying for their food as well as the rent. They wore the new shirts and Vincent had insisted on a uniform haircut, almost a crew cut. It altered their appearances, removing, Vincent thought, any traces of decadence. Before they left for Kent on Saturday morning he lined them up in the garden and briefed them.

'You may have wondered,' he said, 'why I was so insistent the other night. It was because I had knowledge of an impending crisis which threatens us all. And if the Party is to remain strong, if it is to have a future, I must be sure that I have the unquestioning loyalty of its closest members. That is why . . .' he paced the path in front of them, '. . . I needed your allegiance, that is why I am holding you to it now. Tonight we shall be facing a major crisis. When I call upon you I want you to act decisively and if necessary ruthlessly.'

'What's up then?' asked Jessop.

'You will see tonight, but this is to be a testing time for us all. You will see,' Vincent stopped pacing and faced them, 'the qualities needed in a leader. Dismiss.'

Fayers drove them to the house, and immediately Fox sent the boys upstairs and ushered Vincent into the living-room where Patterson and Dobson were waiting. He shut the door and said to Vincent, 'This is very serious. I'm afraid you are in for a nasty shock.'

'We have been harbouring a viper in our bosom,' said Patterson sarcastically.

Vincent lifted the dog off the chair and sat down, crossing his legs and smoothing the crease in the right leg of his jeans, pressing it deliberately between his thumb and forefinger.

'I am never shocked.'

'I think you will be today.' Fox shook his head. 'I must own to being shattered, horrified. Yes, horrified. Patterson has a first-hand account, so I'll let him tell you.'

'I told you Judy was assaulted, didn't I?' said Patterson. 'She was raped by friend Jessop.'

Vincent's face remained impassive. 'Yes? Well?'

'Isn't that enough?' demanded Fox. 'Our most trusted member behaving in a way that disgraces British manhood.'

'He raped her,' said Patterson, 'and then held her while his two henchmen forced themselves upon her too.' Vincent thought Patterson's eyes revealed a vicarious enjoyment.

'He must be sacked from the Party,' said Fox.

'You could do it at the meeting,' suggested Dobson.

'Yes, I could, couldn't I?' Vincent looked round at them in turn. 'Don't worry. I will deal with it at the meeting.' He stood up. 'Let's go.'

The coach was in the drive, and Patterson called down the boys from upstairs. There were fewer than usual, because some were away with their parents for the summer holidays, and others lived too far to attend meetings. They climbed up into the coach and sat in the seats at the back. Vincent and the committee followed and took the front places behind the driver. Fox counted, and told the driver they were ready, and the boys started the usual singsong, beginning with the Party song. They arrived at the church hall, and the Vicar hurried out as he had before. This time he looked worried and apprehensive.

'It's just been brought to my notice,' he began, holding out a newspaper clipping.

'The usual press misinterpretation,' said Fox breezily.

'I'd like to sit in on your meeting, to satisfy myself.'

'With pleasure.'

'I'm responsible to the PCC with regard to whom I rent the hall.'

'Of course.' Fox nodded and smiled.

They took their places on the platform, and Vincent sent one of the boys for a hassock to stand on behind the wooden lectern. Fox, Patterson and Dobson sat on chairs at the back of the platform, and Vincent asked the four boys of the *corps* to stand either side. The hall filled rapidly. Dobson had publicised it efficiently, managing to buy a half page advertisement in the *Gazette* at the last moment, and by distributing duplicated handbills. Delage sat in the front row and looked up at the platform with a patron's possessive smile. Vincent came down and shook hands with him and talked for several minutes. Then he mounted the platform and stepped up on to his hassock and banged his hand hard on the lectern for silence.

'Our meeting tonight is an auspicious one,' he said. 'During the past weeks the Britain First Party has gathered strength at a rate that the most optimistic of us had not dared think possible. And yet we should not have cause for surprise. After all, the Party was formed because I rightly sensed that the mood of the people demanded a virile leadership to lift the country from aimless decadence to heights which equal those great peaks of our past. And yet, if one is not surprised at the immediate response that we have received, one is nevertheless gratified that the people of Britain are so ready to meet the challenges of our time.'

As was becoming customary, Vincent was beginning to pace himself; the words rolled on and on and, like an actor, he was learning to vary the speed and pitch of delivery. He usually started quietly and as he warmed to his theme – surprised himself at the ease with which the words came – he moved through a vocal crescendo as he hammered home each point. Then he would drop his voice again dramatically and start building again towards a climax. He was moving towards a climax now.

'Challenges on two levels, to build for ourselves, first of all, self-respect and self-discipline, while at the same time we learn to act ruthlessly against those malignant intruders which feed on the fibres of our society.' He shouted the last part of the sentence. 'I myself am facing a particular challenge tonight and I intend to act ruthlessly.' Fox looked at Jessop. 'This Party which is so young, which is only now gathering strength, is itself threatened by a traitor who hopes to manoeuvre into a position of power for his own devious and dissolute purposes.' His voice suddenly rose to a shriek. 'I have proof of corruption. I have proof of treachery. One person whose secret hopes of infiltrating the youth of the Party with his own brand of political poison has plotted against me, has plotted against the Party, has plotted against the future of our country.' Vincent turned suddenly and faced Fox, whose face was blankly uncomprehending. Vincent pointed dramatically. 'There he sits, the spider who hoped to spin a web that would entangle us all with his vicious obsessions. A man who lives in a world of private fantasy, of idiot idolatry, worshipping at the shrine of a discredited country, a man who keeps in his house a loathsome collection of pornographic paraphernalia, the relics of a nation many of you fought against.'

Fox had risen. Vincent turned to the boys on the platform. 'Seize him. Throw him out,' he screamed. 'Seize this pervert, this traitor.' Patterson tried to speak, but Vincent's voice continued to scream loudly, directing Jessop and Yates who now had Fox by the shoulders. Vincent pounded the lectern, his voice cracking with hysteria. 'Traitorous pervert,' he shouted. 'Corruptor of our youth. Defiler of our country. Get out. Get out. Throw him out.'

The boys surrounded Fox, pushing and frog-marching him out of the hall. The audience stood and one or two tried to stop him being evicted, but Winters hit out and knocked the outstretched arms away. They flung Fox out of the door and slammed it after him. As they marched back along the aisle to the platform, ten or twelve people threw open the door and ran out to Fox. Others crowded round the platform and shouted at Vincent.

'What proof?'

'What's he done to you?'

'Good riddance.'

Vincent held up his hand for them to be silent. Before he could speak the Vicar shoved through the hecklers, and jumped up beside Vincent.

'I am very disturbed by the un-Christian behaviour here tonight. I was misinformed as to the nature of the meeting and

I regret deeply that I was misguided enough to allow violent and unworthy people in our church hall.'

'You're out of touch, Vicar,' Vincent retorted, grinning round. He was elated and stimulated and triumphant, he couldn't keep still, his hands, shoulders, feet moved as he talked, his eyes were bright from the discharge of adrenalin in his glands. 'Your church doesn't offer the people what I can, they flock to me, not you, your pews are empty.'

'Colonel Fox is a very respected member of this community,' said the Vicar. 'I am shocked at the way you tried to defame his character. He is a man who served his country nobly and well.'

'And dotes on Nazi achievement,' Vincent shouted. 'Have you seen his collection, Vicar? Have you seen the photographs and guns and medals and propaganda locked away at the top of his house?'

'I must ask you to leave,' the Vicar said, stepping down, 'our dance is beginning in ten minutes.'

'I don't normally drink,' said Vincent, 'but I think there's something to celebrate tonight.' He jumped down after the Vicar, and his *corps d'élite* fell into position round him. Vincent raised his fist and, staring insolently at the Vicar, brought his arm up sharply in salute. Then he gave an order and he and his boys marched briskly down the aisle and out of the door and over the road to the pub.

Reporters from two local papers followed him.

'What made you do it, Mr Wright?'

'Do you know Colonel Fox intends to bring an action for slander?'

'The police here will prevent you from holding further meetings. What do you intend to do?'

'Colonel Fox won't dare to bring an action which would only result in a complete revelation of his unwholesome habits,' said Vincent. 'And I will no longer be holding meetings in Kent. My headquarters are in London. All future activities will be directed from there.' And he took the glass of beer Jessop held out to him.

For the first time since the manoeuvres Vincent slept in his flat.

Before he went to bed he played the Ride of the Valkyrie at full volume, conducting the last part of it in front of the glass. Then he lay on the sofa in sudden exhaustion, the whole effort and excitement of the day combining in a moment of overwhelming tiredness. He half fell asleep there, and then pulled himself off the soft cushions and undressed in the bedroom, not even attempting to hang up his clothes, and edged himself between the tight sheets into his bed.

He slept until after ten, and when he had had breakfast he went out for the Sunday papers. He restrained himself from looking through them as he walked home, and waited until he was sitting at the kitchen table before he opened them in turn. His photograph, about an inch square, was in the centre of the page. He stared at it, first in astonishment, then joy and then apprehension. Did he want to be recognised? What would Mr Fowler say? His mother? Vincent had relished the double identity, the cloak his new name had given him. Now there could be no deception, it was as if he had acted in some irredeemable way, it was undeniable. He read the reports of Fox's sacking from the Party and his own comments. Two of the papers reported him wrongly and treated the episode light-heartedly, as if the inner politics of a minority party were humorous. A third gave a serious account, and was headed British Fascists in fight. It was this paragraph that his photograph illustrated, captioned, Party Leader Vincent Wright.

Mrs Pearman arrived shortly after two o'clock. She always read her Sunday papers after lunch, and Vincent, who had been imagining her with her shoes off and feet up on what she called the poof, was not surprised when there was a ring at the door. He opened it and she stared at him tearfully, reproachfully, across the width of the coconut mat.

'Hallo Mother,' he said calmly. 'Come in.'

'Oh Vincent.' She gave a sob as he closed the door.

'For goodness sake,' he said irritably. 'What is there to cry about?'

'Now I know why you're always wearing those awful clothes,' she said, her voice tremulous.

'Come in here, Mother, and sit down.' He went into the sitting-room and she followed him and sat down heavily in his armchair. Vincent looked at her dispassionately, unaffected by her confusion and shock. He did not doubt that he could convert her in a matter of minutes; he had convinced highly intelligent men of his ideals, there was no problem in changing the mind of a stupid woman.

'I read the account in the paper,' said Mrs Pearman. 'Why are you ashamed of your name? Why did you take another name?'

'Because it sounds Jewish. That's why I was ashamed.'

'Oh Vincent, you've made me so upset.' She pressed her hands together on the lap of her beige rayon silk coat.

'Why should you be upset? I should have thought you would have been proud.'

'Everyone will know it's you, with your photograph in the paper. And being the leader, starting such a wicked thing.' Her glasses suddenly clouded over and she took them off.

'Listen mother, I started the Party because I am utterly certain that our country is in need of help.' He used phrases he thought she would grasp immediately. 'I think I can help. You know that you're always saying how terrible the young people are nowadays, no manners and so immoral? Well, I agree with you. I want to direct them to more useful activities than bingo halls and bowling alleys and dance halls.'

'It isn't being useful to ape the dreadful things the Germans did, is it?' She stood up. 'You've made me nervous Vincent, I need to spend a penny.'

While she was gone he remembered those countless occasions when, as a child, he had accompanied her to the ladies' lavatories in parks, on promenades, at the zoo, Madame Tussauds, almost all the places they visited together in the afternoons. He recalled standing, miserable and revolted in indistinguishable cubicles with walls that reached neither to ceiling or floor, feet visible on either side, a smell of disinfectant, an attendant with an evil cloth that rubbed each wooden seat perfunctorily; his mother pressing home the brass bolt so that it said occupied outside, hanging her bag on a hook on the door, arranging a careful horseshoe of lavatory paper round the seat for hygiene and finally spending the penny, or worse still, twopence. And always, always it was when they were on the point of doing something interesting or exciting, about to descend to the Chamber of Horrors or have a ride on an elephant or go along the pier.

She returned to the room, having made up her mind to be calm. 'I don't like the word fascist,' she said, sitting down again. 'That's what upset me.'

'Fascist is another name for being very conservative,' said Vincent. 'You've always voted conservative, haven't you?'

'Oh, but Vincent, our conservatives aren't like that.'

'Our conservatives are just another useless party as far as I'm concerned,' answered Vincent, his voice rising. 'Real conservatism, real right wing policies are what I am trying to propagate, to make England a place worth living in.'

'Don't shout at me,' said Mrs Pearman. 'I'm allowed to have an opinion, just as you are.'

'Yes, but you don't allow me to have an opinion. You've come round here to blubber at me and tell me how miserable I've made you. You aren't interested in my ideas or why I have them.'

'But where did you get them from, Vincent?' asked Mrs Pearman desperately. 'We never taught you to hate Jews.'

'Didn't you?'

'Certainly we didn't. Your father always made a point of having a chat with Mr Ross on his way back to the shop after lunch.'

'Ross,' sneered Vincent. 'That's a good name isn't it? Useful in business to have a name like Ross, because no one can really know, can't be sure.'

'That's not being fair. We know, and your father liked him. He found him very interesting. He liked to discuss things with him.'

'Very gracious of him, wasn't it?' said Vincent. 'And you tell me you don't agree with me. Of course you do. We never had Jews to the house, did we?'

'It's not because of any feeling against them, it's simply because they're different. They don't eat the same things and they have a different Sabbath. They wouldn't want to come to us if we did ask them. They keep among themselves.'

'Exactly. They aren't any use to us, or to Britain. They band together and open businesses and employ wholesome English workers for the purpose of exploiting them.'

'I'm sure that isn't true. Mr Ross . . .'

'Rosenblat. Rosenblat. Mr Rosenblat, mother!'

'He's very good to the girls in the shop. They stay there, so that proves it.'

'No it doesn't. Oh God, you're so irrational. You're so stupid. It's people like you, that have made England so vapid and morally bankrupt. But I'm going to change that.' He stood up and stood very close to where she was sitting. She tried to sit further back in the chair. As he shouted he could see specks of his saliva flying down on to her discreetly blued hair. 'I'm going to make the washed-out, feeble, so-called *tolerant* fools like you grovel on the ground in front of me and admit that I'm right. Because I am. I am right. Anyone with intellect and ambition could see that. But you can't, can you mother?' He shouted out the word mother so violently she jumped. She pushed him away and stood up.

'I don't know what's happened to you,' she said in a shrill voice. 'But you're not the boy who left home. I think you're ill. I think you ought to see a doctor.'

'How dare you,' he bellowed. 'Leave my home. I can't bear your ignorant crass observations. Leave. Leave!'

'Very well. I don't want to stay.' She ran down the little hall and struggled with the front door latch. Vincent rushed after her and she cowered. He thrust the door open and stood aside in silence as she hurried out. Then he slammed the door and stood pressed against it, listening. He heard her ring for the lift, and then a noisy intake of breath. The lift clanked to the floor and the iron gate was heaved back. As the lift descended he heard her gasping sobs recede until they were quite faint.

He knew that Miss Glass would have seen the paper too. But now he looked forward to facing people, he had enjoyed the row with his mother, it demonstrated his own clarity of mind and vocal power. There was a gasp from the girls and Miss Glass as he walked into the bank. He took his place behind the counter, and turned to the girls behind him.

'Good morning all.'

'Good morning Mr Pearman.'

He savoured the words before he spoke them. 'The name is Wright.'

'I knew it,' said Miss Glass. 'I guessed it when you gave me those things to type.'

Mr Fowler stepped in through the swing door.

'Good morning everybody. Pearman, I'd like to see you in my office at once.'

Vincent walked behind him into the dark little office with its view of a back yard and tube of fluorescent lighting that flashed on and off blindingly as Mr Fowler seated himself behind his desk.

'I suppose you read your Sunday papers,' he said. The light came on.

'Of course.'

'Do you wish to comment?'

'I hardly see why I need comment,' said Vincent. 'They were concerned with my private life.'

'Mr Pearman . . .'

'I wish to be known as Wright. As you have the name plaque I should like to have it on display as from today.'

'Mr Pearman,' repeated Mr Fowler firmly, 'I find these aspects of your private life disgraceful. If they impinge in any way upon your professional life you know the consequences.'

'We do not always agree with one another politically or on religious matters or on many other topics,' said Vincent, 'but that is hardly a reason for sacking me, which I believe is what you are trying to suggest. Recently, Mr Fowler, you accused me of altering my books and defrauding the bank. You referred to all my work here for the last four years and found it accurate and perfect. I am a highly efficient and trustworthy employee, and I repeat that what I do at the week-end, whether it is reported by the press or not, is entirely my own business.' He pulled back his shoulders. 'The bank is opening in twenty minutes, I would like to prepare my till.'

'Very well,' said Mr Fowler. 'But one slip and you're in trouble.'

Vincent went out of the office and shut the door sharply. The letters had been a brilliant idea, they had made his position invulnerable. He had a sudden longing for Madame Vera, and then told himself he was managing very well without her.

People were obviously coming into the bank to look at him. A stream of local customers came in on flimsy pretexts, cashing cheques for a pound, asking for their statements, or for details of some foreign currency exchange. He caught Miss Glass mouthing 'I wasn't surprised' at Mrs Burgess. At lunch the waitress said, 'Fancy you being mixed up in that kind of thing.' He decided to wear his uniform every day from now on. Fowler would probably object but by the time he had set the wheels of protest turning Vincent would be ready to quit the job anyway. He could always plead victimisation, that Fowler had a down on him, had tried to trump up charges of fraud.

When he arrived in his uniform and set up the new name stand Miss Glass couldn't control herself.

'I would never have believed it of you, Mr Pearman. I always thought you were a gentleman, and I used to say so to mother. But I don't mind telling you, I feel ashamed to be working beside you. You look really common in that uniform, and how you can prefer it to a well-cut suit I can't imagine. We're all of one mind here, we don't like your Nazi ideas. We didn't fight the war to have Hitler here.'

'I'm sure you speak for the great liberal English people,' jeered Vincent.

'I'm sure I do. If you get on in politics, if that's what you like to call it, then England isn't what I thought it was, and I wouldn't be proud of it.'

'And are you proud of it now?'

'I certainly am,' said Miss Glass hotly. 'I think it's a wonderful place.'

'Here, here,' said Pamela.

'I think it could be,' said Vincent, 'which is where we differ.'

He continued to wear the uniform during the next weeks, but half conformed by putting on a collar and tie under the jacket, which he removed during working hours. Over the counter he looked conventional but he loved walking to work in the Party clothes, and people knew who he was and pointed him out. At the end of the summer holidays he went back to live at Windermere, and made Yates, Winters and Wood escort him to the bank and collect him at the end of the day. Jessop had spent part of the holiday with them, and part with his parents in Portofino. He came back tanned dark brown, and Vincent said, 'One tone darker and I'd have kicked you out of the Party.'

'I'm going to keep it going,' said Jessop. 'I've bought a sunray lamp. I'll leave it here for the week-ends.'

He spent two days at the house before returning to school for the last time, and left transformed from Party member to schoolboy, in grey suit and house tie, his blond hair bleached almost white under the soft felt hat that was uniform for the fifth and sixth forms. For the first two week-ends of term he was not allowed home, but on the third he arrived at Windermere. He came into the house and took Vincent's arm.

'I've some news for you.'

'Interesting?'

'Very interesting.'

'Is it good or bad?' He was afraid. 'I hope Party activities haven't got you into trouble at school.'

'No. They don't even know about them. They watch me seducing all the little boys with iced lollies, and listen to them singing the Party song, and think I'm running a choral group.'

'What is the news then?'

'Fox has dropped his plans for suing you for slander.'

'Of course. It wasn't slander. It was true. He would have lost the case.'

'He wrote to me,' said Jessop. 'He asked me to desert the Britain First Party and to join the Great Britain Party. He's reforming his group. With himself as leader.'

Chapter 11

HALF a dozen members defected to Fox. Vincent was unperturbed. They were part of the original group and Vincent was convinced that Fox had no talent for leadership beyond organising cross-country rambles. He might attract a few boys who enjoyed military discipline, but he could never appeal on a national scale. Vincent had received a letter from a woman's club in a Midland town, pledging support if he could do something about the Indians who were moving into the area and lowering its tone. They lived in filth and crammed numerous families into one small house, wrote the club chairman with much underlining. As mothers and citizens they wanted strong action to provide a healthy future for the children of the town.

Vincent went down to speak to them and was disappointed to find there were only fifteen members. But their rapturous applause and passionate discussion afterwards compensated and he returned home enthusiastic.

'I think we should make a special drive for women members,' he said to Patterson suddenly one evening, when they were discussing something quite different. His mind was so full of Party affairs these days he found his thoughts speeding from one thing to another.

'What?' said Patterson, bewildered.

'Oh, you're so slow, Patterson. I always seem to be one thought ahead of you.' Of course, Patterson lacked Vincent's agile mind. 'I would like you to produce a monthly news sheet with family appeal. I want to have the Mothers of Britain on our side.'

Although Dobson was still officially in the Party and had anxiously disowned any affiliation to Fox, Vincent didn't trust him. He lived too close to Fox for safety. Vincent let him handle the funds and some advertising but he was giving the main jobs to Patterson, and had this morning created him Chief of Propaganda, and now Editor of the News Sheet.

Vincent wondered about Delage too, who had always kept in touch with activities through Fox. What was going to happen now that friend Fox had formed a splinter group? Would Delage try to wriggle out of the covenant, or attempt to transfer it to Fox's party? If so, where would they find more funds? Vincent remembered seeing Delage at the meeting when he had denounced Fox. He recalled a single image of Delage's pink face as he marched close by it down the aisle in such triumph. Had Delage been impressed? Had he thought Fox shamed or victimised?

One evening, very late, Delage's allegiance was revealed. Dobson, who hated the telephone and spoke into it in a flat stilted voice which was always distant because he held the receiver away from his ear, had been prevailed upon by Delage to make the call to London. The message was conveyed that Delage would like to see Vincent the next day – a Saturday – on an urgent matter.

'What for?' asked Vincent sharply. 'Did he say?'

'He's got some ideas about the by-election. He thinks you ought to go down there.'

Vincent had not realised he had been holding his breath until he breathed out the air in a soft gush which steamed up the telephone mouthpiece.

'I'll see him.'

Dobson gave Vincent the name of a London hotel where Delage would be staying, and asked Vincent to be there tomorrow at six o'clock. Vincent disliked the proprietary order from Delage but realised it would be foolish to assert himself. He needed Delage's money.

He sat on the edge of his bed and thought about the relationship with Delage. He was, of course, a patron, and his wishes had to be deferred to for the time being. Later he could be discarded when the Party was paying for itself. If his ideas were good then he might be co-opted on to the executive in place of Fox. Certainly Vincent had not considered the by-election a useful place for action. It was a safe constituency, there was no racial problem, it seemed an integrated and straightforward area. The elderly member who had held the seat for twenty years was to quit the Commons for the Lords. The young and popular politician who was standing in his place was bound to be elected. What could the Britain First movement do to further itself? Wouldn't it, in fact, do its image harm if it interfered where it could only be ineffectual?

Delage was staying in an hotel close to Park Lane. Vincent took a taxi from Marble Arch Underground in order to arrive in the correct manner. He had been undecided whether to wear his uniform or his best suit, a navy blue pin-striped one. He put on the uniform. It was as Party Leader that Delage had summoned him.

The commissionaire, in a long greatcoat and fancy dress hat, opened the door and Vincent, who had paid the taxi through the internal window, stepped out and walked in a military manner into the foyer. Delage was waiting for him in a deep brown leather armchair. Beside him, the receptacle level with his chin, was an enormous ashtray on a tapestry covered stalk. He saw Vincent and stood up, extending his hand.

'Good of you to come, Wright.'

Vincent thawed. Yes, it had been good of him. Busy as he was he had found the time.

'I was very interested to have your message from Dobson.'

'I've been meaning to get in touch ever since . . . shall we have a drink?'

'I don't drink, actually . . .'

'Another crank are you? Has Fox been getting at you?'

'I never enjoyed it,' said Vincent tersely.

'You don't mind if I do, I hope?'

'Not at all.'

'I can talk better if I'm drinking.' Delage lead the way through a revolving glass door into the bar, which was empty except for themselves and the barman. A waiter came in immediately. Delage sat down and ordered a whisky.

'You're sure?' he said to Vincent.

Vincent nodded. 'I'm quite sure.'

'Have a crisp then?' Delage pushed a glass dish of crisps towards him. Vincent took one and nibbled it. He liked crisps.

'The reason I asked you to meet me,' said Delage quietly, 'is because I am prepared to finance you further.'

'Really?' Vincent took another crisp quickly and kept his eyes down. He felt they were shining.

'Certain ventures are bound to require more funds than you have at present. Dobson has submitted to me monthly accounts of your expenditure and I am well aware that mundane items like stationery and armbands and the like absorb an awful lot of money. Your manoeuvres weren't quite the success I had hoped . . .'

'No. Unfortunately Colonel Fox . . .'

'Fox is a soldier, a bloody good soldier, but he could never make a Field Marshal. He needs the ultimate orders from above.'

'Did you support me the other evening?' Vincent could not resist the question.

'I felt it was probably necessary to purge the Party in this way. Naturally I was sorry . . . you know, of course, he's reformed his group?'

'Yes.'

'He came to me for money.'

'Did you give him any?'

'I am a business man,' said Delage. 'I only invest my money where it will be of benefit either to myself or society.'

Vincent ate the crisps, leaning back on the plush chair. He had never been to an expensive hotel – a hotel for ladies and gentlemen his mother would call it. Delage was a gentleman. This was his kind of hotel. He was quite at ease, you could see by the way he flicked his ash into the huge ashtrays and ordered the drinks. Vincent realised that once he became nationally famous he would come to this kind of hotel as a matter of course. He would be asked to the homes of important people, rich and talented people, he would buy a large house and invite the people to visit him.

'My plan is roughly this,' said Delage. 'I'm sure you will be able to add ideas of your own. Let us say you are the carpenter, I am merely supplying you with a sound piece of timber.'

It was absurd to have a mental picture but Vincent did imagine a piece of the birds-eye maple that topped his mother's book cabinet.

'The by-election is, of course a foregone conclusion. Hurst will get in with the usual majority. Poor old Medenham Smith, shoved upstairs to make way. He's gone with tears in his eyes, but the Prime Minister wants Hurst and there you are.'

'In the circumstances I don't quite see what we can do,' said Vincent.

'We can point out to the electorate that they aren't really having a fair choice. This candidate has been foisted on them. At the same time you can present our Party as the choice of the people. You're the speaker, Wright, and a damned good speaker, if I may say so, it's why I'd back you over Fox or any of the others. You'll think up some ways to get into the press and make good the mess Fox made of the manoeuvres. You have to get back in the public eye in a favourable way. The sooner the better.'

He was right of course. Vincent was furious with himself for having dismissed the by-election as a possible Party platform. 'I had thought of it myself,' he excused himself to Delage, 'but frankly I've been so busy picking up all the ends left by Fox, I haven't had the time to develop any plans.'

'You need a secretary,' said Delage.

Vincent waited for the offer to pay for one but Delage called over the waiter and ordered himself another drink.

'You get out a plan of action,' he said to Vincent. 'I'll keep in touch and if there's any money needed I'll see that you have it immediately. Frankly I'm glad to get in a dig at the Government. I've met Medenham Smith a few times – Lord Medenham, now I suppose – and he seemed a nice old boy. It's a phoney situation. Let's air the dirty washing.'

Vincent decided to take the plan to Patterson and Dobson complete. He wanted the kudos of master-minding it himself. Besides, it was less likely to go wrong if he did it alone. This time he was going to be responsible for all the details.

He went down to the constituency the next day. It was just outside London and he was able to travel most of the way by underground. Election posters were pasted up at the station and as he walked the streets he saw handbills in many windows. Hurst's handsome face smiled from a cross-section of homes. His opponents were less represented. Quite clearly he was a popular man in a popular party. Vincent wondered if, even at this late hour, it would be possible to stand for election himself. But that would mean defeat, and defeat would be fatal. Far far better not to stand, and to make it clear why he wasn't.

It was Sunday but the candidates were making last minute appeals. Vincent saw blue, red and yellow rosettes on the lapels of a number of men, and one car with a loudspeaker was touring the streets.

There were five candidates, a Tory, a Labourite, a Liberal, a Communist and an Independent who claimed he was standing for the teenagers of England. He outshone Hurst in good-looks and his photographs showed him dressed entirely in white.

Vincent made notes of the public meetings billed for the days immediately before the election and returned to Windermere to plot.

The idea was inspired. It arrived in his mind whole and ready, almost surprising him as he sat in the bath – a bath hotter than the lukewarm ones he stipulated for the boys. Yet he shouldn't be surprised, he told himself. This kind of brilliant strategy was the essence of leadership. He would stay away until the day before the vote was to take place. It was too late to start campaigning now. Hurst was due to make a final speech at six o'clock the night before the election. It was to be in the town hall. Vincent would go in as an ordinary member of the public, with his uniform underneath his top-coat. He would have some of the boys with him. He would have a microphone in his pocket, and somehow, he didn't know how yet, he would arrange to have cut the wire leading to the speaker's microphone. The boys must have amplifiers. When the audience was seated but before the candidate arrived, he would throw off his coat, stand up on a chair and address the meeting. What an impact he would make! He would be protected by a bodyguard and although there was no doubt he would be thrown out, he would have a few minutes in which to speak first. If it had been a town with a negro invasion or a Jewish community, then there would have been a point in going earlier to ferment the situation. This, in the circumstances, was a perfect idea, a jewel of an idea, which would glitter forever in the annals of Party history. He wrote to Delage giving him the gist of the plan and asked for the money to buy the microphone and amplifiers and the train fares for twelve people.

Jessop, Yates, Wood and Winters were coming with him. He went through the members index and picked another six boys for their physique and looks. They were going to hit the news and this time there was to be no question but that the Britain First Boys were the kind of boys a country could be proud of, strong, courageous and patriotic, an appeal to the teenagers of England far greater than the youth in white could aspire. The youth in white might even, if one examined his picture closely, have a Jewish forebear or two. His hair was suspiciously dark and curly. The twelfth member of the party was to be a woman. The idea of a Party which encompassed whole families was becoming obsessive. The Midland mothers had sown the seed and it now seemed to Vincent to be of immense importance that women should be represented, every time the press were likely to make a report. He wrote a letter of invitation to Miss Glass, and placed it on her till.

It astonished him that Miss Glass did not reply. Vincent despised her but had always been quite certain that she admired him, would ultimately follow him and in secret desired to marry him. He would never, of course, marry Miss Glass or anyone else. He could not imagine even a Hitlerian crisis in which he would have the allegiance honoured, no, not even if Windermere were falling to pieces around him. But he expected Miss Glass to apologise for her outburst and humbly accept the invitation to accompany him to the by-election meeting.

Half an hour before he was ready to leave the bank and depart for the meeting she still had not spoken.

'Oh, Miss Glass,' he called through the cloakroom door where she was rearranging her shopping in the string bag.

'Yes Mr Pearman.'

'I'm wondering if you read my letter.'

'I did.'

'Are you coming then?'

Miss Glass flung back the door and stalked past him, pushing him as she did so.

'There's no need to be ill mannered, Miss Glass.'

'Mr Pearman.' She stopped and turned to face him. 'My mother is dying, I am devoting all my energies to nursing her through her last days and working here in order to support us. No doubt you think I'm a silly woman, I'm quite aware that you have always considered me to be beneath you. But I am not prepared to enter into a discussion with you concerning your horrible ideas. I am too tired to talk to you. And your invitation was an insult. That's how I took it. As an insult.'

'That's right,' said Vincent. 'Toady to the Jews and blacks. You've got it coming to you, Miss Glass.'

'I will be able to face Our Lord when the day dawns,' said Miss Glass, 'which is more than you will. All people are equal in death, Mr Pearman.'

'Miss Glass,' said the chief cashier, 'could you spare a moment.'

'With pleasure.' She left Vincent standing in the narrow corridor by the cloakroom. He trembled, clenching and opening his hands several times in frustrated fury, then he jerked his shoulders into an upright and soldierly bearing and walked stiffly back to the counter, looking straight ahead of him.

He would make a list. He would have a list of people who must be destroyed as soon as the Party took power. It would take time, of course. Every Jew's name must be entered. Every prominent person who had demonstrated that they tolerated a mixed racial population must be ruthlessly exterminated. If it was desirable to retain some of these men alive because they had brilliant minds which might be utilised, then they would not be sentenced to death but kept alive under strict supervision. Miss Glass's name would be on the elimination list as a point of personal revenge.

'When we get back,' he said to Jessop, who was sitting beside him on the tube train, 'I want you to go through the telephone directories listing Jewish names.'

He would let slip a name or two to the press, give the owners a jolt, make everyone else sit up. No doubt in time there would be a rush to emigrate to the United States. That day would come, it would come.

The boys split up at the station and made their way by different

routes to the town hall. Vincent, with a small microphone in his
pocket and accompanied by his bodyguard disguised as ordinary
voters, went into the hall with the public. They were early and
the seats he intended to occupy were empty. He sat in the centre
of the central row. His bodyguard of four sat either side and in
front and behind. The other boys, who were arriving singly, sat in
the corners of the hall. One, wearing blue denims and carrying
a tool bag walked up to the platform, tinkered with the microphone, tapped a plug or two and cut the wire in full view of
everyone. Vincent grinned uncontrollably. The boy plugged in
two amplifiers either side of the platform and laid a microphone
wire along the row close to Vincent's chair. Then he walked out.
Vincent looked round. There were by now, two or three hundred
people including the reporters from all the daily papers. They
wore press badges and sat together at the back. He looked at his
watch. Several minutes to go. He gave thought to his speech for
the first time. Then he jumped up on to his chair and stamped
his feet down hard. Jessop, Yates, Wood and Winters stood defensively round him. The two boys placed at the front of the hall ran
to the amplifiers and held them aloft like beacons. Yates handed
him the microphone lead and he connected it and switched
on.

'Citizens!' he shouted saluting. Delage came in and stood at the
back of the hall. 'We are here tonight to assist in a rigged election. Everything is concluded upon, signed and sealed, cut and
dried. We know this corrupt government is merely foisting its own
choice upon an electorate, who . . .'

'Sit down. Shut up!' Stewards attempting to reach Vincent were
held back by the boys.

Vincent raised his voice above the noise.

'I am Vincent Wright, leader of the Britain First Party. I would
have stood at this election but for the fact that I would be assisting
in a cynical ritual which is the negation of the freedom we so glibly
talk about. Instead, as a serious, dedicated leader of my Party, I
merely want to point out to you how you are abetting this uncon-
stitutional process by pusillanimously letting these so-called politicians get away with it.'

The scuffle with the boys had developed into a real free for all. Vincent's chair rocked as he spoke.

'Follow me,' he shouted above the din, 'follow the Britain First Party and show your independence . . .' his chair was pulled from under him and immediately his *corps* disengaged themselves from the scrimmage and pushed a way for him through the people. Hands clawed at his jacket as he went by.

'If there are any press men here,' he called, 'I will speak to them outside.'

A steward had run for the police. As Vincent ran down the steps of the town hall, the press reporters flocking after him, he saw the helmets of two policemen approaching from the end of the street. Delage was sitting in his car parked on the opposite kerb. A Daimler drew up obscuring it and the chauffeur stepped out and opened the back door. A lady in a flowered hat put a well-shod foot on to the pavement. Behind her bobbed the candidate's rosette.

'There they are,' shrieked Vincent. 'There's the marionette who will be representing you in the government tomorrow.' He thrust his face close to the startled one under the flowered crown. 'Don't think you represent British womanhood, you are nothing but the dying and decadent remnant of a dying and decadent society, a painted skull.'

'Now then, now then,' said one of the policemen. 'What's going on here?'

'Come on,' said Jessop urgently. 'Don't hang around.'

Vincent ran across the road to Delage's car.

'May we have a statement?' a reporter shouted.

Delage started the engine.

'Where are we going?' asked Vincent.

'House called Doughty Manor.'

'I'll make a public statement in half an hour at Doughty Manor,' Vincent yelled through an inch aperture, then wound the window up.

Delage began to drive slowly through the reporters surrounding the car.

'You must wait for my boys,' Vincent commanded. He saw them still on the pavement outside the town hall.

'They'll have to manage without you.'

'Please stop, Mr Delage. I need a bodyguard.'

'Not in a private house. You can't turn up everywhere with a lot of ill-mannered louts. Lady Allardyce is having a party.'

'We're going to her house?'

'That's right. She's very interested to meet you.'

Vincent thrilled at the title. Delage lived in an upper class world and the real upper class was, if not the whole backbone, a vital vertebra of Britain. Inbred of course, but leaders in their own way. One could dismiss the middle-class lady in the car but not a titled lady, particularly a titled lady whose family controlled a large and vital part of the country's engineering industry. To be invited to the home of someone so influential reminded him of Hitler being invited to the houses of the industrial barons of Germany. He leaned back smiling to himself, pleased.

As the car turned the corner of the street Vincent saw his boys running hard in various directions.

'I suppose they'll make their way back to London.'

'Sure to,' said Delage. 'They're not fools. That was quite a success I thought.'

'How long did you stay?'

'Until it began to get rough. The amusing thing is the reporters won't bother to cover the meeting, yours is the story they'll be phoning back to their papers.'

'I trust Lady Allardyce will allow me to conduct a press conference in privacy,' said Vincent, still relaxing.

'She enjoys this kind of situation.'

'Does she . . . does she support us?' He was ready, if not, to convert her, to make a brilliant and impromptu address to her and her guests.

'To an extent, I imagine. She likes to meet celebrities.' Delage drove into a gateway and up a long drive edged with big bushes cut into the shapes of birds. He parked among several other cars in front of the house which was large, low, mainly Tudor and covered with creeper. Deeply impressed, Vincent was determined to seem casual, in fact as he stepped out of the car, he began to shake.

A servant let them in and took their coats, then announced

them from the door of the drawing-room, very loudly. 'Mr Geoffrey Delage and Mr Vincent Wright.'

Lady Allardyce, wearing a blue lace evening dress, kissed Delage and shook hands with Vincent. She was small and thin but heavily busted and gave the impression of listing which was accentuated by immensely high heels. She was middle-aged and sharp featured with a nose which looked as if it might literally peck Delage's preferred cheek. Vincent thought she was well turned out, which was a phrase used by all the women he knew. He had of course, expected her to be well turned out. Her hair was immaculate, she wore jewels, a large diamond ring and a brooch centrally between the bosoms but curiously, a little to the right of the neck of the dress.

'Well well well, Mr Wright,' she said. 'It is certainly most interesting to meet you.'

A manservant brought over two glasses of champagne on a silver tray. Vincent intended to tell Miss Glass. This would make her change her tune. This was being socially accepted. Allardyce was a name as familiar and as redolent of power as Krupps or Vickers.

'I hope you won't mind if I see some members of the press here,' said Vincent grandly.

'Not at all, Mr Wright. You may use the library.'

'Mr Wright brought off quite a victory tonight, Ruby,' said Delage. 'He deflected attention from the candidate.'

'The candidate who will be elected, in spite of all I said,' said Vincent. 'This is what I want to make clear to the reporters. In spite of the fact that I have revealed a corrupt practice, the people will still cast the vote to support the Government. But I hope,' he raised his voice, 'possibly even by the next election, our Party will be strongly represented. If we do not lead the country we shall have a voice in parliament and I feel sure that at the end of the decade we shall be in control.' The other guests had turned towards him in surprise.

'Do you really think so?' said Lady Allardyce politely. 'As soon as that?'

'Why not?' Vincent gesticulated with his arm almost hitting Delage in the chest. 'I'm afraid a certain section of the public indulges in self-delusion. Our *socialists* who imagine racial integration is a possibility. There are, I am sure,' – he looked around the room – 'no socialists in this gracious home. I ask you, has it worked in South Africa? In the Southern States of America? In Cyprus? In Nottingham or Notting Hill? My dear Lady Allardyce, this is a pipe dream of the long-haired intellectuals.'

He refused a second drink. She seemed, he thought, very interested, very impressed, listened and nodded. The manservant came in to say the reporters had arrived.

'Show Mr Wright and the gentlemen to the library,' said Lady Ruby. As he left he heard the general conversation begin again.

The library had shelves of first editions behind locked and gilded grills. The original stone fireplace had been fitted with a modern slow burning grate of cream enamel, and on top of a brass coal bucket, resting on large chunks of coal, lay a tartan coal glove with a black palm. Vincent and the reporters had met in the hall and entered the library together. Vincent walked swiftly to the fireplace and stood on the raised fender, beside the brass bucket. The manservant came in with a tray of drinks and glasses, which he set down on the large desk. The reporters fell on it, and only when they all held glasses did they return their attention to Vincent.

'Now Mr Wright,' said one of them, a short man with a paisley scarf tucked into his shirt. 'If you felt so strongly about the election, why didn't you stand yourself?'

'There is no point in standing when defeat is inevitable,' answered Vincent. 'In any case I would not be prepared to take part in such a mummery. I don't compete with pop singers and cranks. I am a serious contender for the leadership of the country which one day I shall achieve. *Without doubt* I shall achieve it. But not yet. All I wanted to do today was expose this racket, this Hobson's choice of an election.'

'Surely, Mr Wright, it isn't a Hobson's choice. It is still a free choice.'

Vincent brayed a second's laugh. 'In a safe constituency? For the people here any other choice would be worse than the one presented to them. It's like those advertisements for dog foods. Five plates on the floor. Four of them with lumps of wood painted to look like meat. One with the tinned dog food. The dog would prefer fresh beef. But he takes the only possible choice left to him. The people here will vote as they usually vote, but next time, after a process of re-education, rethinking, they will vote for me or my representative.'

'Do you intend to take part in other by-elections, Mr Wright?'

'Wherever I and my Party may usefully serve the country,' said Vincent, 'you may be sure I shall be there.' He was suddenly bored by the interview. He wanted to return to Lady Allardyce, to the room full of influential people. There was an audience worthy of him. 'You can reach me at my London headquarters tomorrow.' He stepped down from the raised fireplace and walked to the door.

'Do you think her Ladyship would mind if we used the phone?'

'I cannot answer for our hostess.'

'Have another whisky, Paddy?'

'Thanks matey. How about you Bill?'

Vincent shut the door and walked back across the carpeted hall. Even indoors it felt strange to walk alone, without the bodyguard. He joined Delage in the drawing-room. This time as he went in he was aware of the big crystal chandelier and the portraits on the walls. Like a little palace, he heard himself saying to Miss Glass. Lady Allardyce had her back to him, she was talking to a tall man with a long face and narrow bifocal glasses without frames.

'Oh, but such a *boring* little man, don't you think?' she said. She turned and saw Vincent. 'Ah, Mr Wright! How did the press conference go?'

'Very well. Excellently.' Had she been talking about him? She gave no start of embarrassment, no indication that they had been discussing him. But the confidence which had so uplifted Vincent as he had crossed her thick yellow carpet dissipated with a shattering immediacy, leaving him defensive and anxious to leave. This bloody upper class smugness, he said to himself, this arrogant assumption of judgement, this utter certainty that they were the elect was an outrageous vanity. He suddenly recognised the long-faced man as a Labour member of Parliament.

'You must forgive me,' he said coldly, 'if I leave you. I have to return to London at once.'

'Oh, I am sorry. But it was a great pleasure to talk to you, Mr Wright. I hope one day, if you are in this area, you will come and see me again.'

'Are you going?' asked Delage, surprised. 'Do you want me to take you to the station?'

'Use my car, Mr Wright, please. I want you to stay a little while, dear,' she added to Delage.

Vincent's self-esteem returned in the back of the chauffeur-driven car. Of course she hadn't been referring to him. Why should she say he was boring. He was interesting. She had said so, interested to meet him, she had said, interesting to talk to him.

The chauffeur stopped the car, opened his door, and in almost a single gesture climbed out and opened Vincent's. Vincent, uncertain whether or not he should tip, mumbled good night and hurried into the station. He bought his ticket and stood on the otherwise empty platform, wondering if the boys had in fact gone back to Windermere or were taking advantage of his absence and drinking in some pub.

He wasn't even conscious that another person had come on to the platform. When the man made a sudden run at him and with an outstretched fist struck him hard on the mouth, knocking him back against a slot machine and on to the platform, he was aware only of the blow, and the dizziness. The person had gone by the time his vision returned to normal and he was able to pull himself on to his feet as the train emerged from the tunnel.

*   *   *

His mouth was swollen. He had lost a tooth. It was lucky, the doctor said, that it wasn't a front one. But it was difficult to issue orders. He wrote them on pieces of paper and handed them to the boys. The first was an edict that he must never again go out alone. Patterson telephoned the story of the assault to the press, and then to the bank, while Vincent listened on the extension, disappointed at the lack of sympathy. Winters fetched all the day's newspapers. Vincent put his hand over his chin, turned up his collar to minimise the ludicrous effect of his distorted face, and read the reports on the by-election, with Wood on guard at the bedside. Every one gave prominence to himself and his speech. In an editorial the *Guardian* said, *It is a curious anomaly of the British political scene that by our very freedom of speech a fringe politician, leader of a self-confessed fascist group, with whom the people of this country have little sympathy, has pointed up a serious flaw, an electoral contrivance, that we have not so much overlooked as, like the proverbial ostriches, buried our heads in the sand.*

Vincent took another sheet of paper. *Manoeuvres forgotten*, he wrote, *we're on the ascent. Good public relations.* He folded it over, put Yates's name on it and handed it to Wood. While Wood was downstairs delivering it, Vincent, in pain, took another page from the pad and wrote in careful capitals, *Bovril and Milk for lunch. Buy feeding cup with spout from chemist.* He lay back, waiting for Wood to return and wondering whether he would use it alone or if it would be more pleasant to let one of the boys hold it for him.

Chapter 12

THE Birmingham cell had kept in close touch since the manoeuvres. It had an initial membership of fifty and was adding to them all the time. The leader occasionally came to London to see Vincent, and visited him one week-end at the beginning of November when Vincent's swelling had gone, and he was intending to return to the bank on Monday. Jessop and the other boys were upstairs in the bedroom using the sunray lamp. Vincent answered the door himself and was furious when Jessop, who had not heard the bell, came into the living-room wearing only trunks and dark glasses. Vincent left the Birmingham leader and raged into the bedroom.

'Get dressed!' he yelled. 'What kind of an impression do you think you gave the Birmingham section leader. Would Lady Allardyce keep a servant who entered a room almost naked? What story do you think he will take back to Birmingham about a dissolute house of narcissistic boys?' He pulled the plug of the sunray lamp out of its socket, wrenched it from the wire and flung it through the open window into the garden. Then he hurled the lamp into a corner and went out, slamming the door. It was Fox's fault. He had inculcated Jessop with an obsession for healthy physique.

Ten minutes later the four boys came down to the sitting-room, immaculate in their uniforms. They saluted the man from Birmingham, who jumped up from his chair and saluted back.

'Section Leader Wilkins has something very interesting to say,' said Vincent. 'I would like to hear your views.'

'The situation is this,' said Wilkins. He was a thin nervous man with a bloodshot right eye. 'There's a rich Yid with a big gown shop, and right on the top floor, over the shop, the attic really, he has a caretaker, who lives rent free just for being on the spot. There were several break-ins before he had the idea of a living-in burglar alarm. Well, the caretaker died, leaving a wife and three kids, who have nowhere to go. The Jew-boy wants them out, so that he can put someone else in, but she won't budge. It means she'll have to get a room and the children might have to go into homes. There's a budgie too and a dog. Our papers have made a story out of it.'

'I get it,' said Yates, 'a story with heart that condemns the wicked landlord, even though the law is on his side.'

'That's right,' said Wilkins. 'I thought we might get it into the London press too.'

'Section Leader Wilkins has suggested that by playing up the unfeeling Jewish landlord aspect, we can get sympathy for the Party by moving in against him when he forces an eviction.'

'Is he going to?' asked Wood.

'Next week,' said Wilkins. 'He's giving her another week to find somewhere else. If she hasn't gone – and she won't go – he's going along with the police.'

'How did the husband die?'

'Driving the boss's van.'

'The landlord's, the shop owner?'

'Yes. Here's this poor widow, left homeless and penniless, and a rich Jew kicks her out. He could afford to employ a night-watchman in the shop.'

'Great,' said Jessop. 'It's a fantastic opportunity for the Party.'

'I'm glad you agree,' said Vincent. 'I want to send two of you back to Birmingham to organise protection for the woman. Use local members. As soon as you have the eviction date, inform me, and I'll come up. Under no circumstances let her accept alternative accommodation. Convince her that it's a matter of principle to stay where she is.'

'That's what I'm afraid of,' said Wilkins. 'You know what it's like when these things get publicity. People always offer homes, whether it's to a horse or a deserted baby or a widow with kids.'

'Yates and Winters,' ordered Vincent. 'Pack your things. You will accompany Section Leader Wilkins back to Birmingham. Wood, get me Patterson on the telephone. I want him to have this story in the papers by the morning.'

Patterson was glad to earn lineage money to supplement his teacher's pay. He was too late for the Sunday papers, but two dailies had a picture of Mrs Ann Gormley, her three children and their puppy Patch. It transpired that although her husband had paid no rent, he had accepted three pounds less a week for driving the van than in his previous job. 'We were desperate for a roof over our heads,' Mrs Gormley was reported saying. 'We already had two babies and June was on the way.' Another paper published a photo of June, 'Unaware that tomorrow she might be separated from her mother, recently widowed Mrs Ann Gormley.'

Yates telephoned every evening. He and Winters had called on Mrs Gormley and she had been grateful for their encouragement and sympathy. An offer for a home in Monmouthshire had been received, but she had refused it. They had chosen a team of twenty strong young men and were training them. Could they have weapons?

Vincent debated it. He and Patterson met after work, and planned Mrs Gormley's siege. Reluctantly Vincent told Yates they could have no weapons, because it was essential that although what they were going to do was illegal, it was the kind of lawlessness the British people would accept, and there must be nothing that would alienate the public.

The eviction date was fixed. The landlord, enraged by the publicity, was determined to maintain his right to possession of the flat. Yates and Winters had persuaded Mrs Gormley to allow some photographs of the inside of her home, and they had bought a camera with a flash out of Party funds, and taken pictures of a peeling wall in the kitchen which had a bath in it, and a shallow old-fashioned sink with a cluttered draining-board. 'I haven't got enough cupboards for even my few possessions,' said Mrs Gormley. The landlord also gave interviews to reporters. 'I felt I was doing the Gormleys a kindness. They had no home. I need the flat, which is in good repair, for a member of my family.'

Vincent issued an edict that at no point in the campaign was the word Jew to be used. 'His name's enough, and the photograph. Let it be implicit. We mustn't be labelled Jew-baiters.' Two days before the eviction he allowed the Party's name to be associated with Mrs Gormley. Reporters telephoned him at Windermere for his comments. 'The Britain First Party would give its support to any oppressed British citizen,' he said. A popular paper ran a leader the next day, asking its readers to help uncover other cases of so-called rent-free homes and exploiting landlords.

Vincent travelled to Birmingham on the evening before the eviction. The local Party secretary had found him accommodation with a member, who turned out to be the old home guard from the manoeuvres. Vincent was photographed leaving the train, and on a visit to Mrs Gormley, drinking a cup of tea and promising her help if the police attempted force. He attended a meeting at Wilkins' house, fussed over by Wilkins' wife who was overwrought at the effort of entertaining the Party leader.

'We're very honoured, Leader,' she said, shaking his hand, and not letting it go. Although he had wanted to be called Leader, Mrs Wilkins was the only person who used the title so freely and unaffectedly. On every other occasion it had been forced out stiltedly, in embarrassment and under pressure. After an enormous meal, Wilkins drove him to the home guard's house, a huge Victorian Gothic folly in which he lived with his mother of ninety-six, and a posse of ancient maids.

It was late, but Vincent's host was waiting for him with a tray of port and brandy.

'Thought you'd like a nightcap,' he said. He was upright, active and unbent, but his voice was squeaky.

'I'd prefer a cup of tea or coffee,' said Vincent. 'I don't drink.'

A maid wearing a quilted dressing-gown was summoned from her bed to make coffee.

'I'm on your side,' said the home guard, pouring it. 'Because I am convinced that there has to be a ruling class.'

They sat in his study with a dying fire and well-stuffed scratched leather chairs and books on the Empire, and famous battles.

'When I was a boy,' said the home guard, 'I used to ride my bicycle all over England. But I can't do that now, can I? And if I go into the town I can't move on the pavements for all the Zulus and Jews jostling on it.'

'You're right,' said Vincent.

'My friends who still travel tell me that even in the remote corners of the globe they find the chosen people and lower classes cluttering the beaches. Nothing but noise and crowds, nowadays, noise and crowds. I used to go to France and I was alone except for the Frogs. I wouldn't go now. I stay here. The world's a ghastly place today.'

'That's why we formed the Britain First Party.'

'That's why I joined, young man. I'm for a privileged class.'

Before Vincent went to bed, the home guard insisted on accompanying him to the enormous drawing-room. It was high ceilinged, and the lights, which he switched on all over the room, merely intensified the shadow and illuminated only the occasional tables and china cabinets on which they stood. There was one with a red damask shade on an organ. The home guard lifted the lamp carefully on to the floor and to Vincent's astonishment took off his shoes and sat down at the organ, pedalling away softly with his stockinged feet. At first the music seemed to consist of arbitrary phrases, but suddenly Vincent realised that he could pick out the melody of Land of Hope and Glory. When it ended he shook his host by the hand and said how much he had enjoyed the interlude, and they both saluted in the gloomy hallway, before the home guard showed Vincent to his room.

The bedroom was furnished in mahogany. The large wardrobe was fitted with drawers and shoe rack and tie rail, and a hat rack high enough to take a top-hat. The chest of drawers had brass handles and an inlay of rosewood, and the drawers were lined with yellow newspaper. Vincent lifted out a page curiously. It was from a copy of The Times and dated 1934. He began to read it. *The speech,* he read, *turns out to be reasonable, straightforward and comprehensive. No one who reads it with an impartial mind can doubt that the points of policy laid down by Herr Hitler* – it seemed like an omen, or as if he were suddenly taken back more than thirty years – *may fairly constitute the basis of a complete settlement with Germany – a free equal and strong Germany instead of the prostrate Germany upon whom peace was imposed sixteen years ago. It is hoped that the speech will be taken everywhere as a sincere and well-considered utterance meaning precisely what it says.*

Vincent replaced the paper carefully. If the people had thought that of Hitler in 1934, how ready they must be to receive him now.

He closed the drawer and climbed into bed, stubbing his toe on a stone hot water bottle as he extended his legs. He opened the cupboard beside him to see if that too contained an old newspaper, but there was only a chamber pot covered with forget-me-nots and designed, it seemed, for a particularly large adult bottom. The light on the table had a beige shade with a silk fringe, and strands of fringe had become unlooped and dangled on to a lace mat. Vincent turned out the light and went over the plans. The landlord had now obtained a court order for eviction, and so even in the face of public opinion he would be unlikely to make a last-minute retraction. Wilkins was sure that some of the boys had air guns, and Vincent wanted to make absolutely certain that they weren't carrying them tomorrow. They had two dogs, alsatians, and he wondered if the police would bring dogs too.

The maid from the night before brought Vincent breakfast in bed at half past five. She had not yet put in her teeth and her upper lip was invisible where it gathered over the gum as if drawn tight by an elastic thread. There was a solitary kidney under a metal dome, tea and two slices of toast with the crusts off. Vincent ate quickly, without being at all hungry, washed in the flowered bowl which matched the pot, and had a moment of nausea as he poured the cold soapy water into the bucket under the washstand, and a dead fly floated up on the scum.

His host was up, and in uniform, his tin hat on his head, hung with a small piece of camouflage netting that looked as if it had been cut from a table-tennis net. Vincent was irritated. He didn't want to have this old fool with him when he arrived at the meeting in Mrs Gormley's flat. As they left the house Vincent saw that a Union Jack hung from a pole over the front door.

Wilkins was waiting with Yates and Winters in a car outside, and Vincent climbed in with the excited home guard. The streets were empty and barely lit. It was only just six o'clock. They parked in a back street and walked the last half mile to the flat. As they walked they were joined by other boys in uniform, making their way singly to the meeting. No one spoke, except to say good morning. Vincent marched a few paces ahead, Yates and Winters at his side in their green shirts. Mrs Gormley opened the back door of the

shop and they climbed the stairs to the flat. There was carpet on
the lower floors because the stairs led to an upper sales floor and
the fitting-rooms. The last flights were covered with lino, and there
were no shades on the lights, only low watt bulbs on long flex.

There was a smell of wet wool – a cardigan had been drying in
front of a paraffin heater – and a faint odour of urine. The baby was
asleep but the two older children were having breakfast. Porridge
was smeared on the table and on the little girl's chin and hands.
Vincent turned his back on them, and addressed Mrs Gormley.

'We're going to leave you in fifteen minutes. As soon as we've
gone, lock the door and push heavy furniture against it and against
the windows. Don't be afraid. Remember that the Britain First
Party is here to protect you and you will not lose your home.'

'I wish Mr Wilkins hadn't made me turn down the cottage in
Monmouth,' she said, wiping the child's mouth with her apron. 'It
sounded lovely. It was on a farm.'

'You would only be letting yourself in for more trouble,' said
Vincent. 'You would have merely found yourself in the same situation again.'

'He sounded very kind in the letter,' said Mrs Gormley wist-
fully. 'The man from the paper said he'd make sure it was all right
for me.'

'Probably a press gimmick,' Wilkins assured her. 'They just
want the publicity for themselves. The cottage didn't exist. They
wanted a story, that's all, to prove the milk of human kindness.'

'Are you prepared for several days' siege?' asked Vincent. 'You've
bought enough food with the money we gave you?'

'Oh yes.' She opened a cupboard to reveal three tins of corned
beef and six of high grade pink salmon. 'I've got bread too, and
oranges for the kiddies.'

'You may not be able to emerge for several days,' said Vincent.

'We'll be all right, won't we?' Mrs Gormley appealed to the children. The baby cried in the bedroom.

'We'll leave you now,' Vincent said, before she had time to fetch
it. A feeding bottle with milk stood in a saucepan of water on the
table. 'Good luck, Mrs Gormley, don't weaken.'

As he went downstairs, followed by Wilkins and the rest, he

heard her pushing the wardrobe along the passage to block the front door.

There were twenty boys to prevent Mrs Gormley's eviction. Two of them hid on the upper sales floor and two in the lower part of the shop in case the door of the flat was forced in and they were needed for on the spot fighting. These four were big, aggressive and working-class. Yates had told Vincent that in this area the support was almost entirely working-class, whereas in London and Kent they had a large proportion of middle-class and even upper-class members. Vincent considered Jessop was upper-class. His parents lived in a big house with several fields that were rented out to local farmers, had two cars and servants including a gardener. Other boys from Jessop's school were equally favoured. Yates, Wood and Winters, although they had disassociated themselves from their homes and backgrounds, were all the sons of professional men. In this district, as in Paddington, the lower-classes resented the immigrants and the threat to their homes.

'They breed like rabbits,' said Wilkins. 'In ten years they'll be calling the tune, not us, if we let them get away with it.' Anti-semitism was less violent. The cell had gained strength on the colour issue, not the Jewish one. But the young men who belonged were as happy to join in this organised attack, just as they liked to beat up Negroes when the opportunity arose for them to provoke a scene.

Vincent led the way out of the back of the shop and into the alley behind. He was wondering how to deploy the old home guard, who was as eager as the boys for a fray, but would only be a hindrance when the battle started. One of the men, a lorry driver, had parked his lorry in the alley, and most of the boys climbed into the back. One went off to fetch the dogs, which were in his house close to the shop, and when he returned he put them, muzzled, in the lorry too.

'One thing about these dogs,' he said, 'they can tell whites from coloureds.' He held them on short thick leather leads. Vincent sent Winters up the fire escape so that he could keep a look-out. He had a whistle to blow if there was no time to come down and give the warning.

'Loyal members,' said Vincent, standing in the lorry. 'I wish I could stay with you and help you defeat this pernicious parasite of a landlord. But as your leader I dare not be involved with the police in case the whole Party machine is thrown into jeopardy. Mr Wilkins and I are going to remain at the headquarters in his house, and if we cannot be here in body we are behind you in spirit, ardently championing you in the cause of a free Britain.' He jumped down, and the home guard, who was still standing on the pavement said, 'I shan't let the bastards in,' and took a revolver out of his pocket. Vincent snatched it away before he had time to contemplate the danger. Then he handed it quickly to Wilkins.

'Sorry, no weapons,' he said. 'We want the people on our side. We haven't come armed.' He and Wilkins helped to heave the old man up into the lorry. 'Find a job for him,' Vincent ordered Yates. He saluted, they saluted back and closed the canvas flaps shielding the interior of the lorry. Vincent and Wilkins walked swiftly back to the car and drove through the now active streets to Wilkins' house, where Mrs Wilkins was waiting for them.

Yates had had the brilliant idea of putting the home guard into the telephone booth facing the shop. There he kept Vincent and Wilkins informed of events. He phoned every quarter of an hour, and Vincent telephoned him back when he was a few minutes late making his report. But by lunchtime nothing had happened, and he imagined Mrs Gormley opening the first of the tins of corned beef.

'The newspaper men are here,' said the home guard. 'They must have had a tip off from the police. There'll be action any minute now.'

The afternoon passed and still no one came. At half past five the shop closed, the four boys inside undiscovered. No one had looked inside the lorry. At six o'clock the home guard said shrilly, 'They're coming. There's a police car drawing up across the road.' He rang off, and Vincent dialled the number of the box in a frenzy, but there was no reply.

'The fool must have gone out,' Wilkins said. 'He thinks he can join in. He'll be knocked down like a ninepin.'

'Old people are useless,' said Vincent, dialling again, 'I'd have

them all put down like dogs instead of giving them a pension.
What do they do for the country?' He listened, the receiver pressed
to his ear. 'He's left his post. How dare he disregard authority.' He
paced the little hall, and Mrs Wilkins came out of the kitchen and
replaced the telephone cover, a legless spanish doll with an arch
expression and a black lace fan.

'Don't do that,' shouted Wilkins. 'Our leader wants to keep in
constant touch.' He swept the doll off the telephone, and Vincent
dialled once more.

'I want a taxi,' he demanded suddenly. 'We'll drive by. We must
keep informed. I might need to make a sudden decision.'

Mrs Wilkins looked up the number of a car hire firm, and telephoned while Vincent stalked up and down the hall, chewing his
knuckles and slapping his hand to his brow.

The car took ten minutes to arrive. Vincent instructed the driver
to take them past the shop, and sat leaning forward and staring
out.

About thirty people had gathered on the pavement outside the
shop, holding banners and placards which read *Fight for the Widow's
Mites* and *Britain First for Britons* which was now being used as the
Party slogan. There were policemen trying to move them, and two
police cars parked at the kerb-side.

'Drive down the alley behind the shop,' Vincent said to the
driver. His heart was beating quickly, and his breath was short, not
from asthma, but with excitement.

The car drove along a little way and then turned in the road and
went back past the people with their banners. There was a scuffle
now, and two policemen were holding a man by his arms. The taxi
turned slowly down the side road and past the alley.

'Slowly, slowly,' Vincent said, his face pressed against the side
window.

Police were advancing down the alley towards the back door of
the shop. A small crowd pressed behind them. One of the policemen turned and shouted at them.

'Stop,' said Vincent tensely to the driver.

'I don't want to get mixed up in anything,' said the driver in a
broad Birmingham accent.

'You'll be quite all right here,' said Vincent. 'If they come too close you can drive off.'

The police, five or six of them as far as Vincent could see, drew level with the entrance. The canvas at the back of the lorry was suddenly flung back and his men jumped down from the lorry one after the other like paratroopers leaving a plane. There was struggling confusion and the din of shouting and barking and blasts on the police whistles, which sent the two policemen at the front of the shop running round to the alley. To Vincent's horror he heard the sound of a shot, people came running from all directions and became embroiled in the fight. The bells of other police cars were heard approaching.

'Drive on,' ordered Vincent. He watched out of the back window until the taxi turned the corner, then he lay against the seat, panting.

'Quite a brawl,' said Wilkins. 'I wouldn't like to be in the middle of that lot.'

'How many police?' said Vincent. 'Were we outnumbered?'

'Depends on the reinforcements.'

'I don't care if they get her out now. We've made our capital. The country knows which side we're on.' His momentary panic and nervousness had gone and he was jubilant and smiling.

'Who had the gun, do you think? One of ours or theirs?' asked Wilkins.

Vincent dismissed it. 'We'll sack any member who carried a gun. We'll make it clear we issued an order forbidding weapons. We fight clean, with our fists.' He shook a fist close to Wilkins' face.

A few minutes after they were indoors again in Wilkins' house the telephone rang. It was Yates to tell them the fight was over and that Mrs Gormley was still inviolate in her flat.

'They've arrested five of the Party,' he said, 'and carted them off. Winters has gone down to the nick to find out the charges. The reporters are shouting to Mrs G. through the letter box. She's moving the blockade.'

'Good. Good,' said Vincent. 'Tell the press they can reach me here for the next hour. I'm returning to London tonight.' He sat in the Wilkins' living-room, chuckling and patting the chair arms, his cheeks pink with success. 'That gave the police a surprise,' he said. 'They didn't expect dogs. They didn't bring any, did they? They didn't expect such a solid mass of support either. Wait till the papers tomorrow morning.'

'Oh Leader,' sighed Mrs Wilkins.

The home guard had been arrested for carrying an offensive weapon. He had had a second revolver, which he had fired into the canvas flap of the lorry. Another boy had been arrested on the same charge, his weapon was a razor blade. Three more were accused of disturbing the peace and making an affray.

'More publicity when the cases are heard,' said Vincent happily.

He slept on the train, and as soon as he arrived in London took a taxi to Fleet Street to collect all the first editions of the papers and then asked the cab driver to take him to Windermere.

Patterson and Wood were up, dressed, waiting for him. Yates had telephoned from Birmingham with the news. They took the bundle of papers and his suitcase from him and escorted him to the sitting-room. Vincent sat down in a chair and closed his eyes.

'It's been very tiring,' he said, 'but a great moment in the Party history. Read them to me, will you?'

'Here we are,' said Wood, opening *The Times*. 'It's headed Fight over Widow's Flat.'

The Times gave a factual account in a four inch column but in a leader questioned the emergence of a new fascist party, recalling the fights between the fascists and the communists in the East End before the War. The *Guardian* Editorial said *Under the guise of defending a widow, this group of thugs had used the situation as a lever in an anti-semitic campaign.* The *Telegraph* referred to *A disease which has lain dormant for many years and is once again revealing ugly symptoms.* There was an article on racial hatred and anti-semitism in the *Sun*, another in the *Mirror* (*Old evils raising their heads*) and in all the popular press news stories spotlighting the human angle. After the fight the budgie was found dying at the bottom of the cage. Were the boys defending Mrs Gormley a bad lot, or were they in fact demonstrating the warm-heartedness of British youth? There was a small cartoon showing a street fight, with the ghost figures of Hitler and his henchmen looming in the sky. Ann Gormley's own story was promised as Sunday reading.

Vincent was very satisfied. 'We must be geared to receive thousands of new members,' he said. 'This widespread attention will raise hope for many people dominated by repressive employers and councils.' Yates and Winters returned to London with accounts of two more riots outside the flat and the landlord's defeated acceptance that for the time-being he could not force the eviction. The home guard was being kept in custody until there was a medical report.

'He'll either be locked up in an asylum or sent to prison,' said Yates. 'Poor old bugger. Not much of a choice.'

'Trigger happy maniac,' Vincent retorted. 'He might have brought the whole Party into disrepute.' He was eagerly looking forward to the Sunday papers, the more reflective comment in the serious press, and Mrs Gormley's own story which was going to be illustrated, said Winters, by a photograph of the children looking out of the window supposedly under barricade. In fact they had been taken before the fight, and Winters believed that Mrs Gormley had signed a contract at the same time. Vincent stayed at Windermere on Saturday night, so that he could mull over the papers with Jessop and the boys. Jessop arrived for the week-end, bitterly regretful he had missed the excitement in Birmingham. He carried the papers under the arm of his black cotton dressing-gown and brought them into Vincent's room on Sunday morning. Vincent was asleep and Jessop dropped the papers on to Vincent's face to wake him.

'Wake up. Mrs Gormley's revelations have come through the letter box.'

Vincent sat up knocking the papers on to the floor. Jessop picked them up, found the page with the photograph and handed it to Vincent.

'My Ordeal,' he read aloud. 'Mrs Ann Gormley speaks.' Jessop sat down on the bed. 'Go on!'

'I was only a few days widowed when I received the bitter news that unless I left the only home my children knew, I would be forcibly evicted from the humble flat my husband and I had shared.'

'Christ!' said Jessop.

'I was in despair until I received a call from two young men who said they had come from London to help me. George and Bill, as I came to know them, promised they would stand by me, and that they had behind them the support of a million people who belonged to a movement called Britain First.'

'A million,' said Jessop, grinning. 'She over estimated, didn't she?'

'It will be a million,' said Vincent, 'now that the public knows about the Party.'

'It's a long way to go,' said Jessop.

Vincent frowned and went on reading. 'This movement had been formed to aid unfortunates like myself, and I must admit to being astonished when a few days after they had sipped tea with me in my shabby kitchen, I found that I was written about in the newspapers, and that I was known to many readers. I received several small gifts of money and – my God!' shouted Vincent. 'The stupid woman. Look!' He held out the paper to Jessop, his hand trembling. Jessop steadied it with his own. 'There,' said Vincent, pointing to the italics under a heading *Offer*: 'I was offered a new home in Monmouthshire. A gentleman, signing himself a friend, was giving me the opportunity to start life afresh in a five-roomed cottage situated on his farm. I thought of the roses the country air would put in my kiddies' pale cheeks and of waking each morning to the crowing of a cock. But George and Bill explained to me that by thinking of myself I would be letting down the Britain First leaders who had spent so much money in championing my cause and needed to take it to its conclusion so that others might not be exploited too.'

Jessop stood up. 'She said a mouthful there.'

Vincent was shaking all over. He gritted his teeth to control himself, but it was as if he was shivering from cold. The telephone began to ring. He made a movement for Jessop to answer it. When Jessop came back, saying, 'That was the *Express*. They want a comment from you,' it rang again before Vincent could speak.

He dressed and shaved, and Wood gave him a tranquilliser. Wood took them himself every day.

'Get me a train timetable,' said Vincent. 'These pills don't work.'

'It will,' soothed Wood. 'Why? Where are you going?'

'Mind your own business.' Vincent was going to see Madame Vera. Her own words came to mind; he was at a crossroads, an impasse. He ordered a taxi, and urged the driver to hurry to the station. The pill began to have effect as they passed Buckingham Palace, and by the time he was on the train he was in a soporific state and fell into a bemused sleep. His dreams were bizarre and horrifying and he woke frequently to become aware that he was on a train, before going to sleep again. He dreamed that Madame Vera shot him in the leg while he talked to a child in a frilly dress; that he and Fox crawled through a railway tunnel with chalk sides; that he was alone in an air-raid shelter in a street in Muswell Hill, with incendiary bombs bursting in front of the entrance; that his father collapsed in a field and that police cars rushed across the field and ran over him. He awoke at the station he wanted, and jumped out of the train in a panic, sweating and feeling sick.

He knew Madame Vera's address, although he had not written to her. He endured terrible guilt as he thought that it was only now, when things were going wrong, that he had come to see her. With her penetrating insight she would know that he hadn't consciously thought of her until this morning.

He asked the way and was directed to a street close to the station. The house was in the middle of a terrace built at the end of the last century. Stone plaques engraved Victoria Cottages, 1890, were on the walls above the doors of every other house. The address Madame Vera had given Vincent was Shangri-la, number thirty-one, Victoria Cottages, and with relief and a sense of meeting his destiny he opened the gate and walked between the stone gnomes and mushrooms and herons edging the path to the shiny blue front door, set in bricks painted a bright terra-cotta and picked out with cream-painted cement. The knocker was a one-legged leprechaun. He held it and banged it against its brass base until Madame Vera herself opened the door and asked him to come in.

'Well, I am surprised to see you, Mr Wright. I was just reading about you.' She led the way into a living-room where the paper containing Mrs Gormley's terrible confessions lay open on a table. A man sat in a chair by the fire with an imitation bear rug round his legs.

'This is my sister's husband,' said Madame Vera. 'This is the Mr Wright I was telling you about, dear.'

'Oh yes,' said the man, staring at Vincent.

'Now you're here I expect you'd like to sit down,' Madame Vera said, sitting down herself.

Vincent remained standing and said urgently, 'I want to see you alone, Madame Vera.'

'Don't mind him. He's not been right since his accident.' She jerked her head towards her brother-in-law.

'Are you sure? It's very personal.'

'He got sucked half a mile along a sewer and hit his head twelve times. He's still got the little lumps,' said Madame Vera.

Vincent sat in the only chair which allowed him to have his back to the man with the fur rug. Instead he faced a wall with a poker worked wooden panel saying 'A spot of cheer to your near and dear makes many a long day bright.'

'Go on, then,' said Madame Vera.

'I need your . . .' began Vincent.

'Before you say any more I have to tell you what I feel, Mr Pearman . . .'

'Wright.'

'Oh, sorry, Wright. One does forget. I just want to say, dear, that being here and devoting myself to him – my sister's in no fit state to do a thing, she's so upset – I've lost touch with the occult. I don't think I can be of much use.'

Vincent took both her hands between his own and pressed them up and down like bellows. 'Madame Vera, you must help me. Don't let me down, I've sat on a train all morning. I don't know what to do. The phone never stopped ringing, they all wanted my comments, but I couldn't say anything until I'd consulted you. You've always guided me, I need your advice, I need your help, Madame Vera.'

'Vee,' said the man by the fire suddenly, in a deep voice. 'Get me a cup of tea.'

'In a minute, dear.' She smiled falsely at him. 'Mr Wright, I don't like to delve too deep. I think you've touched evil forces, and I'm not capable of dealing with them. Besides, I don't want my name in the papers.'

A woman's voice called faintly down the stairs.

'How about a cup of tea, Vera?'

'In a minute dear,' she answered, cupping her hands round her mouth. 'I'm sorry, but there it is, Mr Wright. I'm not attracted to the evil influences.'

'How can you say such things,' Vincent said, tears coming to his eyes. 'I'm not evil, I work for the good of mankind.'

'The evil may be taking possession,' said Madame Vera, struggling to free her hand.

'And some cake,' added the man in the corner.

'This is a crossroads,' pleaded Vincent.

'Have you put the kettle on?' called the woman's voice.

'I am lost, I don't know which is the right direction, I need the steady hand you have always given me. I beg of you, look at my palm.' He released her hands and spread his own, palm upwards, level with her neck.

'They want their tea,' said Madame Vera. 'No, Mr Wright, I'm sorry, but there's nothing I can do. If I had the power I would, but it's gone, and that's all there is to it. I can't do anything without the power.' She stood up. 'I expect you'd like a cup of tea too after your journey.'

Vincent stood and knocked her back on to the chair. 'You've betrayed me,' said Vincent violently. 'You've betrayed me at my hour of need, but don't worry, I'll see you're punished. Don't think I can't manage without you. You may have lost the power, but I've still got it.'

'Do put the kettle on, Vee,' said the man impatiently. 'It's after four.'

'You're being silly,' said Madame Vera getting up. 'You shouldn't get excited like that.'

'You've let me down and you'll suffer for it. Just wait.'

As Vincent walked along the road back to the station her meanness, her injustice, her denial of him burnt his mind, and enraged him so that he would have liked to have hit her and hit her until she fell sobbing on to the ground. Beside this flagrant betrayal, Fox's devious endeavours to overthrow him were like a schoolboy's game.

Chapter 13

FROM the station he reversed the telephone charges to Wilkins' house. When Wilkins answered in a smarmy voice Vincent shouted abuse.

'You fool, you idiot, it's your fault. You mismanaged the thing from beginning to end. It's your fault she shouted her mouth off. Now what? Now what?'

'It wasn't my fault,' said Wilkins hotly. 'It was your London boys. She quoted them, didn't she? I didn't make mistakes. Don't blame me.'

'I do blame you. Every paper in the country has been telephoning me, we're a laughing-stock. You're sacked from your position, Wilkins. If you wish to remain in the Party it is as an ordinary member. You are untrustworthy and incompetent, in short, a bloody nincompoop.'

It was a strange word to use. As Vincent slammed down the receiver and burst out of the hot little booth on to the littered platform he wondered why such a dated, alien word, should have come to his mind. Who had called *him* a nincompoop? He thought it was Binky's mother when he had tried to lubricate Binky's pedal car with olive oil.

'You are a nincompoop, Vincent, you really are.' Or was it his father? 'You are a nincompoop sometimes, how do you expect me to buy an ice cream when it's early closing?'

At Windermere Patterson was waiting with the first copies of the news sheet.

'I've tried to make it appeal to all the family as you suggested,' he said. 'Here's an article for boys on rock-climbing as a means to a healthy body. And here's one for older women with a recipe for Lancashire Hot-pot.'

'A what?' said Vincent disbelievingly.

'I thought a really traditional British recipe each month . . .'

'Well I don't!' Vincent was tired, fraught and hysterical. 'What other gems have you thought up?'

'There's Party activities, which I've given prominence on the front page. I've covered the Birmingham venture fully . . .'

'Have you read the papers today?' Vincent demanded, pressing his top back teeth so hard against the lower ones they hurt.

'Yes. But I wrote this before today. I've been writing it all week.'

'You can't write *news* all week, can you? News has to be vital, it has to be hot and lively, not the stale rubbish you've scrawled down here.' Vincent tore the paper and threw the halves across the sitting-room. They fluttered in the air and descended gently on the bookcase. 'I've just demoted Wilkins and if you dare to waste my time with any more crap like this I'll have you kicked out of the Party too. Get me a national daily on the phone.'

'Which one?'

'I don't care which one. Any one.'

'Well, I haven't got the numbers of all the papers.'

'Find them then.' Vincent picked up a telephone book and hurled it at Patterson's legs. 'I'm going to tell every paper in London about Wilkins and how he tried to turn the people against my Party. It was deliberate sabotage. It was a calculated, cold-blooded traitorous attempt to make the Party ridiculous.'

'Here's the number of the *Mail*,' said Patterson. 'Shall I dial it for you?'

'I ordered you to. How dare you ask me again?'

'Honestly,' said Patterson soothingly, 'if I were you I'd wait until tomorrow. I think it would be a mistake, you'd be sorry later. You're het up now, this isn't the time to speak to a news editor. You'd make bad news for yourself.'

'I know when to speak and what to say.' Vincent thumped his chest. Then a second of indecision and despair changed his angry certainty to a mood of anxiety. Why had Madame Vera deserted him? All the decisions he had made since her departure may have been wrong, everything he did in the future might be wrong too. If he could have consulted her before Birmingham, would he be in this precarious position between success and ridicule? Hitler was a butt for humour until he became too autocratic and strong to make it dangerous to laugh at him. Everyone had made a joke about Hitler's hair and little moustache until they became symbols of an empire. There was no question of doubt. He must stand and rally against jibes in tomorrow's press, because the Party would survive, it was political evolution, a necessary progression and it wouldn't collapse because of a Mrs Ann Gormley's foolish utterances to a reporter who wanted a story angle. This was the moment when he must reject Madame Vera because he didn't need her. He had become superstitious. That had been his only error. He was capable of living without recourse to his palm or the stars or a pack of grubby cards. He was a born leader, *that* was in his stars. That was all he need remember. He could lead. He would lead. And one day he would be in a position to punish Madame Vera for her betrayal, and dispense with Patterson, as he had dispensed with Wilkins and Fox. One day, his Party would be the only party, there would be no opposition. He would lead and rule.

He had not been to work since his trip to Birmingham. On Thursday morning he decided to go to the bank. He wasn't afraid of being in public view, he hadn't scuttled into a burrow because of what had appeared in the newspapers. What was more he would go to work in his uniform and remain in it, not conceal it during working hours, as if he was ashamed.

He arrived late because Yates, unaware that he wanted to be up early, failed to wake him in time.

'I'm sorry and all that,' he said, when Vincent shouted at him, 'but I'm not a mind reader. If you want me to wake you at seven you'll have to tell me.'

It was after ten by the time Vincent had dressed, eaten and walked to the bank. Miss Glass was working alone at the counter, and a queue of women drawing their week-end housekeeping money waited while she stamped cheques and asked 'Ones?' When she saw Vincent she started and stared, and then began to count again fervently, her eyes down. The chief cashier hurried into Mr Fowler's office.

Before Vincent could hang his coat on his peg in the cloakroom, the chief cashier came up to him and said smugly, 'The manager would like to see you.'

Vincent didn't answer, but walked past him and into Mr Fowler's office without knocking.

'So you've deigned to come into work, have you?' asked Mr Fowler sarcastically.

'I have been concerned with state matters until today,' said Vincent haughtily.

'So we saw in the papers. I have to tell you that we want your resignation.'

'That's exactly why I came,' said Vincent. 'I haven't time to work in a menial capacity when the nation needs me.'

Mr Fowler picked up his pen. He looked at Vincent and half-smiled. 'No one needs you, Pearman. You're a raving lunatic.'

He's Jewish, thought Vincent triumphantly. That's it, he's a secret Jew. It accounted for his behaviour. Otherwise he would have kept Vincent in the bank and let him work there when he wanted. He would have helped the Party.

Of course he was a Jew. Didn't he wear his hat in the office sometimes, and no British gentleman, as his mother had told him since the first day he possessed a school cap, ever, ever wore a hat indoors? What did he eat for lunch? Vincent couldn't recollect him eating ham salad on any of the days they had coincided at the Toro. He was dark too, his eyes were Jewish looking, and his nose was big. He might have had his nose altered. His sort, the Judy sort who wanted to keep things quiet, often resorted to plastic surgery, like criminals after a murder or a robbery. They didn't want to be recognised for what they were. Vincent gathered saliva rapidly in his mouth and spat into the gutter on to the dead autumn leaves.

He walked along the pavements of East Finchley. The branches on the trees were almost bare and the sky above blue with fast moving clouds. It was very cold. He turned the corner by the pub and walked briskly towards Windermere. He was glad to be free from routine work, now he could devote all his time to the Party. This morning he would go through the membership cards and select a leader to replace Wilkins. If there was no one suitable in Birmingham he would introduce a member from outside. The Birmingham cell needed careful handling. Morale would be low, less devout supporters would drop away in the confusion following the press reports. Yates was familiar with the area and knew many of the members. Yates was a brilliant choice. He might not want to leave London, but his duty to Vincent and the Party would influence him. Eventually every key town might have a leader chosen from the *corps d'élite*. Vincent would have liked to detail Patterson to take over the difficult Birmingham cell, but unfortunately Patterson had acquired a singular position within his own recruited group and his removal might result in equal chaos there. Vincent disliked Patterson, now, he felt Patterson's very presence in London, with his old allegiance to Fox, was a threat. In any case, Patterson hadn't the qualities to adapt himself to the Birmingham conditions.

Vincent opened the gate of the house. The boys always did the housework directly after breakfast. When he stayed there he waited in his bedroom until the sound of the hoover ceased, then he would go slowly downstairs to the dusted living-room, the windows wide. He remembered that first introduction to the living-room, with the dust and dirt and full ashtrays. He had soon changed that. Now the furniture shone and there was plenty of fresh air. As he walked up the path he saw that the living-room windows were closed.

He put his key in the lock and turned it quietly. He did not close the door, he did not want to be heard. He tiptoed into the living-room and saw that it was as they had left it last night, with dented cushions, used coffee cups and the newspaper cuttings they had been studying lying on the floor. What was going on? Carefully Vincent crept up the stairs, waiting on each step. He stood on the landing outside Yates's door. He could hear the murmurings of voices, Yates's voice and a girl's.

Controlling the impulse to fling open the door and confront them, Vincent stood absolutely still, listening.

'You're quite fabulous,' he heard Yates say. And the girl answer, 'Well, you're not so bad yourself.' Then the silence, while they kissed. In his imagination Vincent saw them lying in the unmade bed. Was it prearranged? Had the girl arrived the moment he left the house, or had Yates telephoned her and said, 'He's gone. Come on over.' Why, why did they do it? Why did they have this compulsive sexual urge which made them disloyal to the Party? He could understand it in the early days before the consuming interest and Party discipline. Then their whole lives had been decadent. But surely now, with the exercises at the gym and the exciting activities, the daily routine of housework and office work, surely now there was no need for these physical indulgences?

I won't go in there and make a scene, thought Vincent, I won't humiliate him in front of the girl, he's too hot tempered, it would be dangerous. But I'll make sure that he's so tired at the end of each day, so intimately involved with the Party machinery, that he won't want to ask her here again.

He went downstairs, less silently, convinced that Yates would not hear him whatever noise he made. As he reached the bottom step, Wood came in through the open front door with a string shopping bag full of food. He stopped when he saw Vincent. His mouth opened.

'Well?' said Vincent sharply.

'I've just been shopping,' said Wood feebly.

'I'm not blind. Nor am I deaf. Who has Yates got upstairs?'

'Yates? Oh, some bird. I don't know.'

'This is the time of the day allotted for housework,' said Vincent. 'Does this occur every time I leave the house? Do I have to supervise you? Are you incapable of carrying out my orders?'

Wood came in, and walked past Vincent to the kitchen. Vincent followed him as he put the shopping bag on the table and began to unpack.

'Is that for lunch? For her?'

'No,' said Wood sourly. 'As a matter of fact it's for your evening meal.'

'I thought you might make the orgy complete with food and drink at my expense.'

'No. We don't go in for orgies. We just need sex occasionally.'

'I doubt that it's occasionally.' Vincent began to shout. 'I believe that every time I go out girls are lured into the house. You aren't fit for my *corps*. You disappoint me. Your promiscuity disgusts me.'

Vincent slammed the door of the kitchen and stamped up the

stairs to his own bedroom. They had let him down. They were using the house for their own lust, misusing his generosity by feeding their women on his food. Was everyone false? Were they all, like Madame Vera and Wilkins, less than his hopes for them? Was no one utterly loyal and trustworthy? Vincent had intended returning to his flat tonight, but now he decided to stay at Windermere. He would let the boys fall asleep and then he would wake them and take them on a midnight exercise. He would march them until the early morning. He would defy them to feel any desire but the desire for sleep this time tomorrow.

Yates appeared at noon, and was warned by Wood that Vincent was at home. By this time Vincent was in his office composing the *News Sheet*, which he had decided to write himself until he could discover someone more able than Patterson. Yates made sure that Vincent was nowhere about and then led his girl-friend down the stairs and out of the back door. He kissed her on the cheek and said he'd ring her, she had better not come round in the mornings for the time being. Winters had spent his morning at the Y.M.C.A. gymnasium, and arrived home for lunch hungry from the exercise.

'Do you think my muscles have improved from the weight-lifting?' he asked, showing his biceps.

Vincent came into the kitchen.

'The only one of you who spends his mornings productively, I see,' he said to Winters.

'I hope so,' said Yates, smiling.

'Don't try to be funny,' snapped Vincent. 'I was very distressed when I came back early. The house was filthy, and you were in bed with a whore.'

'If I'd known you were coming back I'd have cleaned the house first,' said Yates. 'Phone me next time.'

'How dare you be so insolent,' Vincent said, his voice raised. 'I forbid you to have any more girls in the house. I forbid you to indulge your depraved tastes under this roof.'

'We're over twenty-one,' said Wood.

'But I pay the rent. Where would you be if it wasn't for me? When I met you you couldn't pay the bills, could you? I paid them, didn't I? I paid the rates and the rent and the electricity and the gas, and I'm still paying for them. I bought you your uniforms, and I give you pocket money. I'm the piper and I call the tune.'

'This isn't Hamelin, and we aren't forced to follow. It was a bargain, remember?'

'Yes,' said Winters, 'and our side of the bargain was to join your Party. We agreed. But we didn't agree to stop screwing birds. We'd never have agreed to that.'

'Boys,' said Vincent, sitting on the edge of the kitchen table. He realised that he must appeal to them, that giving orders of this kind produced an explosive situation which they would all regret later. 'I chose you because I could see your potentialities. I made you the first members of my *corps d'élite*. You are not the boys you were. Then you were nothing short of wastrels, layabouts. You were glad enough when I suggested you worked as full time members. I like to think that over the months we have been together and watched the Party grow from those small beginnings, that you have developed with the Party, and what you may have taken on because you couldn't pay the bills has in fact become an integral part of your lives, and the very core of your being, as it is mine.' He looked at each of them in turn. 'You have become physically fitter, and morally stronger. You have acquired a code of living, unshakeable beliefs. I want you to believe me now when I tell you that the loose morality you are practising is harmful. Self control strengthens the character. That is why I am asking you now, to give up this casual, amoral way of life. You will respect yourselves for the abstinence. You will become better men, better fitted to serve the Party. I am not forbidding you, that would be stupid. I am asking you to consider what I have said, and I know that your decision will be the right one.' He jumped off the table and went over to the stove. 'Well, what have we got for lunch, Wood? It smells very appetising.'

'Fish fingers,' said Wood sulkily, 'and ice cream.'

Vincent stayed indoors all day and kept the boys busy. He completed the news sheet and Winters typed it laboriously with two fingers in the afternoon. Yates and Wood cleaned the house and Vincent inspected each room when it was done, making them stand to attention while he looked closely for specks of dust. They had supper together and looking at the other two, Yates suggested that they go to the cinema. At once Vincent said he felt like playing cards. They sat round the kitchen table and played gin rummy until eleven o'clock, and then the boys yawned and went to bed. Vincent stayed in the kitchen, savouring their surprise when, in an hour's time, he would wake them and lead them on a march. There was no question who was in command now. He demanded instant obedience.

At twelve he stood up and stretched. Then he pulled on his boots that he had taken off when he played cards, and splashed his face with cold water at the sink. His grip on the boys was to be restored. He went upstairs into Yates's bedroom.

The window was closed and Yates was completely hidden by the bedclothes. Vincent stamped across the room and flung the window open, then pulled the blankets to the foot of the bed. Yates leaped up, swearing.

'Get up,' said Vincent. 'We are going on a night march.'

'You flaming, bloody fool,' shouted Yates. 'This is the time for sleep.'

Vincent controlled his temper. 'Don't speak to me like that, I am your leader. Will you get up and dress immediately. I will see you in the hall in ten minutes.'

He walked out, leaving the door open, and went to wake Winters and Wood. They swore too, and Winters tried to pull the covers up as Vincent jerked them down. For a moment there was a tug of war. Then Winters sat up. 'You're crazy,' he said, 'what's the point of getting us up at this hour?'

'I am illustrating the point I made earlier.'

'What point, for Christ's sake?'

'The point concerning self-discipline. You must learn to overcome the desire for sleep as you must overcome your other bodily cravings. Only then will you be fit to hold your positions within the Party.'

He marshalled them in the hall. They still grumbled.

'I want you in single file. I will keep pace on your right. Are you ready? Quick march!'

He marched them down the path of Windermere and through the ship's wheel gate. It was a bitterly cold November night, with a full moon. No clouds had come up during the day and all the stars were visible. The trees looked one dimensional and as they turned into a main road, the pavements were lit by orange lamp lights.

Vincent's energy increased as he walked, the feeling of tiredness that had overcome him in the kitchen was completely dispelled. Very softly he began to sing the Party song and told the others to join in.

'Quietly. We don't want to be stopped for disturbing the peace.'

A policeman did in fact stop them as they reached Muswell Hill and asked them where they were going. 'Just walking, officer,' said Vincent. He stopped the boys singing and the policeman kept close behind them as they marched towards Highgate. Then he decided they were harmless and left them to proceed homeward along the Archway Road. They reached Windermere again at two o'clock.

'I expect you'd like a drink of cocoa,' said Vincent cheerfully. 'I'll make it for you.'

'Quite frankly all I want is bed,' said Wood.

As they walked upstairs, Vincent put his hand on Yates's arm. 'I've some exciting news for you.'

'Yes?' said Yates disbelievingly. 'What's that? Another march tomorrow night?'

'I'm serious. I have decided to send you to Birmingham to take command of the cell.'

'You've what?'

'This is an exciting challenge for you. I will promote you. It is your big chance. I am overlooking your behaviour this morning.'

'Big deal,' said Yates, as he went back into his room and closed the door.

Vincent woke and looked at his watch. It was half past eight and Winters – it was Winters' turn on the rota – had not brought his breakfast. Just because he had been on a midnight march was no reason to lie in bed and neglect his duties. Vincent was tired too, but when one was healthy, tiredness was natural. He had intended allowing them a rest after lunch, if they worked hard this morning, but now he wasn't sure.

He put on his dressing-gown and went across the landing to Wood's bedroom. It was empty. The bed was made. Then they were up after all. But the room seemed bare. He looked at the door. The dressing-gown which usually hung behind it gone. Vincent pulled open the wardrobe. It was empty. There were only some cigarette ends in an ashtray by the bed. He went out on to the landing and called their names in turn. No one answered. They'd gone! They had left him! He gave a small cry and ran into each bedroom in turn. He dragged open every drawer but all he could find was a contraceptive sheath in a miniature envelope on Yates's dressing-table. He knew Yates had left it deliberately. It was as if he was standing there with his thumb to his nose.

Vincent sat down on the bed and put his head on his arm. They had deserted him, these three closest members, his select *corps*. They were traitors. He was surrounded by treachery. Madame Vera was a traitor, Wilkins was a traitor, Fox was a traitor. And Patterson, too, would turn on him. He had never trusted Patterson. He would sack Patterson today before he could cause trouble. Perhaps the boys were with Patterson, they were banding against him. In a way it was his own fault, he had picked the wrong type. He had deluded himself that he could change their behaviour, but they were obviously as corrupt and decadent as when he had first met them. When had they planned to go? Was it after he forbade them to bring girls to the house? But he had been right. He was right not to relax his moral principles, whatever the outcome, and even if he had known that his demand would make them quit the Party, he would still have made it because it was right. Sexual laxity was disgraceful and harmful. When Jessop came tomorrow they would together replace the three boys and strengthen the *corps d'élite*. He must, this time, be certain of absolute integrity. But a sense of failure persisted in spite of this resolve. He searched the house once more to see if there was a letter of explanation, but he found nothing. Something at some point had gone wrong, it wasn't merely the girls, it was more fundamental. He sat on a chair and put his head back and stared at the ceiling struggling to discover the reason. He examined every event of the day, beginning with his conversation with Mr Fowler in the morning, and his loathing

of Fowler suddenly erupted. What Fowler needed was a jolt that
would shatter his complacent managerial world, and make him
realise that when he sacked Vincent he had made the big mistake
of his career, not only for himself but for his *people*. There was no
doubt, now, of his origins. He had underestimated Vincent and the
strength of the Party. He was going to be taught the lesson of his
life.

Vincent chewed his cuff. What could he do? Then he realised
that of course he had a public duty to perform by revealing that
Fowler was a Jew. He wondered how he had failed to recognise
the truth during the years he had worked at the bank. They had
all been taken in; oh yes, Fowler had been very clever with his
Christmas gifts tied with religious labels, Christ in the manger,
the kings under the star. And no mention of Saturday being his
Sabbath, he had come to work like the rest of them.

He would publish an indictment in the *News Sheet*, and telephone the papers too. They listened to him now, they asked for his
views, printed his comments. He was a national figure, they would
take notice when he denounced Fowler. He would do it tomorrow.
This very action would begin the leverage of Jews from official
positions. The people were afraid to revolt now, but when they
heard of Fowler being uprooted they would turn on other Jewish
masters and prise them out of their positions; out of the schools
and the banks and the shops and the civil service.

Vincent dressed with care the next morning, polishing his boots
and pressing his trousers. He had barely slept but didn't feel tired.
He telephoned Patterson before he left for the bank.

Before Vincent had a chance to dismiss him, Patterson said, 'So
you've lost your boys!'

'I knew they would come to you,' shouted Vincent, 'you're all
traitors.'

'They haven't come to me. But they told me they had left.
Believe me, I'm on their side. You're too bloody possessive.'

'You're out too.' Vincent slammed down the receiver and stalked
out of the house. He had decided to walk the two miles to the
bank but he found that after a short while his feet ached because

of last night's march, and he began to look for a taxi. He hailed one near the underground station and stopped it a little way from the bank. It was only twenty minutes past nine and he had planned to wait until the bank was open before making his public denunciation. He imagined them inside, Miss Glass opening her till and counting the notes and weighing the coins, a rubber thimble on her index finger; Mr Fowler reading his mail, unaware. Vincent went next door to the newsagents and bought a packet of children's chalks. He took the yellow one out of the packet and held it in his palm. He began to march up and down the pavement in front of the bank, stepping higher and higher at each turn until he was goosestepping. People stopped and looked at him, astonished. He ignored them and kept his eyes ahead. He goosestepped from the chemist's down the road to the butchers and back again. Then, as he was passing the bank he heard the scrabbling as Miss Glass unlocked the main door. He gave her a few moments to return to the counter and then he strutted up the steps and flung the two doors inward and stood surveying them from the inset mat.

'Mr Pearman!' said Miss Glass nervously. Vincent stared at her contemptuously. She was nothing but a twittering spinster. She had not even borne a child for her country. He marched the length of the bank to Mr Fowler's door and with his right hand, still swinging the left and marking time with his feet, he turned the handle and pushed the door wide open. Mr Fowler sprang up from his desk.

'Jew,' shouted Vincent. 'I denounce you as a Jew.' He ran over to the desk and pulled and plucked at Mr Fowler's lapels. 'When my Party is in power I will have you tarred and feathered and dragged through the streets behind the rubbish cart.'

'For heaven's sake,' yelled Fowler, 'are you quite mad?'

The chief cashier grasped Vincent's arm from behind and tried to drag him away from his hold on Mr Fowler's pinstriped jacket.

'Jew, Jew,' shrieked Vincent at the top of his voice. 'This man has tricked us all. He is a Jew. He must be removed from office.'

The chief cashier managed to jerk him back. 'Pamela!' he called tremulously, 'Merle!'

Vincent kicked and struggled and burst free. He had crushed

the yellow chalk but a small fragment was usable. He ran down the bank to the door and began wildly to draw a Star of David. The bank staff gathered round.

'It's all right,' he heard Miss Glass sobbing. 'I've rung the alarm.' And he became conscious of the jangling bell and knew it was also ringing in the police station down the road.

He dropped the chalk and flailing his arms he knocked the people aside and tore out of the doorway and up the street. His head pounded, his breath wheezed; he saw a taxi, stopped it and leaped in, and rode home to Windermere crouching down on the back seat.

He was waiting for Jessop. He sat in the locked house not answering either the door or the telephone, and when it became dark soon after four o'clock he did not turn on the light. He hadn't eaten since the boys left. When he went to look for food he found only half a bottle of sour milk, solidified, and the end of a loaf of bread as hard as a biscuit.

He needed Madame Vera. He sat with the glass container of his inhaler in his hands and from time to time he put it in his mouth and pumped the rubber bulb. Why had she rejected him? He had acted blindly, in a wilderness, any path had seemed the right one to take. His stomach ached from hunger and so did his back from the persistent attack of asthma.

He must control his body, he thought. He could do it by sheer willpower. Only he in the whole country had this iron strength of will which fitted him for leadership. But the people were not worthy of him. The country was not worthy of him. He had been betrayed on all sides by little men manoeuvring for their own petty ends. He knew now what he must do, but he needed Jessop to help him.

Jessop had a key and let himself in at half past four. He found Vincent still at the kitchen table with his inhaler in his hands.

'What's the matter?' asked Jessop, throwing his hat on to a chair. 'Aren't you well?'

'Perfectly well,' said Vincent raising his face. It was the colour of newly rolled pastry.

'You look ghastly,' said Jessop.

'I have been waiting for you. I am going to kill myself. Then I want you to burn the body.'

Jessop switched on the light. 'Are you serious?'

'Absolutely serious. Will you promise, loyally, to carry out my orders?'

'I suppose so.'

'Will you telephone the press and the police to come round after you have set me alight so that they can actually see and photograph the flames?'

'Yes, but why?'

'Because only by this act will the British people be brought to their senses, will they realise what they have lost.'

'Don't you think that Britain needs you alive?' asked Jessop kindly.

'They have rejected me. They must be made to see that they have thrown away their chance of greatness and I myself wish to escape the shame of the nation.'

'I see,' said Jessop.

'I want you to arrange to have my ashes scattered on Dover Cliffs. Then you are to shoot Miss Glass. As I sat waiting for you I realised in a flash of insight that Miss Glass's betrayal was the ultimate treachery. Then you will kill yourself. I don't care how you do it. It may be a painless death.'

'Thank you.'

'But first make absolutely sure that the papers have the full story.'

'Yes.'

'Go and buy me some aspirins so that I can take an overdose.'

While Jessop was gone Vincent contemplated dying without any horror or sadness. It was glorious to die in this way. Hitler had died in the bunker. Rather than give up he had chosen to die and to have his body burned. Vincent took the aspirin bottle and glass of water from Jessop and asked 'How many?'

'The whole bottle will knock you out. You won't know a thing.'

Vincent tipped the aspirins into his hand and drank them down, one after the other. They made his mouth sour and burnt the inside of his throat and seemed to stick at the top of his chest. Jessop took him upstairs, his arm round Vincent's shoulders. He pulled off a bedcover.

'Lie down here.'

'Are you going to burn me on the bed?' asked Vincent trustingly.

'No, I'll take you out into the garden. I don't want to set the house on fire. It would destroy the Party records.'

He went downstairs leaving Vincent numbed and detached, extended on a paisley eiderdown.

'Fox?'

'Who's that? Jessop?'

'Yes. I'm at the house. It's happened.'

'You mean Pearman?'

'You were quite right. He's played himself out. He's just taken an overdose. The ambulance is on its way.'

'Why didn't you let him die?'

'What's the point. He's nothing. Nothing. Just pathetic, comic. Let them pump him out. Are you listening?'

'Yes.'

'Well, we've got quite a salvaging job to do. I want you to handle the press. As soon as the ambulance men remove him I'm going up to Birmingham. You can report to me there. All they need is the right leader.'

The bell on the ambulance, growing louder, stopped outside the house. It was replaced by the urgent ringing of the door bell. Jessop went to answer it.

Mrs Pearman crossed the bedroom and drew the curtains.

'It does get dark early, doesn't it?' She smiled at Vincent lying back on his pillows. 'You remind me of when you were a little boy. You were always in bed with your chest. I can see you now, leaning up on your elbow on all those pillows, wheezing away. Shall I bring your supper?'

'Thank you mother.'

She had bought new curtains for his return home but otherwise the room was the same. He could still see the frieze of soldiers underneath the paint of an earlier renovation, and at night, when she had gone to bed too, he heard the cars pass by in the road and watched the pattern of light from the window move up the wall and across the ceiling. His mother was right, he had often lain there for hours as a little boy, and at night he had watched the reflections from the headlamps just as he did now. He could hear her coming upstairs again, slowly, because she was carrying a tray. She came in and put the tray down on the dressing-table, then she helped him to sit up.

'That's right darling. There we are. Bon Appetitie as Daddy used to say.' She went to the door.

'Mother.' He commanded.

She stopped. 'Yes, darling?'

'Mother, you've forgotten!' He rose imperiously in the bed and the tray slid down his knees.

'Oh dear. Wait a minute.' She hurried to the wardrobe and took out his uniform jacket. She held it out for him as if it was a bed-jacket and he slipped his arms into the sleeves and fastened the buttons.

'Don't forget again or I shan't allow you to retain your position in the Party,' he said, and began to spoon his soup.

ALSO AVAILABLE FROM VALANCOURT BOOKS

WHAT CRITICS ARE SAYING ABOUT VALANCOURT BOOKS

'Valancourt are doing a magnificent job in making these books not only available but – in many cases – known at all . . . these reprints are well chosen and well designed (often using the original dust jackets), and have excellent introductions.'

Times Literary Supplement (London)

'Valancourt Books champions neglected but important works of fantastic, occult, decadent and gay literature. The press's Web site not only lists scores of titles but also explains why these often obscure books are still worth reading. . . . So if you're a real reader, one who looks beyond the bestseller list and the touted books of the moment, Valancourt's publications may be just what you're searching for.'

MICHAEL DIRDA, *Washington Post*

'Valancourt Books are fast becoming my favourite publisher. They have made it their business, with considerable taste and integrity, to put back into print a considerable amount of work which has been in serious need of republication. If you ever felt there were gaps in your reading experience or are simply frustrated that you can't find enough good, substantial fiction in the shops or even online, then this is the publisher for you.'

MICHAEL MOORCOCK

TO LEARN MORE AND TO SEE A COMPLETE LIST OF AVAILABLE TITLES, VISIT US AT VALANCOURTBOOKS.COM